COBB'S LANDING

By

Duane Schwartz

A-Argus Better Book Publishers, LLC
North Carolina~~**~~New Jersey
www.a-argusbooks.com

Cobb's Landing

A-Argus Better Book Publishers, LLC

For information:
A-Argus Better Book Publishers, LLC
Post Office Box 914
Kernersville, North Carolina 27285
www.a-argusbooks.com

ISBN: 978-0-9819075-5-0
ISBN: 0-9819075-5-5

Book Cover designed by Dubya

Printed in the United States of America

DEDICATION

For my wife Betty, who suffered through many readings on my behalf and never expressed less than whole-hearted encouragement.

Chapter One

September 1931

"Sheriff Morgan shot her," Frankie Beletucci told his friend, Jake.

"I know," Jake said. He brushed at a fresh tear. It had been Amelia, his Amelia, who had been shot. The last he saw of her she was being carried, bleeding and sobbing, to a waiting airplane. "Let's go find Jonah Cobb. He'll know what to do."

Frankie began to think about everything Jake had told him earlier, that he (Frankie) was now a top target of the mob since his father had botched the hit on Angelo Petruzzi. Petruzzi was fine. Frankie's dad had missed, but miss or not, it made no difference. Petruzzi's wife was down, Frankie's dad was dead and, as Jake had put it, no one was going to let Frankie live long enough to avenge his father's death—not now—not ever. "Won't Jonah Cobb want to kill me? Ain't he mob, too?"

"If he knows all that has gone down he will," Jake said. He studied Frankie's expression and a thought surfaced in his mind. There they were, him only seventeen, Frankie even younger, and today they had become men, men seasoned by war, men seasoned by killing. And they were both all each of them had at that moment, all that they could trust. "Best you stay out of sight," Jake cautioned. He had already lost Amelia. He did not wish to risk losing Frankie too.

The two boys continued their hurried pace towards the bridge where Jake figured Jonah Cobb had gone to

1

defend the Landing against an attack by the vigilante gang from town. When they rounded the last bend in the road, just before the bridge, they came upon the sheriff's overturned truck and the grossly twisted and bloody bodies of its dead passengers. Then they saw the sheriff. He was standing there, his back to them, his arms held straight out in front of him, both of his hands tightly gripping a pistol. They stopped dead. The sheriff's gun fired. The boys flinched. The back window of the truck ahead shattered into hundreds of tiny pieces and settled like rain into its bed. The driver slumped over the wheel, his foot pushing the accelerator to the floor, and the truck sped onto the burning bridge. Fiery timbers gave way and metal and wood fell together into the rapid waters of the creek below. The boys watched as the sheriff, now utterly drained of his once incontestable vigor, labored precariously towards the ravine. They saw Tommy Delaney edge up over the bank. He stood, stunned from his fall into the drink, only to come face to face with Morgan's speeding bullet and have his lifeless body knocked back into the ravine he had just emerged from. Then Sheriff Morgan turned to face them. He raised his revolver, blood dripping from both of his arms.

Jake and Frankie - simultaneously - pulled back on the hammer of their guns and took careful aim.

Chapter Two

September 2001

An incredibly polished and proper Adam Belle shot the crude and arrogant Leonard Morgan a peculiar glance. Their friendship, if one could truthfully call what they shared a friendship, confused Adam. They were nothing alike. Take this moment for instance. Adam had gone to a shop and rented the appropriate attire for this dive, wet-suit, swim fins, proper fitting goggles, etc, and there was Leonard, adorned in a lumberjack shirt, goggles with black elastic crossing the temple on one side of his face, white elastic on the other, swim-fins of two different colors and styles. Funny he didn't swim in circles, but then Adam really didn't know for certain that he didn't. So far Leonard had been the only one to dive.

"What're you gawkin' at?" Leonard asked.

"Can't you at least pull the goggles off? You're not in the water and you look ridiculous," Adam told him, then continued the gaze. Leonard was the kind that made Adam examine himself quite often, whenever they were together as a mater of fact. They had become friends largely due, Adam guessed, to some mysterious force of nature he failed to comprehend as much as he failed to understand their unbreakable friendship. It was a love-hate sort of thing. Right now, as he studied Leonard, it was clearly hate, or maybe it was embarrassment, or possibly Leonard's cocky expression, or even more simply, it might have been the fact that the crack of Leonard's ass showed every time he bent over.

Disgusting! Whatever it was, it did prompt a question; what in the hell made him choose such creature to help him retrieve Jonah Cobb's old truck from the depths of Jesse Lake? Circumstance! That was the answer. Leonard owns the only barge in the county, at least the only one equipped to pull a '29 Ford truck from the lake's floor where it had been since 1931.

Leonard tugged at the goggles. Water spilled from beneath them.

"Christ, Morgan! They aren't even air-tight."

"Water-tight."

"What?"

"Water-tight. You mean-water tight, don't you?" Leonard insisted.

Semantics, Adam thought silently. Leonard was like that. No matter what someone said, he had another way of saying it.

Leonard Morgan understood his connection to Adam Belle even less than Adam did. Truthfully, he had always tried to discourage their friendship, but, on occasion, he could not stop himself from liking the guy. He recalled their first meeting. It was on the day Adam had come home to Cedar Ridge for his grandmother's funeral. The tiny airport on the outskirts of town, just across the highway from Cedar Ridge Ford where Leonard worked, did not rent cars, so since Cedar Ridge Ford did rent cars, and Adam desperately needed one, the two of them were destined to meet.

"What-cha need?" Leonard asked when Adam approached the counter at the dealership that day. He was generally more courteous to customers, but he knew who Adam was and that he was coming. It was a small town with a fast and accurate rumor mill. Adam was a Belle and a descendant of an age-old Morgan family enemy, and him being that, Leonard was not of a mind to be hospitable.

"I need to rent a car," Adam said.

"What for?"

Adam's eyes narrowed. "That would be just my business."

Leonard propped his elbows on the counter, rested his chin in his palms, and stretched his neck to place his face within inches of Adam's in an effort to intimidate. "And these just would be my cars!" he said.

Adam instinctively pulled back. "I need to get to a funeral, if you really must know. Look! I'm already late. The plane ran behind, so if you don't mind?"

"Driver's license?"

Adam handed it to him.

"Chicago," Leonard grumbled as he read. "Land of mobsters."

"Excuse me?"

"Leonard! Just rent him a car," someone shouted from a back office, ending his fun.

Nowadays they get along, he and Adam Belle. Leonard did not know why or how, but they did. He shot Adam a brief, questioning look as he watched him circle Jonah Cobb's old truck now sitting in the middle of the barge. Adam let out a tiny smile.

"What?" Leonard asked.

"Nothing, really." Adam reached out and rattled the truck's loose bumper. "It just occurred to me, you were the only one around to rent me a car when I got here, and now you're the only one with a barge. Why is that, Leonard?"

"Coincidence. Luck, maybe."

"Luck?" Adam's lip curled at the thought.

"Yeah. Luck. Luck put you an' me together, for times like this, times when you need help from a guy like me."

Adam hated to admit it, but Leonard was right.

"Well...we done here? Or do you want us to dive in and see if we can find Jonah Cobb down there?" Leonard asked.

Rumor was, Jonah had been trapped and drowned. "We'll look," Adam said.

"Okay. Can't be much left though. Been down there

5

since prohibition. What the fish ain't got, probably washed into the deep water long ago. And what the fish did get folks fishin' this lake ate a long time ago."

"Christ, Morgan! You are one crass son-of-a-bitch. You know it?"

Leonard's chest swelled. He grinned. To him, the observation was a compliment, not an insult.

Adam unbuttoned his shirt as he walked by the driver's door of the truck. He glanced inside. *A wallet.* He leaned in through the broken window and picked it up. He opened it; nothing, save a couple of worn-thin dollar bills and a picture with the face washed away. On its cover the letters "J C" appeared. It was Jonah Cobb's, alright. If Adam hadn't been eager to dive before, he certainly was now. He stooped and unlaced his boots. He took them off and stuffed the wallet inside one of them. "Let's go!"

Leonard pulled his oxygen tanks back over his shoulders and lowered himself into the water. He bobbed, waiting for Adam to join him. But as Adam slid out of his pants and into his diving gear his mind traveled back six months to the crisp March day of his beloved grandmother's funeral—and his reintroduction to the north. It was there he reunited with his grandfather, Jacob Belle, who he had not seen in seventeen years, and Maggie, the girl to whom he had become totally devoted. Jointly they were the reason for this adventure. Jonah Cobb, the man who was the target of this dive and the driver of the truck he and Morgan had retrieved from bottom of the lake, was from his grandfather's past. He was also thought to be Maggie's great uncle.

~*~

Jacob Belle had met Adam at the door of St. Michael's Catholic Church on the day of the funeral. It had been a long time. Adam nearly failed to recognize his own grandfather.

"Still standing," Adam commented.

"You mean me?" Jacob asked.

"The old church. It's still here. Would have thought they'd have replaced it by now."

"What? Replace it with one of those new-fangled buildings? God! I hope they never do that. I find turn-of-the-century architecture interesting and most enchanting. And the modern look?...sterile! Don't you?"

"It's been a long time," Adam said, as he offered his grandfather his hand.

"Too long," Jacob said. "I'd guess maybe twenty years."

"Seventeen," Adam corrected. "Mom and Dad's funeral. Might have seen me at my graduation a couple of months after that. too. I don't know. I don't remember." He didn't know his grandfather well—never had. Something had happened when Adam was young—about six years old. His parents stopped all contact with his grandparents and he was never told why. They considered him too young to understand at the time, and when Adam left Cedar Ridge, it was only months after his parents died in a car accident so he never found out what that problem was. After a time, he didn't care. "I was just eighteen when I left; I'm thirty-five now. It seems a long time ago—in a different life."

"I'd say we have a void to fill, Adam," Jacob offered.

After the accident that orphaned him, Adam stuck around just long enough to get his high school diploma and that was it. He had been traumatized by the event, and, as hard as he sometimes pressed himself, his memory of that time was sketchy at best. More often than not, he preferred it that way, but for now he did not wish to hurt his grandfather's feelings with unneeded truth; not at his wife's funeral. "Maybe," he agreed.

"There's a reception in the basement of the church," Jacob said as he led Adam around the side of the building after the service.

Familiar, Adam thought as they approached the stairway to the basement. *I've been here. When I was young? Religious instructions.* The door swung wide. A pretty, blond-haired woman, mid-thirties Adam guessed, stood in the doorway.

"Will you stay long?" Jacob asked Adam.

He looked at the girl. *Maybe,* he thought "Not long," he said.

He looked again at the girl.

"Maggie, Maggie Buckley," his grandfather quietly whispered.

"Excuse me?"

"The girl you're breaking into a sweat over. Her name is Maggie Buckley."

Maggie handed Adam a glass of punch as she planted her soft lips on his cheek and held the kiss for several seconds, then said, "It's been a long time—too long."

She felt...so...familiar—comfortable. *Who is she?* Adam found himself wondering. Then he began to remember. *Maggie! Little Maggie from up the street.* He pictured her as she had been as a child. Her teeth were crooked. Her hair was reddish and ratty, and she wore it in pigtails. But now? Today? *Wow!*

"How long will you be staying?" It was his grandfather's question, only asked differently.

He gave the same answer. "Not long."

He doesn't remember me at all, she thought. A tear came to her eye.

"Are you alright?" Adam asked.

"Fine," she said. "Just sad for your loss."

"Thank you." Adam wondered if she knew. He really couldn't remember his grandmother, so felt no loss. "Thank you," he said again.

"Grandfather Belle," Maggie said, "I'm going to steal Adam for a bit. That is if you don't mind. I want to show him off."

Jacob waved a hand, his sign of approval.

"Come," Maggie said as she tugged at Adam's arm. "Let's reacquaint you with some old friends." She leaned her head over until it just touched his shoulder for an instant. Then she led him through the crowd. Her touch excited him, yet, put him oddly at ease.

"You know you broke my heart," she told him once they were alone.

"I did? Well... I apologize."

"I forgave you a long time ago."

"What did I do?" Adam asked.

"You left. I was in love with you and you left."

"So what did you do?"

"I married Bobby Bartell." She smiled.

"I remember him."

"You should. You were best friends," Maggie reminded him.

Adam could picture the guy, all right. He just couldn't recall them being best friends, he didn't recall ever having a best friend. It was something he had learned to live with. A doctor had once explained it—*cause and effect*. His parents died...together...in a bloody car crash when he was young. His mind blew a gasket and blocked the time out. *No big deal.* He always figured the door slammed shut on that little piece of his history for a reason, so why try to open it.

"So, you're not Maggie Buckley," he said. "You're really Mrs. Bartell."

"The widow Bartell. Bobby died. Ten years ago now—cancer."

"I'm sorry."

Maggie had loved and lost. She had moved on some time back, and now what she saw was opportunity. She and Adam had been an item throughout their high school days. It wounded her deeply when his memory of them died with his parents that fatal night, but she did not hold him to blame. After a time when she finally accepted that Adam was gone for good, she set aside the dream of the two of them living together to old age. She married

Bobby Bartell, but, as much as she tried over the years, she never really got over Adam...not by a long shot. Now that he was back, and she was no longer attached, she was determined to keep him, no matter what it took. She did not want his sympathy. She wanted him.

"Just remember that when you go to look for my number," she said.

"And when should I look? Tomorrow?"

Yes! She thought. "Tomorrow would be perfect," she said.

She brought him to his grandfather's table, and explained that she needed to see her aging father home. She kissed the tips of her fingers and pressed them to his lips. Then she was gone.

"I see you've made a friend," Jacob Belle said.

"I think I've made a date," Adam said.

~*~

"We divin'?" Morgan broke in. "Or you just gonna stare off at yesterday some more?"

"Yeah! Yeah! We're diving." As Adam pulled his tanks over his shoulders, he wondered how long he had left Leonard bobbing in the water. "I'll be right there."

He jumped in. "Shit!" He gasped. The icy water of Jesse Lake stopped any further attempt to speak for a time. All he could do was shiver.

Burley Leonard studied him briefly, and then smiled. "Pussy," he said. Then he dove.

By the time Adam reached the lake's floor, Leonard had the sand so stirred up seeing was impossible. He felt around, gathering items that did not feel like a rock. Leonard held something large. He pushed it at Adam—too murky. Adam couldn't make out what it was. Leonard signaled that he was going to the surface, then left Adam in a cloud of stirred sand and mud. Adam waited for a time to see if things would settle, but finally gave up and headed for the surface himself.

"What did you find?" Adam asked as he pulled himself onto the barge.

Morgan proudly held the item up.

"Jesus Christ!" Adam screeched. *A skull!* He stood. "Jesus!" he said again, as he backed to the edge of the barge.

" Recon this is ole Jonah Cobb, himself?" Morgan asked.

"I'm guessing it is." He had thought they'd find something, but Jonah Cobb's skull—too much—but it would serve an important purpose. His lady, Maggie, needed more. She was only rumored to be related to the Cobbs. She wanted to know for sure. DNA tests on the skull would certainly tell the story—or so he had been told.

Adam pulled at the drawstrings of the canvas sack he had put his collected pieces in and peered into it. "Jesus Christ!" He jerked on the strings, closing the bag tight.

"What?" Morgan shouted.

Adam tossed him the bag.

Leonard pulled it opened and looked inside. "Jesus Christ!" *A hand. A right hand to be exact.* "We need to dive again. Might be more of him down there."

Adam did not know if he wanted to find more. Jonah's skull and hand would suffice. Finding more bones might be unnecessary. This entire ordeal was beginning to remind him of his first thoughts when his grandfather began his tale of the place called Cobb's Landing. *Gangsters waging full-scale war? Here? Sounds so preposterous!* he had thought. But, it was his grandfather's tale, and he believed it—all of it. Angelo Petruzzi—the Cobb brothers, Jordan and Jonah (whose skull he knew he was presently staring into the eye sockets of)—Anthony Russo, a mob enforcer turned priest—a hit man named Delaney—Brooks, the turncoat pilot. He was, at the moment, just four miles from where he grew up, and now he was looking directly at one of them...at least a piece of him...damn hard to deny. More

11

bones wouldn't change anything.

"You okay?" Leonard asked.

"Let's dive." Adam pulled his mask over his eyes, plugged in the mouthpiece, and lowered himself into the water. Even though he had reservations, if they didn't dive now, he'd feel he hadn't done all he could have, all he had promised to do.

Further searching produced little. They had Jonah Cobb's truck, his skull, the skeleton of his right hand, a couple of other bones neither of them could identify, and a monogrammed wallet. A quick once-over of the truck's interior produced a pocket watch. Rubbing it with the tail of Leonard Morgan's tattered lumberjack shirt revealed an inscription reading, *"To Jonah on Our First Anniversary. With Love, Mae."*

"You and Maggie are really gonna to tie the knot?" Morgan asked.

"Yes. We are."

"I sure wish you hadn't come back here. I had me some plans, and they included that girl."

"You did, did you?" Leonard's desire for the attention of Maggie Bartell sometimes annoyed Adam—sometimes it entertained him. Today...he was entertained. "She doesn't exactly seem your type, or I should say, you don't seem hers."

"Really! What makes you say that?"

"Oh, I don't know, Leonard. The words 'Beauty and the Beast' come to mind."

While Leonard began examining their catch, the carcass of Jonah Cobb's '29 Ford truck, Adam dug into the cooler, popped the top on a cold beer, unfolded one of the lawn chairs they had brought along, settled into it, and began drifting off to the day of his grandmother's funeral and the conversation he had with his grandfather.

~*~

The air between Adam and his grandfather, Jacob,

had grown stagnant with silence; neither man knew how to get the conversation going. Adam decided to hang some words out there…just to see if they would go anywhere. "I thought we'd be going to the cemetery."

"Why?"

"Isn't that what usually happens?"

"Not if you're being cremated."

It didn't add up. His grandparents were Catholics. This was a Catholic church, with a Catholic priest officiating. "A Catholic cremation? That's different."

"You don't approve?"

Adam thought about it briefly, *What the hell do I care? I haven't been inside a church, Catholic or otherwise, since my parents' funeral. And really,—what I disapprove of is Catholics—not cremation.*

"What's the priest had to say about it?"

"He's pissed," Jacob admitted.

"Doesn't that bother you?"

Adam's grandfather did not answer. He just stared off in the distance. When Adam studied him, it came to mind that he didn't appear sad. *Odd. His wife just died. Yet…?* "Can I ask you something?"

"Sure."

"Why were we kept apart?"

"Things that happened at Cobb's Landing."

"Excuse me?" Adam's brow wrinkled.

"It all had to do with my work at the Landing—people I met there, and what I became because of them. Look, Kid, there's probably a lot you'll want to know. But this isn't the time or place. I tell you what. You come over in the morning and we'll get started." As he walked away he waved a hand behind him. "In the morning, Adam," he said.

~*~

The loud splash brought Adam back to the barge. Leonard had been lashing down Jonah Cobb's truck with

13

nylon straps when he lost his balance and fell backwards into the lake. Adam could not contain his laughter. Leonard looked more like a soaking wet cartoon character than a human being as he emerged from the water.

"Pull up the anchor behind ya?" Leonard commanded. He acted as if what had just happened was commonplace. "If we wanna get this truck unloaded at the Landing, we best get a move on."

Chapter Three

Cobb's Landing was no more than a half-mile west of where the barge had been anchored. Adam looked at the lake's surface; it was calm and smooth—clear—not a ripple in sight. If one needed to strap something down to move it the short distance to the Landing, it certainly wasn't on Jesse Lake, not on that day. Then he looked up the small river at the remains of the bridge whose collapse deposited Jonah Cobb and his truck into the once rapid water, sending them to a resting place where they would serve as a kind of gateway to Cobb's Landing from 1931 until now, and he felt sad. He realized that the presence of Jonah and his truck beneath the crystal-clear waters is what drew the eye up the little river, and without them to point the way, no one would notice the remains of the bridge that had played such a significant part in the Cobb's Landing story. Adam scanned the shoreline as the barge made its way to the Landing. He looked for more he might miss without Jonah and his truck there to set the mood, but, as they approached the Landing's shore, he discovered the mood could not be broken—only delayed, maybe even enhanced. For now, as the barge touched the sand of the beach, he could close his eyes and see flappers and gangsters dancing the Charleston around the bonfire in the cool of a 1931 summer evening. He could hear the music. He could smell—almost taste—the contraband whiskey.

Leonard had brought along two dolly sets for moving wrecked cars, a long length of chain, a come-a-long, and a pair of ramps. Moving the truck to land was almost effortless, but positioning it where Adam wanted it proved difficult. He saw the old truck in a certain spot, the exact location (as near as he could figure from his grandfather's tales) where it sat until Jonah Cobb lit out in it on that fatal morning in the fall of '31. It had been idling, with a dead man behind the wheel, in the main driveway, near the front door of the lodge. Adam thought back to his grandfather's account, and how it had been the sheriff, Leonard's great-grandfather, who had been shooting at Jonah as he peeled off, and he began thinking of an early memory of Leonard himself. Aside from the distasteful experience renting a car from Leonard, Adam had one other early and equally unpleasant encounter with him. It was the morning after his grandmother's funeral.

~*~

Adam was used to the sounds of Chicago's busy streets, so the disturbing quiet of a Minnesota night spent in a less than four-star motel had him awake before sun-up. From the window of his room he watched, as the pancake house across the street came to life, and an old pickup truck pulled into one of its parking spaces. *Why not,* he asked himself. *I'm already awake. Might as well eat.* He dressed and walked out the motel room door into the parking lot. He turned and looked back at the building—something out of the "sixties." On the corner stood a gas station; one he had patronized as a teen. It looked the same. Time, in this little berg, had stood still.

"Christ! It's freezing," he said aloud as he pulled at the collar of his jacket to shield his neck from the wind.

"It's Minnesota."

"What?" He could not tell where the voice came from.

"I said...this is Minnesota." A young girl in a maid's uniform slid out of the shadows to face him. "It's Minnesota and this is springtime. Spring's always a little cold here. It's nice during the day, but cold in the morning and evening—that way in the fall, too."

"How's the food at that pancake house," Adam asked the maid.

"Good, I guess. Haven't heard no complaints about it."

She disappeared back into the shadows leaving Adam to make his way across the street to the café where he chose a booth, rather than one of the many stools that lined a long counter.

On one of the stools, a man dressed in a sports jacket, jeans and a cowboy hat sat slurping runny eggs. He turned to glance at Adam, and then returned to his breakfast. A waitress appeared from behind a swinging door and stood with pen and pad at the ready in front of Adam's booth. She yawned.

"What can I get-cha?" she asked.

"How about a menu?" Adam suggested.

She walked off in the direction of the counter. She returned with a menu.

"Will ya need coffee?"

"Yes. And a glass of water, if you don't mind."

When the waitress returned with the coffee and water, Adam ordered the daily special from the menu.

"You're Belle, aren't-cha?" he cowboy at the counter said, without turning around.

"Yes. I am. I'm Adam Belle."

"Thought I recognized ya."

"Do we know each other?"

"I rented you the car you're drivin'," the cowboy said. He turned and gave Adam a quick glance.

"Of course. I remember you now. How are you?" Adam was trying to be polite, despite the peculiar way he had been treated at the dealership the morning before.

"You from the Cobb's Landing Belles?"

"I don't know. Am I?"

"You're old Jake's relation, ain't ya?"

"I'm his grandson."

"Then you're a Cobb's Landing Belle."

"Just who are you, Mister?" Adam asked, his tolerance thinning.

"Name's Morgan." Then he grabbed a handful of bills from his pocket, dumped them on the counter, and he left without another word.

He did, however, leave a lasting impression on Adam—one reminiscent of an artificial sweetener aftertaste—something that would not go away; and now that he looked at Leonard standing there leaning on Jonah Cobb's truck, the taste returned.

"This about where you want this thing?" Morgan asked.

"I think it needs to be about twenty feet west," Adam told him.

"Just how the hell would you know that?" Morgan objected.

"Because you're great-grandfather's shot hit just above the back window...from there," he gestured towards the building, "in the doorway to the lodge. This close and bullets would have riddled the side window. That's how I know." He tapped his knuckles on the closed passenger's window of the old truck, its glass intact.

Leonard hooked a chain to a tree several yards in front of the truck, and began pulling it the final twenty feet. "Let me know how far." He worked the lever of the come-a-long back and forth. "How'd you and Miss Maggie get together anyway? You know, I been askin' her out for years. She was 'bout ready to go too. Then you come along. I had big plans for her and me."

Adam shook his head and grinned. "So you've said." Then he thought back to the morning in the pancake house. "You know, it's kinda' your fault Maggie's with me."

"How's that?"

"You recall that morning we talked in the pancake house—back in March? You sat at the counter and talked…your back to me," Adam reminded him.

"Yeah? So?"

"Well…after you left, I sat there for a while reading the paper and waiting for daylight. Then I went back to the motel and looked for my grandfather's phone number. Now the shitty meal and the lousy conversation already had me pissed off, so when I couldn't find any Belles in the book, I threw the damn thing completely across the room. I was about to give it up and snag a flight back to Chicago, where I came from, and where I had a real life."

"But you decided to hang around and hit on Maggie, just 'cause I pissed you off that morning. Is that it?" Morgan asked.

"Not exactly, but that did help. After a while, I started thinking. Guess what I thought, Leonard."

"Now…how the hell would I know what you thought?"

"I thought of Maggie. Then I called her and her soft, sweet voice changed my whole mood. She came over to the motel."

"The slut!"

Adam wanted to beat Leonard with his own chain, but he fought the impulse. He faced Leonard, eyes wide opened and cold, brow wrinkled, fists clenched. "Don't you ever talk that way about her again, Leonard. And, for your information, Maggie dropped by rather than give me directions over the phone because she needed to run an errand for her father. She just stopped on her way."

"Cute story," Leonard said ignoring Adam's warning. "But what's it all got to do with you stealin' her from me?" He wrenched harder and faster on the come-a-long.

"Oh! That's coming right up. You see, she waited around until I got in the car, the one you rented me. The goddamned thing wouldn't start. So…Maggie drove me to my grandfather's, and she picked me up later that day. We've pretty much been together ever since. Yes sir,

Leonard, it's all your fault. If you rented cars that run, she and I probably would never have gotten together."

"Bullshit!"

"No bullshit."

"Anything else good happen with her that day?" Leonard asked.

Adam thought back to his conversation with Maggie that morning.

~*~

After the usual pleasantries were exchanged, and unusual annoyance of the rental that wouldn't start behind him, Adam accepted a ride with Maggie and hoped for a better day. He buckled in and Maggie threw the shifter into drive and pulled into the street.

"Rent that car from Morgan?" she asked.

"As a matter of fact, I did," Adam admitted.

"Most of his don't start. You're lucky though."

"How's that?"

"Some don't have brakes either." She smiled, obviously stretching the truth.

"Well then, I guess I am lucky. Who is he anyway? I ran into him early this morning at the pancake place. He's sure a strange one."

"That he is. He's hard to explain. Leonard is crass. He can be rude, obnoxious, annoying and a whole bunch of other adjectives most of us don't care to see in another human being. But Leonard Morgan can also be a genuine good-guy. He's got a heart that far exceeds the average capacity for giving. He's always a contradiction—difficult to understand. You'll see when you get to know him better."

"Do I really want to know him better?"

"Sure you do. The two of you are connected—by Cobb's Landing," Maggie explained.

"Is that why he asked if I was of the Cobb's Landing Belles? What's he know about Cobb's Landing?"

"He might know a lot. His great-grandfather was the town's sheriff when the Landing was in full swing."

Maggie pulled the car to the curb in front of the bank.

"It seems I ought to know him. We're about the same age. Did he go to school here?"

"No. The sheriff, who was Morgan's great-grandfather, died at Cobb's Landing. The family disappeared after that. The old man had some connection with Cobb and it didn't sit well with the town. They moved on. Leonard settled back here a few years ago."

She pointed out the passenger-side window at a door that led to an apartment above the bank. "That's your grandfather's."

Adam opened his door. "Thanks for the ride."

"Call me when you're ready to leave. I'll come and get you."

~*~

Adam smiled at Leonard. He thought of telling him more of the story, but felt the poor guy had probably had enough.

"I learned about your great-grandfather, the sheriff back in the day of Cobb's Landing," he decided to tell him. "Come on," he said. "Let's get this stuff loaded back on the barge and head for home. I'm beat."

"Pussy," Leonard said puffing out his chest.

~*~

On the barge, Adam leaned back and closed his tired eyes. The sun glaring off the water for nearly a full day had taken its toll. He dozed. He dreamt.

~*~

It was back to that first visit to his grandfather's

21

apartment that was above Cedar Ridge's original bank. The stairway leading to its upper floor was narrow and dark. At the top, there was a landing outside a single door. Adam knocked.

Jacob Belle was in pajamas and slippers when he answered. "You found me."

"Am I too early?" Adam asked.

"Not at all. Oh! The pajamas. I stay in them as long as I can these days. Your grandmother raised holy hell if I didn't get dressed first thing. Now that she's no longer here, I do as I please. Does it bother you? Because I can get dressed if it bothers you."

"No. This is fine," Adam said as he looked around the room. Its furnishings seemed outdated but the place was clean and neat.

"Grandma was bossy, was she?" he asked.

"Ridiculously," Jacob said.

"Hard to get along with?"

"She sure wasn't easy."

"Do you miss her?"

"Sure I miss her. I was married to her for sixty-seven years. You spend that much time with the devil himself, and all of a sudden he's gone; you'd miss him, too, wouldn't you?"

"I wouldn't know," Adam said. "I doubt I would last that many years in the first place. But if I did, I don't think it would be with someone I could compare to the devil." *I'm not sure I like him. He seems too abrupt, crude, unfeeling,* Adam thought.

"You're not a practicing Catholic. If you were, you'd understand. You see, Catholics, especially those from my generation, don't divorce. They endure." He stared deep into Adam's eyes for a long moment. "Now let's get on with this. You came here to learn about Cobb's Landing, didn't you?"

"And to learn about you."

"Then you need to hear the whole story of the Cobb's Landing. That's what made me. That's what I'm all about." He paused long, and then added, "The story also holds the reason why your father kept us apart. You want to know that as well, don't you?"

Adam was surprised. He had always thought it was his mother who stopped Adam from seeing his grandparents, not his father. "Yes. I do want to know that."

"Well, then. Let's get started."

Jacob Belle walked into the kitchen and poured two mugs of coffee. He placed them on the table and motioned for Adam to sit. Then he took the chair across from him.

~*~

"I was just seventeen when I went to work for Jordan Cobb. It was 1931, a year I will never forget. Now...the first couple of weeks were uneventful. Fun actually. It was my dream job. I was happy. I came from an unhappy home—not enough food. Depression, you know. Just being away would have done it for me. But my job at the Landing, well... it was more than I dared imagine. Then, early in my third week, Angelo Petruzzi arrived."

Chapter Four

Spring—1931

Angelo Petruzzi spat on the ground. *Mud,* he thought. *It's been a year and the goddamn runway is still mud.* He took a hard look at Cobb, then back at the side-to-side tracks left behind by the plane, and shook his head. *Christ! I can't stand this mosquito infested woods he calls a haven. Haven my ass. Trees...bugs...Shit, give me skyscrapers and concrete. Give me automobiles...not tractors. Cobb's Landing a haven? It's a goddamn jungle.*

He fixed his steely eyes on Jordan Cobb's. His custom-tailored, silk, dark pinstripe suit provided an extraordinary and drastic contrast, not only Cobb himself—standing there in overalls—but to the wilderness that now surrounded him. He looked oddly out of place.

"What were you thinking, Cobb? Why'd you have that green pilot fly me in here?"

Cobb shuddered. He hated having Petruzzi at the Landing almost as much as Petruzzi hated coming here...but...what was he to do? Angelo Petruzzi was the mob boss, not him.

"I thought Billy was better than that."

"Better than what? Jesus! He damn near killed me. And who knows, maybe he did kill my wife."

"You bring Ellen along?" This wasn't good news. Trouble usually followed Angelo, but triple trouble

24

followed whenever he brought Ellen. She was a lush—a lush with hot panties and open-for-business legs.

"You goddamn right I'm 'ere, Cobb. Why the hell shouldn't I be?" Ellen Petruzzi slurred from the plane's open doorway. Then she slipped and fell backwards into the airplane. Her legs flew into the air—no panties at all. Jordan Cobb looked away. It wasn't that she was homely. Hell, the truth be known, she wasn't half-bad, attractive really; but Cobb had already been offered some of that and turned it down. It wasn't safe. When a piece of ass costs a bullet, the smart guy doesn't buy.

"For Christ's sake, Ellen. Just get back in the plane. Goddamn drunk."

"I gotta piss!" Ellen Petruzzi objected.

Billy Brooks came out from under the plane where he had been trying to look as though he was checking things over. Actually, he was sneaking closer to Petruzzi and Cobb, getting a feel for just how much trouble the horseshit landing was going bring.

"Brooks," Cobb shouted. He knew Billy was edging closer. He had been watching out of the corner of his eye. He also knew Billy could hear him just fine… without shouting, but Petruzzi didn't. Petruzzi's back was turned. No sense in alerting him. He'd just shoot Billy and what good would that do? Cobb would be without a pilot to get the Petruzzi's off his Landing…so…he yelled. "Take Mrs. Petruzzi to the outhouse."

"Yes, Sir."

"And hurry the fuck up," Angelo Petruzzi added.

Ellen gave her husband the finger and stuck out her tongue, then turned to Jordan Cobb. "Christ, Cobb, can't you have indoor plumbing like the rest of the world?" It was an admonishment, not a question.

"This isn't Chicago, Ellen. It's the wilderness," Cobb insisted.

As soon as Billy Brooks and Ellen Petruzzi were out of sight, Jordan Cobb turned to face Angelo. He did not like what he saw. The mob boss' expression said trouble. The runway was crude, so he should have known the Landing would be rough, and he probably did, but Jordan Cobb could see in those cold eyes, the man didn't care. He was pissed and nearly as drunk as his wife—bad combination. There would be hell to pay if Cobb didn't think fast and get Petruzzi's mind away from his current state, a hell that would run downhill.

"I know you're not fond of my little hideaway, Angelo, but think about it. The guys appreciate it. They come here to relax. Besides, it's awful handy for getting that whiskey out of Canada ain't it?" The Landing's location was just a hundred miles south of Manitoba.

The mob-boss settled. Jordan Cobb was right. This was, when he thought about the Canadian whiskey side of things, one sweet operation, and, even though he didn't give two shits if his guys had a place to relax, he had to admit it was a great place for them to lay low when the law was closing in on them.

"Three years is a long time. You ever going to get this place finished?"

Three years was a long time. Jordan Cobb had been thinking that himself; just last week he was thinking that, and he had already set his mind. This would be the year.

"Oh, it'll be done before the end of the season. I can promise you that Angelo."

"Landing strip too?"

"Well... that's up to Mother Nature. I've hauled in enough gravel and clay. Now it needs rain—to pack it. Then it'll firm up like concrete."

"Indoor plumbing?"

"Probably next season."

Maybe three years was too long for the Landing to be in the making, but, really, that was Cobb's business; not mob business. This land had been left to the Cobb brothers, and Jordan Cobb had come here to this Minnesota woods of his, to carve out a resort—a retreat actually—for his people, and even though the Landing would cater to a clientele of mostly ill repute, patrons like Petruzzi, it was still Cobb's, and Cobb made the rules. Right now, Angelo Petruzzi was overstepping his bounds.

"You know, Angelo, I put this together for the family; for our guys. Their day-to-day activities from Chicago to Milwaukee to Minneapolis and St. Paul... well... that's a tough life. You and I know that. We did it for years. This resort is the ticket to relieve a bit of that toughness. And it's their safe-haven for when they're on the lam. Now, anyone who comes here can satisfy almost any whim, but it does run with rules; my rules. Not yours. I don't wanna get on your bad side, Angelo, but I just gotta say, a deal like this needs rules and you're not here to enforce them. I do that."

"What brought all this on?" Petruzzi asked.

"I just though, if we're talking completion of Cobb's Landing, we're talkin' expansion. That's dangerous. Might even be disastrous. It will be for sure if I don't keep control out here. Just thought that needed sayin'."

Petruzzi studied Cobb's face. Competence shined and so did courage. Cobb was right. The one always here should be the one in charge. He had always trusted Cobb. He trusted him with his life, why not this?

"I'll stay out of your way, Jordan. I'll try to keep my nose out of the Landing's business." Angelo Petruzzi rarely used an underling's first name, but Jordan Cobb was different. They had come up together; the two of them, through the ranks, and because of that Petruzzi considered Jordan Cobb his friend, not really an underling.

An airplane droned in the distance.

"Ours?" Petruzzi asked.

"Probably," Cobb answered.

"Will he stop here?"

"If he's one of ours, he will. He'll be coming from north of the border with whiskey. Some of it will unload here and the plane will need fuel."

"He going to Chicago?"

"After a stop outside St. Paul."

"Then we'll go with him. You do whatever you want with that Brooks kid. But do something. Or I will."

Jordan Cobb knew exactly what that meant. Let Petruzzi handle it, and Billy was a dead-man. He did see the need for action; Brooks had fucked up—badly! He damn near crashed on his landing; embarrassing for Cobb, dangerous for everyone else. Cobb chose him to pilot this flight so Petruzzi could bet his ass Cobb would do something—but killing? *Nah! A bit extreme.*

Billy didn't deserve to die, not over this. Angelo was overreacting just like Cobb knew he would. He always did when he flew. Everyone knew what no one would dare say. Angelo Petruzzi was scared shitless of airplanes and he always drank heavily when he had to fly, and booze made him mean—unreasonable.

The drone of the airplane grew in volume as it circled overhead. Cobb and Petruzzi watched, as the pilot set it down gracefully on the soft earth of the runway. It slid side-to-side, almost poetically, and then came to a gentle stop, short of the plane Billy Brooks had piloted.

"Now, that man knows how to handle those birds. I'm flyin' with him," Petruzzi said. "How about you have young Billy take the liquor load and this guy take us?"

The door to the airplane opened. A young man seemed to come from nowhere, from out of the brush. He quickly pushed a set of steps to the latest arrival's open door and then he disappeared back into the woods.

A tall, slender, blond-haired woman in her mid-twenties appeared in the doorway. Angelo Petruzzi studied her.

"Pilot?" he asked.

"Yup!"

"Jesus, Cobb!"

"I know."

"The kid?" Petruzzi asked.

"Jake Belle. He come to work for us a couple weeks ago."

"He know who we are?"

"Not yet," Cobb answered.

"Let's try and keep it like that. He from the town?"

"Yeah!"

The blond descended the steps. She pulled off a hat she had been wearing to keep her hair from obscuring her view while she flew. She shook her tangles free and let her hair fall to the middle of her back. The two top buttons of her blouse were unfastened, revealing a hint of cleavage.

"Ellen's not going to like her," Petruzzi whispered to Cobb.

"How was the flight, Erica?" Cobb asked.

"Smooth, Mr. Cobb. Conditions are perfect." Erica looked to the sky, a gentle blue; no more storm clouds. "It's a wonderful day to fly," she added as she approached Cobb and Petruzzi. She smiled, and then extended her hand. "Good to see you again, Mr. Cobb. Some of this load's yours. Still got that kid around, I see. He unloading, or shall I?" She held a hand in Petruzzi's direction.

"Angelo, this is Erica Braun. Maybe you remember her dad, Henry Braun?"

"The trigger-man from Milwaukee?"

Henry Braun had taught them both, when they were young. Henry was only a couple of years older, but had been in organized crime since he was thirteen. He was Angelo's and Jordan's mentor, and he had saved both of their lives on more than one occasion…before he got his.

"When she came to me wanting to be a pilot, and I found out she was Henry's kid; how could I say no? Good pilot, too."

Angelo Petruzzi and Jordan Cobb had been with Henry when he died. They both felt responsible.

Petruzzi took the girl's offered hand. "Good to meet you, Darlin'. You'll fly me back to Chicago. Brooks will

29

take your load to St. Paul."

Erica looked to Cobb.

"He's the boss," Cobb told her.

"I thought you were my boss," Erica said.

"I am. But he's mine. That makes him yours too."

Petruzzi released her hand.

"Now, Cobb. Tell me more about the kid you hired."

"He's just a kid from town."

"Living here or living in town?"

Petruzzi was concerned. Cobb's Landing was a retreat all right, but the mob's real use for it was as a stop-off for liquor trafficking. He did not want the place to spill over into the town. That could mean trouble, big trouble.

"Got him in a cabin. Agreement was that if he came to work for the summer, it was for the summer. He don't go home, not at all."

"Belle! Jake Belle!" Cobb yelled out.

Jake Belle poured out of the thick underbrush at full speed. He took a hard look at Petruzzi. He knew who he was. He had been close enough to hear most of the conversation between him and Cobb. Even more so, Jake knew what Petruzzi was. Dangerous! He looked away. He looked to Erica Braun.

"Want me to unload, Mr. Cobb?" Jake asked.

"Show him what to take off the plane, Erica."

Billy Brooks and Ellen Petruzzi approached the runway. Mrs. Petruzzi seemed better able to navigate than when they set out for the outhouse. The trek must have been sobering. She carried her classy, high-cost, high-heel shoes over her shoulder, like an unwanted garment. Her feet, her silk stockings having been discarded, were covered with mud.

Brooks was smiling—his face...red.

Jesus, Billy, Cobb thought. *Tell me you didn't tap that. Been gone long enough.*

"I need a drink," she said, looking to her husband.

"Not now," Petruzzi said. "We're leaving in a

minute."

"I better get the plane fired up," Brooks said.

"Been a change, Billy," Cobb said. "You're going to take the whiskey load to St. Paul. Erica will take your plane to Chicago."

Ellen Petruzzi glanced toward the steps to the plane Erica Braun had piloted in while she was in the privy. Erica had reached the top step. She swept an arm behind her head, brushed her long blond hair up, and tucked it under a hat.

"Who the hell is that?" Ellen asked, her piercing eyes flashing first to her husband, then to Erica Brawn's perfect figure, then back to her husband.

"That's our pilot."

"The hell it is."

"The hell it isn't. That's our pilot for the ride home. And that's all there is to it, Ellen. Get used to it."

Petruzzi turned his attention to Jake Belle. He was coming out of the plane, pushing a two-wheel cart full of whiskey cases. He thought of objecting to having a local youth at the Landing, and then thought better of it. War was in the air. There was trouble brewing between the outfit and a rival family. Others wanted in on the gang's whiskey connection to the north and Petruzzi had had balls enough to say no. Manpower was at a premium, and Angelo could spare no one right now. Rumor was that the Rosettis or the Polano's were determined to hit Petruzzi—maybe both of them—a compliment, really. No one would mess with him if he weren't doing damage. Besides, he had already agreed to stay out of the Landing's business, so he kept quiet about the boy.

Jordan Cobb had already crossed the bridge of indecision concerning whether or not to hire a local kid to help out, but these were tough times in the little town; people were flat broke. A boy Jake's age, gone from the family food budget for the summer, was a blessing. No one would come looking for him because that would mean they'd have to feed him. It was safe. The boy would cause no harm, no connection with the town.

Billy Brooks came out of the plane with another cart full of cases, followed by Erica Braun. Erica's cart was half-full.

"That's all of it for the Landing, Mr. Cobb," Erica said.

"If you folks are ready," she said to the Petruzzis, "Hop onboard," she pointed to the plane Billy Brooks had flown in. "We'll get you home."

Ellen Petruzzi followed Erica to the plane while her husband studied Brooks.

"Do something about him," Petruzzi ordered Cobb.

Jordan Cobb approached Billy Brooks at a high lope. On his way, he pulled a snub-nosed revolver from the small of his back and held it firmly. He pressed its barrel into Billy's forehead. He smiled. Brooks' brow filled with tiny beads of sweat. Cobb pulled the trigger.

CLICK!

"Let me down again, Billy, and there'll be a round in the chamber."

I'll bet the little son-of-a-bitch is pissing his pants right now, Cobb thought, as he walked back towards Angelo Petruzzi.

"Angelo, I wish you could stay longer," Cobb told Petruzzi.

"Next time. I'll be here for a couple weeks. Wouldn't have seen me today, but I had to protect our business up north. Everyone's trying to muscle in. Better watch your back. Me and you are gettin' way too popular, ya know?"

Petruzzi started to leave, then turned around. "Do something about this freaky airstrip, for Christ's sake. It scares the shit out of me. Plane slides every which way."

"That why you stopped here today, to check out the airstrip?"

"Yep!"

~*~

Jake Belle watched, as Petruzzi got on the plane. He then watched, as Billy Brooks stumbled up the steps to the cockpit of the whiskey plane, his face filled with fear. He watched, with amusement, as both planes taxied down the runway; one right after the other, and took off into the air. He did not quit watching until they were out of sight. Then he looked at Jordan Cobb.

He thought back to the day he first saw the handbill in town, the one advertising for a boy to work at the Landing. *"Room and board–Generous wage"* it had read. Still, it took several days before he would walk the four miles through the dense woods to apply. He was afraid of Cobb. Most of the town was. Cobb's reputation of being mob-connected had spread widely—rumors mostly— rumors that nearly stopped Jake. But…money, in a time when there was little of it, convinced him otherwise. He soon found himself employed, and in his new job he would witness a wide range of activities he would have missed, if he hadn't signed on. Today's was just the beginning.

Jake Belle thought Jordan Cobb to be a man of admirable talents, and because he was in that awkward stage between childhood and manhood, he found himself being molded by Cobb's thoughts and actions; but today's activities would teach Jake that choices had to be made, informed choices on what he found best in the man; for Jordan Cobb, Jake was now discovering, might well be a man of murderous deceits as well. The time to choose which of Jordan Cobb's traits he would take for his own had come. Now, as he thought through all he had witnessed at the airstrip, and pictured in his young mind the episode with Cobb and Billy Brooks and the gun, he chose. *I will someday be a man like Jordan Cobb. I will one day have such power over other men.*

Jordan Cobb turned an eye to his young apprentice. He seemed off in a distant land. "You daydreaming, Boy?" he asked

No response. "Boy?" he said a bit louder. He knew the teenage mind. He was a father himself. He knew teens had to be awakened now and then.

"Boy!" he shouted.

"Yes, Sir!"

"They're gone. Time to get back to work."

~*~

Cobb's Landing consisted of thirty-three buildings, of which twenty-six were for regular guests. Two cabins were reserved for special guests. A two-story house built of logs was Cobb's residence and a lodge, storehouse, greenhouse, and bathhouse rounded out the resort. The summer Jake started work for Cobb was also the year the crude airstrip would gain a terminal and a clubhouse would be added to the nine-hole golf course. They had been working on the latter, when the plane carrying the Petruzzis interrupted them.

The morning's excitement done with, it was back to the task. Concrete had been poured the previous fall, but now that spring was here, new growth was taking it over. The foundation needed clearing before walls could be built, and it was while they were in the process of that clearing that Jake had his first real conversation with Cobb. It began with an answer to Jakes curiosity about their current project.

"You know, this is going to be a nice little place for the golfers." Cobb went on. "I'll bet my brother would enjoy this."

"Will he come up for a visit?"

"No. No, he won't. I guess you could say we're building this in his memory."

"He's dead?"

"Near as I know. I heard he was anyway. We used to do a lot together. Even worked for the same whiskey runners." It was the first anything that might indicate gang activity was mentioned in front of the boy, but he

34

had already gathered as much, so said nothing.

"But….. I came here, he headed west, Reno first, and then, I think, outside of Seattle. Lots of business opportunities on the Pacific Coast, especially that close to the border. Anyway, I got a letter from him…said he was in some trouble. Bad trouble. 'Bout a half a year later, I get another letter. This one's from a lady saying she was his wife, or had been. Called herself Mae, I think. Anyway, she said she had some stuff of his she wanted to send my way. She said that he had disappeared—probably dead. I wrote back but never heard anything else."

Cobb rested on his shovel, like it was a cane.

"Yep. Poor bastard. He surely did like playing golf. Almost as much as he liked gambling on it."

"Might be that's what killed him," Jake offered.

"How's that?"

"Gamblin'…on golf. Maybe he got mixed up with the wrong guys."

Cobb gave the boy a curious look. It reminded Jake of the look his father would give him just before a reprimand or a smack.

"Huh! I never thought of that. That's just the kinda thing that coulda' happened. Pretty damn obvious, all things considered."

~*~

Two weeks flew by between Petruzzi's visit and the final stages of the clubhouse construction, and Jake and Cobb had many conversations. Airplanes came and went like clockwork, bringing in supplies and whiskey, and delivering and exchanging guests of the Landing. Young Jake Belle was getting to know his employer and he liked him; he was settling in to his strange new life rather nicely.

The high point of this new existence for Jake was his outdoor activities. He ran equipment. He was motorized.

35

He knew no other boys his age that could make such a claim. He mowed grass with a power mower. Cobb owned a tractor, an International Titan 10-20, and a 1930 Ford truck with a dump box, and Jake would operate them. He was in the land of miracles, the country of invention—and the airstrip, where guests would arrive and depart...a whole other world to a boy of seventeen...well...almost seventeen.

His duties indoors, however, well...that was a different story. These he would come to despise. In the cabins, he would see his first homosexual act. He would witness a murder. He would see his first naked woman. He would catch a man beating a woman and a woman beating a man. He saw alcohol and drug abuse, and two suicide attempts—one successful—one not, and in the lodge, he was required to serve men who he had seen beating the shit out of their wives; and women who had done the same to their men, and he did not like any of this. What he did like about the summer of '31 at Cobb's Landing, is that he met his first love, and it would be this first love and the duties of his work that would dwarf any experiences for the rest of his life.

~*~

It was early June. Jake and Cobb were nearing the end of the clubhouse project, when dark clouds rolled in from the west. The wind whipped around their faces and the clouds started to spit. The poplars and spruce swayed until their tops nearly touched the ground. The gentle rain turned into a downpour, and they made a dash inside. Once safe, they peered out at the bending trees. Branches snapped and crashed to the ground.

"Going to be a bad one," Cobb said.

"What'll we do? We got suppertime comin'. There's folks to feed in the lodge."

"Well, we can't worry about them. Not if they're fool enough to wander out in this storm. They'll just have to wait."

Jake was relieved. There were only a few guests at the Landing—too early in the season—but in one cabin a couple stayed, who always dined in the lodge. They were two lesbians, and even though they were generous tippers, Jake detested having to serve them. The storm would save him this time. He welcomed the storm if it meant delaying any service for those two.

Hail began to fall. It slammed against the window. Cobb stepped back, then reached out and snatched Jake's shirt collar. He pulled him from the window.

"That glass'll bust and you'll be wearing it in your eye, Boy."

Cobb walked to the bar. He grabbed two glasses and a bottle of whiskey, then filled the glasses.

"Here! This'll thaw you out," he told Jake as he handed him one of the glasses.

"No thanks," Jake said. He had never tried a drink. He always wanted to, but thought his boss might be testing him. "I don't drink," he explained.

"This isn't drinking, Boy. It's medicine against the storm. You don't drink it to get drunk. You drink it to keep yourself from coming down with pneumonia. Now take it and slam it down like this." Cobb put the glass to his lips. He tipped it up and let its contents run freely into his mouth. Then he swallowed without taking a breath. "Just like that, Boy. Now, you do it."

Jake took the whiskey and imitated his employer's method, all but the not breathing part. He choked. He gasped for air. Tears ran freely from his eyes. He tried to speak but no sound came out. Cobb patted him on the back.

"First time, eh?" Cobb said.

"Yeah!" Jake admitted.

He sat quietly, waiting for the burning to subside and a normal flow of air to return to his lungs. Just as he was catching his breath, he heard a strange sound. It was an incoming airplane. Its motor was cussing and sputtering.

Jake and Cobb stepped to the window. They looked off toward the airstrip, which lay just on the other side of a heavy stand of balsams, whose lower limbs had been trimmed so the golfers could have a clear view from the clubhouse. They wiped at the glass to clear it. The craft was coming at them fast, fire shooting from its nose like a dragon.

"It's going to hit us!" Jake yelled, as he covered his eyes.

"No! It's not," Cobb said.

He grabbed the boy and threw him to the floor. He plunged an arm over him, protectively.

"It's not going to hit us. Everything will be okay."

The plane passed close overhead. The deafening sound rattled both of them and shattered the window's glass down on them. Cobb tightened his hold on the boy. Jake began to shake violently.

"It's okay. It's okay," Cobb assured him.

~*~

As the airplane's engine smoothed and its huge mass climbed over the treetops, its pilot wiped at the sweat on his brow.

"Jesus Christ! That was close. You alright back there, Miss?" the plane's pilot asked.

His only passenger did not answer. He prayed she wasn't hurt. Should something happen to her; it would be the end of him. This was Jordan Cobb's daughter, and Jordan Cobb was a mob boss. If she were hurt, he would be hurt. If she were dead, he would be next. He banked the plane left as it climbed, hoping to gain enough altitude to see the runway better.

As he leveled, the girl frantically slid into the seat beside him. She looked stunned but unhurt. He gasped in relief.

~*~

Cobb and Jake rose. They looked out the jagged void where the window's glass had been. The airplane's engine resumed its sputtering for a moment and then it landed, just off the path. Its left wheel took the track and the right should have; the right wheel hit the rough grass beside the runway. The landing gear snapped after bouncing through a large washout that had been created by the heavy downpour. The right wing of the plane dug hard into the soft earth. The craft spun out of control and its wings splintered through the trees. Flames engulfed its nose. Cobb jumped to the door. He flung it open and ran for the airstrip.

"Amelia!" he shouted. "Amelia!"

Jake was close behind and nearly slammed into Cobb when he reached the plane. Cobb was frantically tugging at the door. The flames were snarling in the rain and slapping at Cobb. Jake placed his hands and eyes against the cracked and broken windows, trying to see in. Intense heat pushed him back. He could hear a body slamming against the plane's door from the inside. He needed to do something. He needed to help. Then Jake and Cobb both grabbed for the handle at the same time.

They timed their effort and muscle as one, pulling on the door, and gave it a colossal jerk. It screamed open, and a frantic, pretty redhead sailed past Cobb and landed in the arms of Jake Belle.

"Amelia?" Cobb said.

"Hello, Father!" the young redhead said, still clinging to Jake's neck.

"Move her to the other side of the runway," Cobb commanded Jake. "Anyone else in there, Amelia?" he asked, without taking a breath; it sounded like an extension of his orders to the boy.

Amelia hesitated for a moment, and then answered, "Just the pilot." Turning to Jake, she asked, "Who are you?"

"Jake. Jake Belle," Jake said as soon as he was sure

she had been addressing him. "I work for your father."

He sat her on the ground and turned to help Cobb. Cobb was just coming out of the wreckage, the plane's injured pilot in tow. A trickle of blood flowed from a cut over the pilot's left eye and an arm dangled like it was broken. Cobb's shirtsleeve was on fire. Jake rushed to put out the flame, but the rain beat him to it.

Cobb dragged the dazed and shaken pilot over to the other side of the runway and sat him on the wet grass beside Amelia. He leaned and kissed his daughter on the cheek.

"How's your mother?" he asked.

He talked as though nothing out of the ordinary had happened.

"She's fine. She sends her love."

The four of them sat there in the wet grass, and watched, as the airplane burned to an empty shell.

"I wish that she had come with you this time," Cobb said.

"Oh, Father, you know she hates the wilderness. She'll never come here."

She turned and looked into Jake Belle's eyes. She blinked, slowly, purposefully.

He looked deep into hers. He could not understand all that he saw there, but he knew he was in love.

Chapter Five

"Feel like some lunch?" Jacob Belle asked his grandson.

They had been at it for hours, and Adam had become so engrossed in his grandfather's account of the place called Cobb's Landing that he hadn't given food a thought. But the mention made his stomach growl. And one look at his grandfather told him the old gent needed to eat.

"You want to go someplace?"

"Nah! We can make a sandwich. Got a lot of cold cuts, from your Grandma's funeral. Ladies-aid girls dropped 'em here. Don't know why. Might as well use them up, though."

Jacob went to the refrigerator and pulled out a platter. He placed it on the table between them.

"When do you have to go back?" he asked as he fumbled through a cabinet for a loaf of bread.

"No set time," Adam said. *Shit! Why'd I say that? Now the old man will try to keep me here forever.* "That is, I'm free, until the work gets too piled up. Can I help you find something?"

"Grab the mustard and mayo—in the fridge. What do you do at your job?"

"I write technical manuals," Adam said.

"Maybe you could write the story of the Landing."

"I'm not that kind of writer. My stuff is more how-to. What your story needs is a novelist, or a historian. Not a how-to guy."

Jacob set two places at the table. "Dig in," he told Adam as he spread a generous layer of butter on his bread and chased it with a like amount of mayo.

"Ever heard of cholesterol?" Adam asked.

"You will stick around till we're done with the story, won't you?" he asked, ignoring Adam's comment.

"I'll try."

"All I want is the time to tell you this one story. Then, it's back to the big city for you. No more small-town old guys. Is that too much for an old man to ask of his only grandson?"

Probably, Adam thought, *but what the hell. I'm ahead at my job. I could take months, if I wished. And the story is interesting. And that Maggie?...well...cute.* "I'll see what I can do."

After lunch, Jacob Belle eased his tired body into an overstuffed recliner in his living room.

"Sit." He pointed to an armchair that faced him.

"You look tired," Adam said. "Sure you want to go on?"

"We'll keep going. A little bit further, anyway. Now...where were we?"

"I believe the plane carrying Amelia Cobb was burning beside the runway."

"That's right. It was my introduction to Amelia. She was just this skinny, freckle-covered, redheaded thing," he started. "Hell! She hadn't even grown tits yet. But, to me—I had just turned seventeen the week before—and, to me, she was a knockout." He gazed off into nothingness for a long moment. Then he returned to the story.

~*~

The rain let up. Jordan Cobb had been sitting alongside the runway with the others: Jake Belle, his daughter Amelia, and the pilot who had crashed the plane. He studied the wreckage, feeling grateful that Amelia had come through the incident unscathed. He explored his options. This was unacceptable. Something had to be done. The plane's pilot, a young man named Billy Brooks, the same kid who nearly crashed with Petruzzi in the plane a couple of weeks earlier, would have to be dealt with.

He was just coming around, rubbing at a sore shoulder and feeling the same as Cobb — grateful. Brooks realized that if something —anything— had happened to Jordan Cobb's only offspring, he was a dead man. That's the way things were. This was the mob. Billy Brooks never once diluted that truth. He never allowed himself to pretend that a mistake on his part would be forgiven. He did not work for a forgiving people; he worked for killing people. Still, he wondered as he sat there in the wet grass, what his punishment would be—not if it would be—but what it would be. He only knew it would not be death, and for that, he was grateful. He would soon know. Jordan Cobb gave him a half hour to check himself in and clean himself up. Then he was to see Cobb in his office.

Jordan Cobb did not look up when Billy Brooks entered his office. "I should shoot you now, and get it over with," Cobb said.

Billy Brooks broke into a sweat. He hadn't expected this reaction. "It was the weather, Mr. Cobb. The storm. I did the best I could."

"It wasn't good enough. Maybe if you hadn't damn near crashed last time, we could let it go this time. Maybe if you hadn't had Petruzzi onboard last time we could still overlook this. But that isn't the case, is it, Billy?"

"No, Sir."

Jordan Cobb slid a desk drawer open and pulled a handgun from it. He laid the gun on the desktop, barrel pointing in Billy Brooks' direction.

"You remember what I told you? Remember me saying there'd be a round in the chamber next time? Well... guess what, Billy. The gun I keep tucked in the back of my pants I leave a chamber empty, so I don't make the crack of my ass longer. This one, the one I keep in my desk, is fully loaded."

"I'm sorry, Mr. Cobb," Billy Brooks cried.

"So am I, Billy. But I told you what I would do. If I don't do it, Billy, nobody's going to respect me."

Brooks turned and ran from the room—like rabbit from a fox. Cobb fired once in the air and smiled.

Jake Belle heard most of what was said between Cobb and the pilot, and he heard the bullet crack from the barrel of Cobb's handgun and slam through the ceiling of his office. Once more, he secretly set his sights on becoming like his boss.

He had been setting up for dinnertime in the lodge. The rain had put an end to his outdoor duties for the day, and when weather prevented him from his usual work as groundskeeper, he worked at whatever anyone could find for him to do. Today it was setting up the lodge for the evening meal. To Jake it all sounded like the trouble was over but when Brooks shot by him, he knew he was wrong. Trouble was coming—not leaving. The angry look on Brooks' face told him that much.

"Mr. Brooks."

Brooks turned, looked, then went on running.

Jake didn't care that Brooks didn't answer. All he really wanted was another look at the man's face. He got it. The word trouble seemed inadequate.

Jake was so absorbed in his thoughts that he did not hear the girl approach.

"What time do they serve food around here, Jake Belle?" she asked.

Her sudden appearance startled him. He jumped. He gasped for air.

"I...er...I thought you'd be napping, I mean, what with the crash and all, Miss, ah, ah..."

She laughed. "Amelia," she said. "My name is Amelia—Amelia Cobb."

She snatched a towel from Jake's hand so swiftly and smoothly that the boy barely noticed. She then wiped the table in front of them with a grace and agility that made her movements appear dance-like. When she had finished, she smiled up at him over her shoulder. "It needs flowers," she said softly.

"What?" Jake asked.

"Flowers," she explained. "The table needs some cut flowers." She paused. Then she realized that the young man was simply not getting it. She supposed most young men wouldn't. "Fresh cut flowers so the guests have something soft and beautiful to look upon as they eat."

"Something soft and beautiful?" Jake questioned. He grew up in the north—in the wilderness—in an age where nothing but food, what little of it there was, was placed on the table. To put flowers in the path of the boarding house reach that everyone practiced in order to survive seemed preposterous.

"Come," she ordered as she took his hand in hers. "We'll go cut some."

Her hand was soft and warm. His was damp from sweat. He obeyed. It was that or let loose of the hand, and he was not about to do that.

Cobb watched with a degree of discomfort as the two youngsters disappeared through the door. *Ought to be an interesting summer,* he thought. He hadn't considered that the time of physical attraction, of teenage crushes, of first loves, had arrived. Given the age of his daughter and Jake's age, he should have expected it. Caution and observation would be the order of the day this season. He returned his attention to his work.

Amelia Cobb held tight to Jake Belle's hand while they walked the quarter-mile through woods. Either she did not mind the damp palm, or she simply didn't notice it. "Here we are," she said as they arrived at the greenhouse. She released his hand and grabbed for the building's door handle. She pulled the door open and walked in. "Come on. Let's get some flowers and get back. We don't want to miss dinner."

They harvested the flowers in silence, and when

Amelia decided they had enough, she started towards the door. "You're not much of a talker, are you Jake Belle?" she said.

"Nope," Jake said. They walked into the woods and started down the narrow pathway back to the lodge.

"How ever will we get to know each other then?" She smiled as she spoke. She knew she was embarrassing him. She enjoyed it. It was *power.* Her mother had taught her that she would one day have such power over some young man. She had no idea that it would turn out to be this pleasurable.

"I don't know," Jake admitted.

The youngsters walked on in silence.

"Perhaps, before the end of the summer, I will manage to get a decent conversation out of you, Mr. Belle." Amelia said as they approached the lodge.

Perhaps she would, Jake thought. He hoped so anyway. This silence was uncomfortable. He couldn't understand it. Girls never bothered him before—not like this one anyway, but this girl—Amelia Cobb—was different. He didn't know if it was because he worked for her father, a man to be respected, admired, and feared; or simply that she was a goddess. But with her, everything was different.

"Petruzzi will be here tomorrow," Cobb was saying to one of the kitchen staff. "Make sure we have enough supplies. There'll be a plane through here soon. Get your list ready. Give it to the pilot. But let him know the stuff needs to be here tomorrow. No fuck-up's this time."

Amelia did not react. Jake knew she had heard the vulgar words—she couldn't help but hear—but she had no response.

"Have you met Petruzzi?" she asked.

"I've seen him. But meet him? Not really," Jake said, watching her arrange the flowers in old quart canning jars he had been ordered to throw out the day before. He sure hoped Cobb didn't mind her using them for vases now.

"Well... try not to. He's fat, loud, and dangerous."
She did not look up from her flower arranging as she
spoke. "And I think he's Daddy's boss."

~*~

The sharp ring of Jacob Belle's telephone slammed
both men back into the present day.
"Get that," Jacob said as he eased out of his chair.
"It's for you."
"How would you know that?"
"Because nobody ever calls me."
He was right. The call was from Maggie. She thought
it late and wondered if Adam needed that ride.
"I sure do," Adam told her.
"I'll be along shortly," she promised.
He hung up, and then he looked around for his
grandfather. He found him at the old wooden bay
window that protruded from his second floor apartment
over the bank. He was gazing out at the street below.
"Why the hell do they do that?" he asked.
"Do what?"
"Put the temperature on the sign like that."
Adam walked to join him. He looked out at the sign.
"42 F".
"I guess so folks know how warm or cold it is."
"In Fahrenheit and Celsius?" He looked at Adam
curiously. "Who the hell needs the temperature in
Celsius?"
"Scientists?" Adam asked.
"Well... really. Aren't many of those around here.
Look! Isn't that your young lady?"
Maggie Bartell was pulling to the curb.
"I'd better run," Adam said. "Tomorrow?"
"Sure. Say...you know Tucci's Diner?"
Adam thought for a moment. "Yeah!"
"Meet me there about seven. I'll buy breakfast."

Chapter Six

"Were you waiting in the street long?" Maggie asked when Adam opened the door to her car.

"No. We saw you out the window when you pulled up."

"How was your time with your grandfather?"

"He tells an interesting story." Adam said.

"I wouldn't know. You're the first to hear it."

"Really?"

"Really. Cobb's Landing's a big mystery. Big secrets. Some folks know a little about it, rumors mostly, but Jacob Belle? He knows it all. And now you get to know it all, too. You should be honored." Her hope was that he should feel it also—honored that is—might make him stick around longer. "Tired?"

"Yeah. Hungry, as well. I think I'd like to go to the motel and order in pizza. Maybe catch a cable movie. Care to join me?" *Christ! Did I just ask a girl I barely know to go with me to a motel? That's class! Hope she's not offended. Wait! Does my motel even have cable?*

"I thought you might like to have dinner with me tonight."

"I'd like that. Where?"

"I thought I'd take you home with me—feed you a home cooked meal, then, treat you to a video."

"I am tired of restaurant food."

"Adam?" The time had come. Maggie could wait no longer to tell him what she needed to tell him.

"Yes?"

"I've moved you out of your motel."

Adam felt panic. "Why? Where am I to stay?"

"Your grandfather insisted. I've moved your things into your parents' house."

"But that place went for back taxes. Didn't it?"

"Your grandparents kept it up," Maggie said, "just in case you ever returned."

"Well, that's kind of them, but what makes anyone think I'll stay here?"

"They just hoped someday you might come home. I mean, for good," Maggie explained. "So did I," she added. Then she started her car and pulled into traffic.

That thought, that she might want him around, subdued the panic he had been feeling. He was interested. It was nice to know she was. He glanced at the sign on the bank. "Minus three Celsius," he said.

"What?"

"The sign on the bank. The time and temperature. The old man is right; that is stupid."

"Was he complaining about that again? He's always fussin' over that temperature sign. He even calls my father." Maggie's father served as mayor of Cedar Ridge. "Thinks with his position, he should be able to do something about it."

"What's he want done?"

"He wants the bank to change it—drop the Celsius part."

Maggie suddenly took a left turn. She did not bother to slow down.

"Hold on. I forgot about your car."

The passenger's side door swung open. Adam had to grab at the seat's fabric to stay in. He hadn't bothered with the belt. Maggie quickly snatched the sleeve of his jacket.

"You okay?"

"That woulda' been an E-ticket ride at Disneyland. Now, what about my car?"

"It's still at the motel."

She turned into the motel parking lot and pulled to a

stop beside his rental car.

Adam tried to start the car. No go.

"What now?" he asked.

"I can call the dealership in the morning if you'd like—have Morgan come and get it."

"That'll be great. Suppose they'll have a dependable one for me?"

"We can hope."

She glanced toward the pancake house.

"Look! There's Morgan's truck. Let's stop in and tell him to pick the car up."

She pulled the car across the street and into the lot at the restaurant before Adam could answer. She pulled to a stop next to Morgan's truck.

"Come on," she said. "This'll be fun."

Morgan was seated in the same place he had been when Adam saw him that morning. Maggie walked quietly up behind him, waited for him to put his coffee cup to his lips, then yelled, "Morgan!"

Adam saw great humor in her act. Morgan did not. He wiped at the coffee running down his chin.

"Goddamn it!" he said.

Maggie dangled the keys to Adam's rental in Morgan's face.

"It's across the street in the motel lot. Find him something that runs. Bring it to my place in the morning."

"Why? Is he stayin' over?" Morgan grinned.

Maggie stuck her tongue out, turned, and walked out of the café.

Maggie's home was immaculately clean and exceptionally comfortable. Its furnishings were tasteful and warm and her cooking...well...Adam thought she put out a damn fine meal; best he had tasted in a very long time, perhaps ever. After dinner, she treated him to a movie she had rented, a large bowl of popcorn that filled her living room with the aroma of a theatre, and pleasant conversation that lasted until nearly midnight.

Then she drove him home, or, to the house his parents had raised him in until that terrible night many years before; the night his parents died in a tragic auto accident and he was called upon to identify their bodies.

A deep sadness overcame him as they pulled in front of the place. She recognized it when she looked into his eyes, even in the dimness of her car's interior lighting, she could see it.

"You know, you could sleep on my sofa, or I could bring you back to the motel, that is, I mean...." she stammered.

"No. I'll eventually have to face this place. I might as well get it behind me tonight. I'll be alright."

"Want me to walk you to the door?"

"You mean, like a date?" His mood lightened at the thought. "No, I guess not. Next time we'll turn things around. Then I'll walk you to the door. How's that?"

"Why, Mr. Belle," she said. "Are you asking me for a date?"

"I-I-I guess I am," he stuttered. "Would you accept?"

"Only if I were to get a promise of a good night kiss when you walk me to the door."

He didn't need to be hit over the head. He moved to the driver's side of the car, opened the door, leaned his head in, and kissed her hard on the lips. "Good night," he told her. Then, he turned and walked to the front door of the home he had known as a teen.

The magic of the moment, the delightful taste of her kiss, the faint aroma of her perfume that still clung to his clothing as he entered the house, did little to counter the deep sadness he was to feel that night. He would have thought the loss of his parents so many years before wouldn't have surfaced so vividly. He was wrong. The memory of that night became as crisp as the movie he and Maggie had watched. He did not make it past the living room. He fell into his father's old recliner just as he had done on the night of their deaths. And he slept very little.

~*~

The bang from the old furnace as its forced air fan kicked into action startled Adam awake shortly before five. His life in the city was radiant steam and hot water heat that operated silently. It had been years since he had heard such a racket. His every muscle complained as he attempted to free himself from the broken down recliner. It seemed to take forever to stand. Once he did, he adjusted. Muscles loosened. Pain began to fade. He went to the front window of the house and looked outside. He stood there for more than a half hour drinking in the view. When he glimpsed the first sign of daylight on the horizon, he decided to make his way to the kitchen. *Coffee. I need coffee,* he silently told himself.

On the counter, near the sink, under a vase in which one leafy red rose proudly stood, was a note from Maggie. —*The coffee is set up—just pour the water through—call me when you've had a cup—555-7795—Maggie.* Adam smiled and placed the note back on the counter. He poured the water into the top of the coffee maker, then began a hunt for his cell phone. He found it tucked between the cushion and the arm of his father's old chair. He began to key in Maggie's phone number. A remarkably loud and irritating racket stopped him. The sound was indefinable at first. Then it became vaguely familiar. Finally, downright annoying. It was the ancient black wall phone that still hung on the wall of his mother's kitchen—a grotesque contraption from long ago, whose ring came from a bell, not from a pleasant electronic tone. Its numbers and letters hid behind a cumbersome dial rather than beneath sleek plastic buttons. *Atrocious,* he thought. He picked it up before it could ring again.

"Hello."

"How do you like the phone?" Maggie asked.

"It's got to go!"

She laughed. She promised not to ring it again. She told Adam the phone company would be upgrading the system that day and, by nightfall, he would be brought into the present century.

"Who's paying for all of this?" he asked.

"Petruzzi, I should imagine,"

"Petruzzi? From my grandfather's tales? That Petruzzi?"

"Well... kind of. It's a foundation that's funded with his money. Angelo Petruzzi stashed money, a lot of money, money from his illegal activities back in the days of prohibition. When he died, he left it all to the Cobb's."

"Wouldn't that be the mob's money?" Adam asked.

"Technically, I suppose."

"So why's the mob paying for my phone?"

"Because the money, after Jordan Cobb died, went to Amelia, and Amelia set up a foundation, The Cobb's Landing Foundation, and now Jacob Belle has some control of it."

"My grandfather?"

"Yes. But it's complicated. I really don't know much about it. Only your grandfather does. Speaking of your grandfather, he's an early riser. Why don't you shower and I'll be over to get you?"

"I suppose I'd better. He's probably at Tucci's already," Adam said.

"Tucci's?"

"Yeah. He asked me to meet him at Tucci's Diner. I think he said seven."

Adam thought of the pancake house he had shared with Leonard Morgan one morning ago, and became appreciative of his grandfathers suggestion to eat at Tucci's.

"I'll see you when you get here," he told her. Then he hung up.

~*~

53

Adam had showered and was ready when the doorbell announced Maggie Bartell's arrival. The unseasonably warm temperature contrasted that of yesterday to such a degree it came as a shock. He took off his winter coat and dropped it on the floor, just inside the house.

"I'll bet you forgot how fast it can change in the spring of the year around here," Maggie said.

"It must be seventeen Celsius," he said.

"What?"

"Oh, nothing. It's--ah--my grandfather," he started to explain.

"Right," she said. "The sign on the bank," She recalled. "It's only one of his many pet peeves."

"He has many, does he?"

"Many," she said. "Don't worry though, you'll get used to him. You know, he's really quite a remarkable man. Folks around here can't understand why your parents never allowed you near him when you were young. He's a bit eccentric perhaps, but not bad."

She pulled the car to the curb in front of the diner.

"Remember this old place?"

"I do." Tucci's Diner was a place where their generation hung out as teens—a place where youngsters were allowed to be themselves, and no one got into serious trouble because old man Tucci watched over them. It was also one of the places Adam could get a look at his grandfather. Tucci and Jacob Belle were friends and Tucci's Diner was a place Jacob frequented.

"I remember," he said as he held the door open for her.

They spotted Jacob Belle at a table near the back of the restaurant. He stood as they approached and reached a hand out towards Maggie. She put her hand in his. He pulled her close and kissed her on the cheek.

"I hope you don't mind me joining you for breakfast," she said.

"Not at all. You're family, my dear. You're welcome anytime."

Adam held a chair for Maggie, and then took one across from Jacob. "Good morning," he said. He was not comfortable calling him Grandfather, so avoided calling him anything at all. Breakfast at Tucci's Diner was pleasant. Old man Tucci stopped by the table but not until they had all finished eating.

"It's good to see you again," he told Adam, his Italian accent still very much intact. "I just wish you could have been here sooner, before your grandmother passed." He crossed himself and glanced up reverently. "You would have enjoyed some time with her."

"Were you at the funeral?" Adam asked. He meant nothing by the question. It was just that he hadn't recalled seeing him.

Tucci looked down. "I apologize. I haven't gone near that church for a long time. It's that old priest. He had me excommunicated," he said. "That son-of-a-bitch."

"Why?" Adam asked.

"Mob ties," he explained, "he said I had mob ties, and that was cause for excommunication in his eyes. That son-of-a-bitch."

"Do you have them?"

"Have what?"

"Mob ties."

"Of course I do," he said. "Many of us do, but that's no reason for excommunication. That son-of-a-bitch. If it is, then why ain't the rest of them excommunicated? Why not the Pope? Why not...."

"Well," Jacob Belle interrupted, "it's going to be a long enough day for you as it is, Adam. I suggest we get going."

He stood and reached for his wallet.

"Put that away, Jacob," Tucci insisted. "Breakfast is on me."

Jacob Belle did as his friend requested. Maggie left him and Adam with the promise that she would return at five. The two Belle men walked the three blocks back to Jacob's apartment in silence. Then, Jacob took up the story of his life at Cobb's Landing from the place he had left it the day before.

~*~

The damage done to the young body of Jake Belle seemed nothing short of catastrophic. He didn't know if it was the rain, the crash of the airplane, or catching the girl that was causing the most pain. He didn't really care. He just hurt. It was five in the morning, time to get up, and his body just did not want to move.

Jordan Cobb knew how his young assistant would feel. He sent Nurse Jennings and a bottle of liniment to ease his pain. Jake was shy, but today the nurse could see his naked body and he would not complain, and he was not embarrassed until six... when the tenderness began to subside. For it was then that it hit him. This wasn't just any female rubbing lotion over his naked body; it was one he knew.

"Feeling better?" she asked when he started to squirm a bit.

"Fine. I'm fine."

He reached for his blanket. He pulled it over himself. He took a hard look at Jennings. *She was the one alright.* He had walked into her cabin two days earlier. It was one of those rainy days when his outside duties gave way to indoor monotony. Jennings had been standing in the middle of the room, stark naked, when he opened the door. She made no attempt to move. She did not cover herself. Jake Belle thought he had moved quickly that day. He thought he had closed the door and left the room instantly. But now, he came to realize that some time had to have passed. He could see her clearly. He could picture her nude breasts; firm, with hard nipples. He remembered her slim waist and firm, tight stomach, and her smooth round hips. And her long slender legs. He even recalled thinking she had less pubic hair than he thought she should have. And when he began to picture the room, and the spot on the floor where her panties lay, he knew he had not moved quickly. He turned red.

"Well I guess you remember me don't you?"

"Y-y-yes ma'am."

She smiled. It was a friendly smile. "Don't worry with it, Jake Belle. We were bound to come to this moment, sooner or later. It's no big deal. It was an accident. Don't worry about it."

"Y-y-yes ma'am."

"We best get going," Jennings suggested. "Mr. Petruzzi's airplane should be here any minute."

Jake was grateful. It was time for this to end. But, when Jennings opened the door to his cabin, the sound of the incoming plane began to gain in volume.

"Shit! He's here. Get dressed and get to the runway. Look alive. Look your best," she shouted as she ran from his cabin.

Jake dove for a clean shirt and yesterday's bib overalls. He was still buttoning when he reached the runway and took up his position between Jordan Cobb and Nurse Jennings. Her presence indicated there would be passengers. Someone may be injured or ill.

"No clean pants?" Cobb asked.

"I dressed in a hurry, Mr. Cobb."

"Don't you want to make a good impression on Mr. Petruzzi?"

"But Mr. Petruzzi doesn't even know me."

"He knows of you," Cobb said.

Jake Belle said nothing. Nurse Jennings gave him a glance that said his silence was appropriate. He looked back in the direction of the lodge. *Where's Amelia? I thought she'd be here,* he thought.

~*~

What should I do, Mother? Amelia Cobb asked of a

parent who was not there. She wanted to see Jake Belle as soon she awoke, but remained in her room when she heard the plane land. She did not like Petruzzi. There was something dangerous about him that frightened her—something hidden deep within the man—some ugly spirit. *Why does Daddy put up with that man?* She wasn't afraid of Petruzzi simply because he was dangerous. She knew who he was. He was a mob boss. He had people killed. She had grown up with that. She had even seen Petruzzi and some of his men in action. They were beating a man tied to a chair, and they did it until he passed out. And she did not fear for her father. She knew that he and Petruzzi worked together for years, since before she was born. He might be her father's boss now but it hadn't always been that way. Her father and Petruzzi were friends. Yet, she was afraid of Petruzzi, and she avoided him whenever possible. It just seemed wise. She would stay in her room this morning. She would have to be content to wait for a better time to see Jake Belle.

~*~

Nurse Jennings wore a solemn look. Cobb seemed somehow different to Jake, as though he were worried about something, and it made Jake uncomfortable. Who was this man Petruzzi? What kind of man could scare Jordan Cobb?

"Exactly who is Mr. Petruzzi?" he asked Cobb.

"Don't worry about him, Boy. He probably won't even notice you."

Cobb motioned toward the aircraft's door with a hand that looked enormous to Jake Belle. *Bigger than my dad's,* he thought as the door slowly opened.

"Hold on, Angelo." Cobb said.

He began pushing a set of steps across the dirt runway, aiming it at the plane's door.

"Don't just stand there, Boy," he barked, "grab a

hold."

A large figure appeared in the opening long before the steps touched the body of the craft. It moved into the sun's light. Petruzzi—he filled the doorway—all muscle, didn't seem to have a neck, face scarred from ear to chin—*Knife fight,* Jake guessed. He hadn't noticed last time he saw Petruzzi. *Amelia was right. Petruzzi is scary,* he thought. *No wonder Cobb seemed cautious.*

"Push!" Cobb ordered. Then, "Back up, Boy," he said as the steps touched the plane. "Give him room."

Nurse Jennings approached and stood beside Jake. No one moved until Petruzzi's first foot landed on solid earth.

"How was the trip?" Cobb asked.

"Fucking rough," Petruzzi barked, "just like always. You'll find three puking drunks in there, Helen," Petruzzi told Nurse Jennings. "One of 'em's my wife. See what you can do."

"Yes, Sir," Jennings said as she hurried past.

Petruzzi swung a large clumsy hand at the girl's ass as she went sailing by. He missed. Had he connected, Jennings would have been knocked down.

"Who da fuck is dis?" Petruzzi slurred in Cobb's direction, waving an unsteady hand at Jake.

Jake didn't need the slurring. He knew Petruzzi was drunk. Hell... they always were, all of the passengers he helped from the planes. This one though, he could smell the liquor on. He turned his head aside to get out of the odor's path.

"Jake Belle."

"He the kid was wit'chu last time?"

"He is."

"You a good worker, Boy?" Petruzzi asked.

"Y-y-yes, M-Mister Petruzzi."

A commotion from behind them brought an abrupt end to their conversation. They turned to see a woman slide down the entire distance of the stairs. Helen Jennings was following quickly behind her, trying desperately to grab her. The woman's momentum was too great. Jennings effort was wasted. The woman thumped to a hard landing on the ground at the bottom of the steps.

"For Christ sakes, Ellen, can't ya fucking walk?" Petruzzi grumbled. "Fuckin' lush." He turned away and continued walking.

"Les go get a drink, Jordan, ol' friend,"

"Go help the nurse," Cobb told Jake.

Jake ran back to the plane. When he reached out to help, the woman swung at him. "Get this little pipsqueak away from me," she shouted at Jennings. Jake ducked, but Jennings, with a nod of her head, signaled him to step back in and help her.

"He's creepy," he said, as he and Jennings pulled the woman to her feet.

"You might want to take care with what you say," Jennings warned. "This is Mrs. Petruzzi."

"Somethin' I can do?"

It was one of the cooks. Normally he wouldn't be at the airstrip. Today, though, he needed to collect supplies he had ordered the day before.

"Check the plane. There are more."

Mrs. Petruzzi was looking at Jake. Jake thought she was studying his face so she could report him to Petruzzi for his careless remarks. She was not. She could barely make out his face. Jennings knew it.

"You take Mrs. Petruzzi to her cabin. I'll help the cook with the others."

Jake steadied Mrs. Petruzzi and she vomited the remainder of her bootleg whisky all over his clean shirt. He gagged—violently. The nurse began to gag. They both let go of Mrs. Petruzzi and she plummeted to the ground, landing hard on her backside.

"That's going to hurt when she sobers up," Jennings said. "Let's sit her back on the bottom step and let her come around a bit."

She glanced at Jake's shirt.

"You can go clean up. I'll handle her from here."
Jake did not hesitate. He ran. He ran back to his
cabin, tearing the vomit-soaked shirt from his back as he
ran. He grabbed another shirt and a fresh pair of bib
overalls, and then ran to the bathhouse. He wondered
along the way if Amelia Cobb would be there.

~*~

Amelia Cobb heard Angelo Petruzzi and her father
enter their house. She grabbed a towel with some
toiletries rolled inside, and slipped out the back door. It
was time for her shower. "Where are you, Jacob Belle?"
she asked of no one.

~*~

The cook handled the other occupants of the airplane
without incident, and without the need for Jennings'
help. Jennings cleaned Mrs. Petruzzi as much as possible
at the airstrip and walked her to her quarters. It was not
until they came to a long stairway leading to the resort's
upper level that she had trouble.

"I ain't climbing that goddamn thing," Ellen Petruzzi
slurred.

Quarters set aside for special guests—namely, mob
royalty—were above the rest of the resort's buildings. It
was an age-old custom that high society would look
down on the general population. It had been practiced
for centuries, and it was practiced at the Landing. Her
quarters were at the top of the stairs. Helen Jennings
swung Ellen Petruzzi over her shoulder like a sack of
potatoes and started up the steps. Ellen Petruzzi vomited
down her back.

~*~

The bathhouse at Cobb's Landing had been built on a

61

peninsula. Lake water was pumped into a tank by a small windmill. The tank was kept full, its contents warmed by the sun. From the tank, the warm water flowed inside to a shower adjacent to a small dressing area. Amelia Cobb had no idea she would run into the naked Jacob Belle when she opened that door. She screamed. Jake dropped to the floor. She screamed again. Then she slammed the door. Nurse Jennings ran down the pathway.

"What is it?" she yelled. "What's going on?"

She ran around the corner of the little building and almost into Amelia Cobb. "What is it? Are you alright?"

Jake Belle flew out of the bathhouse, soaking wet and half dressed.

"What the hell is this?" Jennings shouted.

"It's my fault," Amelia said excitedly. "I walked in on him."

"Did you forget to turn the sign, Jake?"

On the door of the bathhouse hung a sign. It read **OPEN** on one side and **OCCUPIED** on the other. There was also a hook type lock inside the door that he neglected to latch.

"What were you thinking?"

"What is that horrible smell?" Amelia asked, before Jake had time to answer Jennings.

"Mrs. Petruzzi puked on me." Jake said.

Jennings remembered. *Poor kid. I shouldn't have yelled at him. If Ellen Petruzzi had done me that way... wait a minute. She did do me that way.* "Just remember to turn the sign and lock the door, Jake," she said. "There are ladies here."

She went into the bathhouse. She smelled Ellen Petruzzi's vomit on her uniform. She forgot to turn the sign. She forgot to lock the door.

Jake walked off in the direction of the lodge. He needed to check in for his daily orders.

"You startled me," he said, as Amelia stepped beside him.

"I saw you naked," she said.

He turned a shade of red she had never before seen.

"What's wrong with you? Can't you breath?"

"Nothing's wrong. I'm fine."

"Why, that's more words than you spoke all day yesterday," she said. "Is that what it'll take to get a conversation out of you, a fright?"

"Maybe."

"So what were you doing in the bath house this time of day? I thought you were up and around hours ago."

"I told you. Mrs. Petruzzi's puked on me."

"How rude!" she said. "She actually threw up on you?"

"I don't think she meant to," Jake said. "I mean, she was sick, or drunk, or both, I guess."

"What are you going to do now?" she asked.

"I have to see your dad. I have to find out what I'm to do today."

"I'll walk with you," she offered.

Small talk filled their walk to the Cobb house. Amelia chose to duck into the bushes rather than to chance a meeting with Petruzzi. Jake went in. He returned quickly.

"What did he say?" Amelia asked.

"He told me to busy myself."

"It'll be that way all week."

"How do you know that?"

Jake hoped she was right. He wasn't lazy or wanting to avoid work; but he did want to spend time with Amelia.

"Because Petruzzi will be here at least that long and Daddy always spends all of his time with Petruzzi when he's here. That's how I know. We're going to have a lot of time to ourselves, Jacob Belle. A lot of time." Her smile filled her young face. "Want to walk me to the bath house? I was about to bathe when I found you there."

When she found me there naked, he thought. He felt

his face turning red again. "I'll walk you. But what about Nurse Jennings?"

"She'll be done by now. Come on."

She handed Jake her rolled-up towel. "I don't mean you have to walk me into the shower." She smiled at his embarrassment. *Mama was right. This is fun.* Her smile broadened. They walked in silence the rest of the way to the bathhouse.

~*~

Angelo Petruzzi stood nearly six feet and weighed in at just less than three hundred pounds. His hair was dark and receding. What remained on top of his head came to a sharp point in front. His career in organized crime started as an enforcer-for-hire. He worked his way up from there, aligning himself with whichever gangs needed his services, and when he realized he could go no higher on his own, he joined with Salvatore Bracco, head of the Bartoli family. Soon, he was second in command. Now he was the 'top-dog', a position he made sure everyone was aware of, including Jordan Cobb.

"I don't give a shit, Jordan. That kid can have the qualities of a goddamn saint. I still want him dead. Do you understand?"

Petruzzi's nose leaned left and sported a permanent swell. Too many direct hits. A deep-voiced Italian accent, which uttered mostly gangland gutter language, only enhanced his menacing appearance. Fear! Fear was his look—and power.

"Billy Brooks is gone, Angelo. He shot outa here like a bat outa hell after the crash. I don't know where he is."

"Why didn't ya just shoot 'im?"

"I shot at him," Cobb said.

That don't add up, Petruzzi thought. *Jordan Cobb is the straightest shot I ever seen. If 'e missed, 'e meant to miss!*

"You see 'im again... you shoot 'im!"

~*~

Adam Belle stood. He looked at his watch. As engrossed in his grandfather's story as he had become, the muscles in his back, stiff from easy-chair sitting, were telling him that the hour was getting late. It was nearing time to go.

"I gotta piss," his grandfather told him.

Adam helped Jacob to his feet, and, while Jacob was gone to the bathroom, called Maggie.

"Can you come for me? Or should I call a cab?"

"I'm on my way. I thought you'd be ready soon. I'm only ten minutes out. See you soon."

"I'll meet you out front," Adam said.

"No. I'll come up. My father's sending something over for your grandfather. I need to deliver it."

Jacob Belle came out of the bathroom. He looked for his grandson in the living room where he had left him. No Adam. *Where the hell did he get to?* he asked himself.

Adam came up behind him. "Maggie will be here in a few minutes. I figure you've had enough for one day."

"I have."

"One more question?"

"Shoot."

"What happened to the pilot... that Billy Brooks? Did Cobb shoot him? Or what?"

"Not right then. Billy escaped. He went into town."

"What'd he do there?"

"He went to church. It was a Saturday morning."

"Saturday? Church on Saturday?"

"How long has it been since you were a practicing Catholic?"

"Aside from Grandma's funeral; a long, long time."

"Then you need a little refresher. In the Catholic religion, priests say mass every day of the week. It was

Saturday and Billy Brooks hiked it into town, and he went to mass. Now, I wasn't there, so some of the story might be off a bit. But it's what I know from listening to others. Anyway, the story goes... Billy Brooks found something he hadn't counted on in church that day."

~*~

"In nomine Patris"— *Look at that girl in the front pew*—"et Filii"—*beautiful blond... seventeen? Eighteen?*—"et Spiritus"—*I hope she's eighteen... it'd be enough to have God after me*—"Sancti"— *don't need the law, too*—"Amen."

Anthony Russo was no priest. But he knew all the right words... in Latin. And he had almost everyone fooled—everyone but Billy Brooks.

Billy was in church that Saturday morning for one reason. Cobb had run him out of the camp—damn near shot him—and he had no other place to go. He had been born Catholic—raised Catholic—and since he was now all alone in a strange town, hundreds of miles from his home, he thought, *what the hell.* He'd go to church. It had been a long time. It had been an even longer time since he saw Russo, and it did take considerable studying, what with the priest outfit and him saying the mass and all, but he was sure of it. That... was definitely Anthony Russo, the hit-man who took out Salvatore Bracco, the family's head before Petruzzi. *What a stroke of luck!*

He sunk down in the pew. He did not want Russo making him. Not yet.

He made the sign of the cross.

Chapter Seven

Jacob Belle pulled himself from his chair and back into today with a yawn.

"I sure miss your grandmother," he said. "Spring is coming on strong. We used to take long walks about this time of evening in the spring, her and I, even when it was a bit cold. She used to insist. *'Button up,'* she'd say. *'Get out in the fresh air. It'll blow the winter stink off of ya.'* I sometimes miss those things."

He walked over to the window and looked out over Main Street. He stood still. Silent. Time passed. Too much time, Adam thought. He worried. Something was wrong. Jacob slid a finger under the right lens of his glasses. He brushed a single tear away.

"I told Mayor Buckley not to let them put that stupid flashing red light on that corner." He pointed to the intersection in front of the bank. "At night that damn thing flashes on and off constantly. It shines right through the curtains. Makes the place look like a whorehouse."

Adam could not hide his amusement. Jacob turned. He saw his grin.

"Think that's funny, do you?"

"Yes, Sir! I guess I do." "Well you try to watch the news with that red light flashing on and off, on and off, on and…"

"I get the picture."

"What the hell did we need a light there for in the first place?" he asked. "We already had a four-way stop. It did the job just fine. We didn't need that annoying piece of shit." He looked at Adam for a long moment, waiting for his input.

"What can I do about it?" Adam finally asked.

"You can talk to your girlfriend."

"Maggie?"

"Yes! Maggie."

"She's really not a girlfriend, at least not mine," Adam told him.

"Sure she is. She just hasn't told you yet."

~*~

Maggie Bartell balanced her load. She had no free hand to ring the bell with. "HEH! JACOB! ADAM!" she yelled. "OPEN THE DOOR!"

"That's her now." Jacob said. "Better get it."

Adam pulled the door open. "Let me take that," he said. He grabbed a wicker basket from her arms. "That's a real lazy-man's load you have going. What should I do with this?"

"Take it to the table. It's your grandfather's dinner."

Adam placed the basket on the table. He opened it. He studied its contents. He breathed in their aroma. "I'm eating here," he said.

"As much as I appreciate the compliment, no, you're not. I'm taking you someplace special. My treat."

Jacob looked inside. He smiled.

Adam whispered, "Why don't you just ask her?"

"Ask her what?"

"About getting rid of the light."

He looked towards the window. Dusk was rapidly approaching. The red glowed through the lace curtains, illuminating the wicker basket on the table.

"Alright, I will."

"Maggie," he started, "you think your father could get that thing out of here?"

Maggie looked at the basket. She knew exactly what he was talking about. He had mentioned it numerous times to the mayor, but no one ever took the complaint serious before. *I guess nobody ever saw the thing in action,* she thought as the basket lit up.

"I'll talk to him," she said. "That's… very annoying."

"I would appreciate that," Jacob told her.

"Speaking of my father." She handed him a manila envelope. "He needs your signature on these papers."

Jacob emptied the envelope and spread its contents out on the table. He began signing pages after a quick review of each of them. Then he came to one page he studied in detail.

"Tell your dad this one will need to be mailed. I can't approve it."

He stuck those he had signed in the envelope and handed her the one he hadn't signed.

Maggie picked up the paper and glanced at it. Then she put it in with the others.

"I'll tell him," she said. "Were you boys about done for the day?"

"Unless Adam has questions we are," Jacob said.

"Nothing that can't wait."

Jacob Belle rifled through Maggie's basket as Maggie and Adam started for the door. When he heard the first squeal of the hinges he turned towards the sound.

"See you both at Tucci's in the morning."

"Oh! I almost forgot," Maggie said. "The lake's opened. We can reach the Landing by water any time you wish."

Jacob Belle perked like a deer at the sound of a snapping twig. "When do you want to go?"

"How about Sunday," Maggie suggested. "The temperature is supposed to climb into the mid sixties."

Fahrenheit? Or Celsius?, Adam thought of asking. He thought better of it. *Get him going on that and we'll never eat.* "We can get the winter's stink blown off of us," he said instead.

"That we can," Jacob said.

~*~

The restaurant Maggie chose was thirty miles away, a distance she was pleased to drive so long as it took them someplace with class. Eateries in Cedar Ridge were adequate, but lacked ambiance. She had made reservations that were to include a table overlooking the river, a view for romance.

"What's the name of this place?" Adam asked.

"The restaurant? River's Edge."

"It's quite nice." He looked around him. "Not really new though, is it?"

"It's been around awhile. Since before we graduated."

"How about that broken-down patch of foundations we passed just before we got here? Was that once a town?"

"That's what's left of Morgan's Junction."

"What happened to it?"

"I don't know. It would be fun to find out though, wouldn't it?"

"How long ago did it exist?" Adam found himself fascinated with old towns these days, since his recent interest in Cobb's Landing began to form and grow. He looked out the window—up river. The late afternoon sun had faded, but left enough light behind that he could still make out the old bridge they had crossed to get to the restaurant. It was at the bridge that the town had been. A couple of its original buildings, paint long gone and roofs caving in, still stood, silhouetted against the setting sun.

"It started back in the thirties."

"I thought I knew all the towns around here."

"You probably didn't venture out this far, Adam. Thirty miles was a long distance when we were kids."

"Got anything to do with old Leonard Morgan?"

"As a matter of fact, it does. This is where Sheriff

Morgan's widow moved her family. It was only a farm at that time, though, owned and operated by the sheriff's two younger brothers. The town just kind of grew from there."

The couple enjoyed their meal, the view, each other's company and delightful small talk that did not quit as they journeyed home afterwards. Maggie suggested they go to her place. Adam did not object.

~*~

Adam awoke just past seven, in an unfamiliar bed, in a strange house, face to face with a beautiful woman he did not remember, until he became fully conscious. As the delightful images of last evening's thrills came clear, he chose to allow ten undisturbed minutes to pass while he watched her sleep. He wanted more but his shoulder, the one Maggie was using like a pillow, began to ache. He tried to reposition himself without awakening her. Luck wouldn't have it.

"Good morning," she said as she snuggled closer.

"Good morning."

"I need coffee," she said.

"I should have gotten up and made you some, but I've been selfishly laying here, awake, enjoying the view. It was thoughtless of me,"

"Don't worry," she said. She snuggled closer. "You're not required to do such things until the second sleepover." She bit gently on his neck. "What time is it?"

"Just after seven."

She bolted to a sitting position and brushed her long soft hair back from her face. "My God!" she said. "Your grandfather. He's probably been waiting at Tucci's for half an hour already." She swung her legs over the edge of the bed. The covers fell from around her shoulders. "I'll shower quickly," she said, as she stood. Her hair fell to the middle of her back and swayed gently from side to side as she walked. Adam watched her graceful

movements as she hurried from the bedroom. *Poetry!*
Magic!

"Can't he wait?" he said as she disappeared around
the corner.

Maggie peeked back at him through the doorway.
"You're getting to know him. Does he strike you as
someone who'll wait?" She waved a hand. "Bye!"

Adam leaned against the headboard. It seemed like
only seconds before he heard her say, "The shower's
yours. I'll make coffee and call Tucci's."

After a quick shower, Adam dressed in the clothes he
had on when he got to Maggie's the night before.
Maggie came around the corner, coffee cups in hand, as
he was buttoning his shirt. The two top buttons were
missing.

"Maybe we need to stop by your place and let you
change." She glanced at her watch. *Eight-fifteen.*
"Maybe not!"

The drive to Tucci's was fast. There was little time
for talk, but Adam did manage to tell Maggie that he
needed to make it a short day with his grandfather. He
had to check in with his work. He had left things
dangling. "Could you pick me up at three?" he asked

"I should be done by then."

"Big day planned?"

"Enormous. I have to see if I can solve Grandfather
Belle's dilemma with the flashing red light at the
intersection by the bank."

She pulled the car to the curb in front of Tucci's
Diner.

"It's about time you two got out of bed and showed
up for breakfast." Jacob Belle shouted across the dining
area as Adam and Maggie entered. He was at his usual
table, the one where he and old man Tucci had been
having their morning coffee together for decades. They
seemed to like the back corner.

The sound of his greeting was resounding. Most of
Tucci's patrons turned to look at the newcomers.

Embarrassed, Maggie and Adam made their way to Jacob's table and sat down.

"Good morning Grandfather Belle," Maggie said.

"Tell me all about your date," he said.

"We had a very nice time. It was a very good meal," Adam said.

The waitress took Adam and Maggie's order after placing a cup of coffee in front of them.

"You had much more than a good meal." He reached across the table, put a finger at the lowest of Adam's missing buttons and flipped upward. "Tucci. This look like the same shirt he had on yesterday?"

"Nope! That one had buttons."

"For Christ sakes," Adam said. "Could you two just leave it alone."

He turned to face Maggie. She blushed. He chose to change the subject—throw the ball back in his grandfather's court.

"You going to tell me all about you and Amelia Cobb in the shower this morning?"

"I'll bet you're the kind who reads the last chapter of the book first, aren't you?" he asked. "You'll learn all there is to know on that and many other subjects, but you'll learn them in order." He paused for a long moment, then looked at his wristwatch. "I don't know how much you'll learn today though. The day's half gone."

Adam glanced at the clock on the wall over the counter. A memory. *Maggie and I once shared a milkshake under that clock. Two straws. We were teens.* "9:37".

"Would you look at that time? The day is almost gone. Whatever have we done, Maggie?"

"You'll see when you reach my age and there's little time left," the old man said. "You'll understand the value of the morning's first few hours then. Now eat up and let's get to the apartment. I have a lot to tell you today."

The side of his face started to twitch slightly. His skin started to pale.

"Are you okay?" Adam asked.

"I'm fine," he said.

"Are you sure? Because, I mean, you're a bit pale."

"I said I'm fine," he said, a bit louder. Droplets of sweat formed above his lip.

"He has a little con……"

"Shut up, Tucci," Jacob cut the other man off in mid-sentence.

"You have a condition?"

"Let's go."

He stood. He reached into his pocket, pulled out a wad of bills and tossed it on the table.

"Let's go," he repeated.

The color had returned to his face.

"Take your money, Jacob," Tucci called out.

"Give it to that pretty young waitress you just hired," he said. "She'll earn it before she's done putting up with us."

Outside the diner, Maggie excused herself and promised to return for Adam at three. As she got into her car, Adam realized his grandfather was watching her.

"You're a lucky man, Adam Belle," he said. Then he turned and began his slow walk to his apartment.

Adam followed.

Once inside his living room Adam thought his grandfather's breathing seemed more labored than it had been yesterday—noticeably more.

"Are you sure you're alright?"

"Did you know the bank downstairs once got held up?" he asked, ignoring Adam's question.

"No. I didn't. When was that?"

"Oh, it was a long time ago. I was just a kid. A lady got killed right here in this very apartment."

He rose from his chair. "Come on. I'll show you."

Adam followed him to the kitchen where he flopped back the corner of a rug under the table.

"See?" He pointed out a small flaw in the hardwood floor. "That's the bullet hole."

"Did it have anything to do with the Landing?"

"Everything." He turned silent. He leaned back in his chair and closed his eyes.

"Tell me about the holdup."

He smiled. He opened his eyes. He chuckled.

"Did I tell you about Amelia saving my life?"

"No."

"Let's do that. The holdup is a bit more into the story."

"So why bring it up now?"

"To keep you curious."

"I'm curious enough."

He smiled. "Does that mean you'll be sticking around for a while?"

"I haven't ruled it out. Now, can we get on with the story? Please?"

~*~

"Amelia," he began, "had been right. Jordan Cobb's entire time was devoted to Angelo Petruzzi when he was at the Landing."

It was a week of sunshine. Young Jake Belle was fortunate indeed. The boss was busy. Warm, dry days kept him from inside work for the most part. He loved his job. He loved his life. And he was rapidly learning just what it would be to love a girl.

Jordan Cobb had his issues. Billy Brooks was still at large, and Angelo Petruzzi was relentlessly applying pressure. He wanted Billy Brooks found. He wanted him dead. And he demanded that Cobb make it all happen.

Further complicating his week, Cobb was tied to Petruzzi. It left him with no time for keeping a vigilant eye on his daughter—and that would lead to real problems. He would lose control. Teen-aged hormones would take over. He knew Amelia wanted to spend all of her time with the young man of her dreams, and that was something he would never willingly allow; but now, with Petruzzi and all of his demands in the picture, Cobb grew more and more powerless as the week played out. It was discomforting.

Amelia knew Jake would be out of her father's sight all week. She would see to it that he would be in hers.

~*~

Jake always rose early. It had become his habit over the years. Back home it had been the safe thing to do—rise before anyone—be out of the house and out of sight before his father rose. It wasn't that he had an extraordinarily mean father; it was just that he had been born into hard times. Folks had trouble making ends meet just feeding themselves and their families. Jake's father was no different than most fathers of the day. Depression begat depression, and depressed fathers sometimes took things out on their children. It was the way things were—the law of the time. It was in the boy's best interest that he got out early. He would do all that he could to help feed the family, but he would keep his distance. Then, and only then, did he get along with his father.

At five AM, Jake was at the airstrip with a tractor and a logging chain. He was determined to clear the wreckage of Billy Brooks' downed airplane. The tractor idled. Jake struggled to tie the chain to a large chunk of metal. With no holes in which to plant a hook, he wrapped the chain around the piece and hooked it to itself. He got back on the tractor. He gave it a little throttle. When he slipped the clutch the tractor's front wheels jumped completely off of the ground. The chain popped loose. The hook sailed past Jake's right ear and smashed into the hood of the tractor, leaving a baseball-sized dent behind.

"Are you trying to kill yourself, or kill me, or just kill

the tractor, Jake Belle?" Amelia's voice came from beside him.

"I didn't see you. Where were you? That chain could have killed you," Jake said excitedly.

In his excitement he jumped from the tractor, neglecting to put the transmission in neutral. Its front end once again left the ground. He chased the machine, trying to get back on, and nearly ran himself over in the process.

Amelia grabbed for Jake's shirt, clamped hard into its material with strong fingers, and stopped him short of the large rolling steel wheel. The tractor barreled off into the thick woods, uprooting tree after tree. Finally, it plowed into a huge, immovable oak. Its wheels dug up dirt until the tractor's engine gave in and sputtered to a stop. She watched as Jake's look changed from excitement to terror.

"It's only a machine," she said.

"But it's your father's machine."

"Actually, it's Petruzzi's machine, the mob's machine," Amelia corrected.

"Petruzzi's? The mob's?"

"You didn't know?"

"Know what?"

"The land's my dad's. Everything else is the mob's."

Jake looked at the dented tractor. He winced. The nasty scar on Petruzzi's face came into focus. He shuddered.

"You okay?" Amelia asked him. She had grown up mob. Jake's reaction she found strange. "You scared of them?"

Jake thought for a moment. Petruzzi's menacing frame came to mind. Damn right he was scared. "Not so much," he lied. "What are you doing out here this early anyway?" he asked.

She was out early because she wanted to see him. But she would not tell him that. That would be far too bold for a lady, even one who was mob. "I was on my way to the bathhouse. Will you walk me?"

He took a good look at her. He supposed it had been the commotion with the snapping chain and the runaway tractor that kept him from noticing that she was wearing a thin nightgown and had a towel draped over her shoulders. The sun behind her shone through her gown—just a bit. Breasts—they were small, but they were breasts. *Had she grown them overnight? Had she grown them just for him? Of course he would walk her to the bathhouse.*

"You know, Jake Belle, you're in the mob too," Amelia said as they approached the bathhouse.

He thought it through. He guessed she was right, after all, he had made a choice to be a man like her father and he was mob. "I know," he agreed.

~*~

The early morning banging on Cobb's door startled him awake.

His week had been tough: days filled with meetings and planning and Petruzzi, nights filled with entertaining until well after dark. This morning's plan, now that things were finally calming, had been to sleep in. He had not set an alarm. He sat upright and swung his legs over the side of the bed. He reached for his pants. Within seconds he was at the door. It was Petruzzi.

"She's O.D.'d!" he shouted. He was dressed in underwear. "It's Ellen. She's overdosed herself. She drank almost all night. Took some pills, too. She's on the floor, flopping like a goddamn fish. Do something, Cobb. Fuck!"

"Get Jennings," Cobb told Petruzzi. He pointed at her cabin across the courtyard. "I'll meet you at your cabin."

Cobb ran for the stairway that had been cut into the bank. He took the steps two and three at a time. The Petruzzi were in the largest of the units. Cobb entered. Ellen Petruzzi was still flopping, just as Petruzzi had described, like a fish. Her convulsions had been so violent that she had managed to open a nasty gash in the back of her head. She was bleeding all over the floor. Her silk robe had fallen completely open. She was naked under it. Cobb had no objection to the nude female form, but one that was flopping was hideous indeed. Instinctively, he covered her. The weight of the quilt he had used seemed to slow her movement. He wondered if what Jennings had once told him was true. She said sometimes people having fits bit their own tongue off. He hadn't thought it true but decided not to chance it. He looked around for something he could stick between her teeth. He spotted a pair of her underwear. He grabbed them, wadded them up, pried her mouth open, and inserted them between Ellen Petruzzi's teeth.

The initial plan for Cobb's Landing had included a full medical staff with an onboard physician. The doctor who showed had some small disagreement with Angelo Petruzzi and disappeared without ever treating a patient. Helen Jennings, the Landing's nurse, was the entire medical staff now. Helen was good. She could handle the average medical emergency like a pro. But when it came to a half naked, middle-aged wife of a mob boss convulsing on the floor of her cabin? Well... Helen was at a loss. The situation towered over her abilities. She stood there by Cobb. She stared at the Petruzzi woman. She rocked from side to side, tugging at her own hair until Cobb, quietly and gently, leaned close to her ear and whispered, "Do something, Helen, or we're both dead.*"

Jennings took a deep breath, and then dashed to the flopping woman's side.

"What is this in her mouth?" she asked.

"Underwear," Cobb said. "I thought she might bite her tongue or something."

"You were right," she said, "but let's get something a little more solid."

Petruzzi and Cobb began looking around the room.

79

Jennings grew impatient. "A stick," she shouted, "a twig—anything about the size of your finger. Move!"

Both men flew through the open cabin door. Within seconds, they were back with a half-inch diameter twig about a foot long. Jennings took it.

"Help me pry her mouth open."

She traded the underwear for the twig. Then she ripped a long piece of cloth from the bed sheet. She tied the twig in place so the woman's convulsions would not shake it loose. Once that was done, Jennings tended the bleeding wound on Ellen Petruzzi's head.

Mrs. Petruzzi started to calm. Soon she was still.

"Is she coming out of it?" Petruzzi asked.

"I don't know," Jennings said. "She's lost a lot of blood. She might just be too weak to flop."

She continued to dress the wound. She wanted the woman to snap out of it. Maybe she wouldn't. Maybe it was too late.

"I wish we had a doctor here," Jennings said.

"Why the fuck don't we have a doctor, Cobb?" Petruzzi demanded.

"Because you ordered the doctor shot," Cobb said. "Remember that?"

"Alright!" said the nurse. "That's enough. We don't have time for this. We have to get this poor woman to a doctor. We need to take her into town."

"No!" both men shouted at the same time.

Nurse Jennings stared at them in disbelief.

"We can't do that, Helen," Cobb said. "We can't take the chance of alerting the town. The law will be out here. All hell will bust loose. They'll be trying to shut the Landing down. It'll be war, Helen. We can't risk it."

"But this is Mrs. Petruzzi," Jennings said, thinking it might make a difference.

"We won't risk it," Petruzzi said.

That was too clear for Jennings. She knew who she was. She was mob. And she knew wherein her loyalties must lie, but this was a human life, and one of them.

Helen Jennings did not like Ellen Petruzzi, but to let her die, when death was preventable, was wrong. It was crossing a line that Helen did not want to cross, and it did not settle well. Petruzzi could see it in her eyes.

"Don't even think about it, Darlin'. Do anything like's on your mind right now, and the only thing that will happen is there'll be two dead women instead of one. You got that, Darlin'?"

"Yes, Sir," she said.

Ellen Petruzzi began to come around. She sat up, slowly…carefully. She began to vomit.

"Help me get this thing out of her mouth. She'll choke to death."

She fumbled with the knots. Cobb pulled a knife from his pocket. He cut the cloth. Mrs. Petruzzi jerked to the side when she felt the cold steel touch her cheek. The twig fell from between her teeth. Ellen Petruzzi started coughing and spitting. Jennings patted her back. Then Ellen calmed.

She glared at the homemade devise.

"What am I," she slurred, "a goddamn horse? Dija havta put a fuckin bit in my mouth?"

She tried to stand, but fell back. "Christ!" she said. "I'm dizzy!"

"You've lost some blood," Jennings explained.

"Who the hell are you?" Ellen Petruzzi demanded, unable to recognize the nurse who had helped her from the airplane to her cabin earlier in the week.

She detested having been handled by a stranger. She swung a hand at Jennings. In her current state, however, she missed Jennings by nearly a foot.

"Get this pathetic creature away from me, Angelo," she demanded.

Her speech was getting better. Jennings took it as a sign. The incorrigible woman was on the mend. She moved back out of reach.

"She'll still need medical attention," Jennings told Petruzzi. "She still needs to be seen by a doctor."

An airplane engine sounded in the distance.

"That's one of ours coming in." Cobb said. "It's ahead of schedule. Shouldn't be here for several hours."

"When will it take back off?" Petruzzi asked. "We'll take this old broad out of here. Get her to see a doc someplace else."

"The pilot will need some rest. Several hours," Cobb said, "Then he can safely fly again. I like them to get at least eight off, and a good meal."

"Haven't you got another pilot?" Petruzzi asked. He did not feel that an eight-hour delay was in his wife's best interest.

"Brooks is the only one we'd have. But we haven't found him yet."

"Well, when you do, you do what you're supposed to with him. We'll wait. Jennings, you stay with Ellen. Give the pilot a couple hours. Tell him to sleep fast."

Cobb looked at Jennings. She rolled her eyes back. *Better than having her here permanently,* she thought. *Or... Even worse! Having her die at the Landing.*

"You aren't taking me out of here," Ellen Petruzzi objected.

"Yes I am," her husband told her.

"Are you flying with me?" she asked.

"Yes, Ellen, I will be with you." He was becoming aggravated. "What kind of husband would I be if I didn't go with my ailing wife? What the hell would people think if you died on the plane and I sent you alone?"

"What about your little friend?"

"What little friend?"

"Your little faggot friend," she said. "You know very well who I'm talking about, Angelo. That little son-of-a-bitch: Tommy Delaney. He's coming in on that plane. You know damn well he is. And so do I."

When she drank to excess, Ellen Petruzzi accused. It could be anything. Truth? Seldom! But always, Angelo was the recipient.

"I should imagine you'll want to stick around—be

with him."

"Ellen!" Petruzzi warned.

"Oh, don't 'Ellen' me, Angelo," she said. "Just put me on that plane. You and your little faggot have yourselves a gay old time. I don't want to be around either one of you. Just stick me on the goddamn plane and forget about me." She laid back flat on the floor and turned away from her husband. "And when I end up laid out with quarters on my eyes, you and little Tommy Gun, isn't that your pet name for him? You and the little queer can live out you're simple lives without any concern over me."

Petruzzi walked out of the cabin, leaving his wife in Jennings' care. He had business to take care of—urgent business.

~*~

Jake Belle had been sitting outside the bathhouse, waiting for Amelia Cobb to finish her morning shower. He prayed for two things. First, he pleaded with God to somehow turn his head should the girl suddenly appear from the building naked. Second, should Jordan Cobb happen along at the wrong time, that God would also turn Cobb's head. Jake Belle had no intention of turning his.

The anticipation that he felt as he heard the shower stop was agonizing. She would be coming. He could hear her stir. He saw the handle of the bathhouse door move. There hadn't been time for her to dress. He was to get his wish. He looked around. No Jordan Cobb. No Nurse Jennings. No one at all. He sighed in relief. He concentrated. He was paralyzed.

Then came the sound of an airplane engine. It was coming in fast. It was his job—he had to go. Even the prospect of seeing the beautiful Amelia Cobb, the forbidden nectar of his life, naked, would not get in the way of him doing his job. He would run, not walk, to the airfield.

"Where are you going?" Amelia yelled at Jake Belle's back, just as it disappeared into the thick underbrush. She had emerged from the building in a hurry because she too had heard the planes roaring engines. She was stark naked, dragging her towel behind her. He did not turn to look. He had missed the very sight she had wanted him to see.

"I have to get to the airport," he shouted back through the brush. He dared not turn around for fear he would poke his eye out on a low-hanging branch like one of his school chums had done. "The plane is landing."

Amelia turned, stomped a bare foot on the ground, and dragged herself and her towel back into the bathhouse. She would go to the airstrip when she was dried and dressed and tell the young man what he had missed. *That's what Mama would do,* she supposed.

~*~

The first passenger to get off the plane was a young, slender, blond-haired man in his mid twenties. Another man, darker-haired, with a moustache, followed him closely. The second man was a skinny, pale, sickly specimen. He looked odd—out of place. Jake did not know why, but he instinctively knew two things. There was reason for concern with this strange individual, and he did not like this person.

"He's a druggie," Amelia whispered in Jake's ear as she walked up behind him. She had watched him studying the guy with the moustache. "You can see it in his eyes."

She had a lot of experience with drug users. There were many of them in the mob. They were generally those who did some sort of undesirable task within the organization, killing—torture— prostitution—like that. She had always reasoned that the purpose of the drugs was so that these people would not have to dwell on their sins.

"Best stay clear of him," she warned.

"I don't see anything in his eyes," Jake said.

"That's what I mean. There's nothing to see. They're hollow." She paused briefly. "Kind of ghostly, isn't it?" Jake couldn't disagree.

The two men approached Jake and Amelia.

"Are you going to take our bags, Boy?" the first man asked, his voice, feminine, disconcerting. They didn't wait for Jake to answer. They dropped their bags on the ground and set out for the main complex. Jake picked up the bags and began a labored walk to the Landing's main check-in lobby, which was located in the same building that held Mr. Cobb's office and the dining room. Amelia followed behind him. She walked close enough so he could still hear her when she whispered to him.

"You missed it," she said.

"Missed what?"

"Sh!" she said. "Do you want the whole camp to hear our private conversation?"

"Are we having a private conversation?" he asked, his voice lowered.

It was a silly game—he knew that, but she was a girl, and girls were prone to play silly games. At least that's what one of his uncle's once told him.

"Yes," she whispered. "Now, do you want to know what you missed or not."

"I guess so."

"Slow down," she said. "We're gaining on them. I don't want them to hear us."

He began to slow. The two men did not. Soon they were out of earshot.

"Stop," she whispered.

Jake stopped. He stood still. Amelia came up close to his back. He could feel her body heat. He could sense the warmth of her sweet breath on his neck. He felt her small, firm breasts brush lightly against his back as she stood on her tiptoes to reach the height of his ear. She whispered. "I came out of the shower naked and you missed the whole thing." Her kiss on the back of his neck sent a shiver down his spine. He broke into a sweat. The two bags dropped to the ground with a crash.

Amelia Cobb giggled softly, then ran off past the two men they had been following, the owners of the bags that had just hit the ground. She veered left around the corner of the lodge building and out of sight. The two men heard only the sound of their luggage hitting dirt. They turned around, dodging the girl as she skimmed by them.

"Fucking clumsy teenagers," the light haired man said. He started toward the boy.

The other man, the one with the moustache, laid his hand on the blonde guy's arm.

"Come on, Tommy," he said, "I'm beat. Let's get checked in and get some sleep. The bags will be fine."

Chapter Eight

Jacob Belle—his story-telling finally done for the day—edged his way out of his chair and moved to the bay window. He gazed out over the street. "It's 2:45," he said. "Your lady will be here soon." He made no comment about the time and temperature sign, the flashing red light or any of his other pet peeves.

His silence troubled Adam. He felt compelled to break it. "Was it your mob involvement that caused my father to keep me from you?"

He did not turn to look at Adam. "No," he said. "He knew how I got involved with the mob, and he never held it against me."

"Are you're still in the mob?"

"Yeah. Once you're in, you're in for good."

"Why?" Adam asked.

"It's that proverbial crossed line; the one with no return."

"If you had it to do over, would you still join up?" Adam asked him.

"Probably."

"Because of Amelia Cobb?"

"Not really. It was never intended that she and I would actually be together. That happened out of circumstance—not by plan. She was, I grant you, a key to why I really didn't fight joining up, but the real incentive was the times. Jobs for poor kids like me, well… they just didn't exist — not back then. For a young fellow like me the mob was salvation—a way out. It was a way to avoid the inevitable life of destitution. It came down to Cobb and Petruzzi and the mob, or starvation. Those were my options. Yep—for me, it was the mob or become what my father became."

"What was that?" Adam asked.

"A starving man—old before his time—died without ever finding happiness. I consider myself fortunate. Amelia Cobb or no Amelia Cobb, I would have made the same choice." He turned to face Adam.

Adam studied his face. It was a sad face at that moment, and Adam wondered why. Was it because he was missing his wife? Was it because he was thinking about Amelia Cobb? Was it because he was an old man looking back on a more favorable time? Adam wanted to know. He wanted to know, but he didn't ask. He did not wish to disturb the sadness on his grandfather's face. For in it he found an odd beauty—inexorable truth—and he did not wish to interfere.

Adam answered Maggie's knock on the door while Jacob returned to his silent study of the traffic in the street.

"Is he okay?" she asked Adam. For Jacob Belle to ignore a new arrival to his apartment was uncharacteristic.

"I think he's tired. We should go." Adam said. Then, "Tomorrow?" he asked his grandfather.

"Early," Jacob said without turning around. "Seven. At Tucci's."

"I'm starved," Adam said as they stepped onto the street. "Any dinner plans?"

"I thought we'd eat in tonight," Maggie suggested, "at your place."

"At my place? I have no groceries."

"We'll get some…after you call your work," Maggie said.

"I doubt my appliances work."

"Let's test them," Maggie said.

They drove to Adam's place so he could make his call. He was a private contractor, not actually employed by anyone, and it happened that he received news of his grandmother's death at a time when he was ahead of his workload. All he needed now was to check to see if he was still ahead.

"I've got some bad news, Adam," his client told him. "We're cutting back. Orders from above." Shock at the news prevented him from replying. "Adam? You still there?"

"Well... that's... ah... I don't know what to say. What the hell happened?"

"It's just cutbacks. Slow business. That sort of thing. I'm told the bosses want to buy you out of your contract."

"How?"

Maggie gave him a curious look. "What's happened?" she asked.

"I've been fired."

"You haven't been fired, Adam. You've been cancelled. It's cutbacks. And they're going to pay you," his client said.

"How much?"

"What do you think is fair?"

"You guys honoring your contract. That's what I think is fair."

"Look, Adam. I'm authorized to offer you what you'd make off of us for a full year. Would you settle for that?"

Adam did not answer. He still had two years on the contract.

"Adam?"

More silence. He was thinking. *One year's pay. No work. Two years pay. Work.*

"Adam?"

"Yes. Yes. I'm here. I'm just thinking."

"Well what do you think? Do we have a deal?"

A year's income, without doing anything? Sounds better. Maybe I will write about Cobb's Landing, he reasoned silently.

"Deal." He said goodbye and hung up. He looked at Maggie.

"What just happened?" she asked.

"They're going to pay me for a year."

"And what do you have to do?"

"Nothing. Spend my time with you. Spend time with my grandfather. Maybe write a book."

"Are you good with that?" Maggie asked. She certainly was. She wanted all the time she could get with him, but a year? That was more than she imagined. *Perfect,* she thought.

"I'm great with it. Every day it gets warmer. Might even be able to live here in this God-forsaken land." *At least for the summer,* he thought.

Adam looked around his parents' house for a moment.

"You know, Maggie. Maybe I should consider staying here permanently. My last few months in Chicago, well... I've been getting more and more fed-up with the city...and technical manuals? It's writing directions for people who won't read them, except as a last resort. Not very rewarding, when you think about it. I'd have given it up long ago if it didn't pay so well."

"Well here's your chance. You get to give it up and still get paid."

Maggie considered his face. He did not look sad. "I'm starved," she said. "Let's go shopping."

~*~

Maggie pulled her car to a stop just outside the front doors of Carl's Market. The store looked run down. One of its enormous front windows had a crack running diagonally, corner to corner. Duct tape held the two pieces of glass together.

"Is this a good place to shop?" Adam asked.

"It's a family owned market. They have great fresh vegetables."

"Vegetables?"

"Vegetables. And fruit. Come. You'll see." She got out of the car. Adam followed.

A worn, thin rubber mat triggered the doors. It had been years since Adam had seen anything like it. He found it amusing. He chuckled.

"You making fun of my favorite market?"

"Not at all. I'm finding it... quaint."

Just inside the entrance were a dozen or more rusty carts. Adam's struggle to free one of them seemed endless. Maggie stepped in. She easily pulled one loose.

"How'd you do that?"

"You have to know their secrets." She pushed the cart in front of him. "Follow me."

When Adam began pushing the grocery cart down the first of the store's narrow isles, it protested. The one wheel that was not squealing wobbled, and caused the cart to pull left.

"There must be some sort of salvage yard one can take these things to when they become this disabled," he told Maggie.

"Sh!" Maggie said. "It'll hear you and quit on us completely." She reached out and patted the cart sympathetically. She grabbed a couple of cans of creamed corn and placed them into it.

Adam thought he heard a quiet moan. *Probably just metal rubbing on metal,* he reasoned.

"Did you know that the Landing was run by the mob?" he asked.

"Yeah," she said. "What do we want for dinner?"

"Whatever you'd like," Adam answered. "Was that common knowledge?"

"Was what common knowledge?"

"The mob involvement."

"Pretty much," she said.

"I must have led a sheltered life when I grew up. This is all news to me."

"You just left here too young. None of us were told

anything about it until we grew up. Our parents all had some sort of pact to keep it from us kids. They figured we didn't need to know. It was a thing of the past."

"Did you know that my grandfather was involved?"

"Do you like fish, Adam?"

"I love fish."

"Then fish it is," she said. "How about a nice salad with that?"

"Sounds wonderful. So… did you know Jacob Belle is connected to the mob?"

They came to the end of the isle. The back wall of the store was filled with open topped white refrigerator units. Maggie approached the one containing heads of lettuce. She picked up several, giving each a slight squeeze before selecting the right one.

"I knew," she said.

It occurred to Adam he had been doing something wrong most of his life. He had always taken the first head and tossed it into the cart. He never considered they might not be all the same.

"Many of the older men in town have some sort of connection to the mob," Maggie went on.

"Your father?"

"Yes." She moved to the cooler filled with vine-ripened tomatoes. She picked up a batch. They hung like grapes.

"He's always been a zealous advocate of the mob. Their money supports this town."

"The papers you had my grandfather sign?"

"Exactly."

"The one he couldn't sign?"

"Too much money. Funding for a new park. A project of that size needs Chicago's approval."

She began pulling each of the tomatoes loose from the vine. She put the tomatoes in the cart and casually threw the vine back into the cooler.

"Why'd you do that?"

"Do what?"

"Throw the vine back?"

"They charge by the pound," she explained. "You don't want to buy the vine do you?"

She started towards the meat counter. She selected the perfect fish for their meal. Then she continued on.

A young girl—fifteen or so, Adam guessed —overweight—with far too many body piercings tended the till. As she slid from the counter, the black conveyor belt began to move. It started with a squeal and a groan. Adam wondered if it had come from the same place as the carts.

Maggie looked at him and grinned. "Why don't you choose a movie for us," she suggested, pointing out a horseshoe-shaped area containing a few hundred current releases. Adam selected one, brought it to the counter, then paid the teenager, while Maggie bagged their catch.

Outside the market, Adam placed the bags on the back seat of Maggie's car.

"Can I drive your car?" Leonard Morgan hadn't replaced the rental and Adam missed being at the controls.

"Sure," she said.

Adam opened a door for her, and as she slid in, a noisy old sedan pulled close beside them. Its window came down and the three occupants let out simultaneous wolf whistles. Then they shouted profanity aimed at Maggie, in mock Mexican accents.

"Eh, baby. Ju wan to fuck?" one said.

"Ju like to sit on my face?" said another.

Adam stood. Powered by rage and adrenalin, fists clenched, he turned and walked towards the intruders.

The driver looked directly at him. "Let's get the fuck out of here," he said.

The old car's noisy engine started, then pealed away, tires squealing and leaving black marks in the pavement behind them.

"What was that all about?" Adam asked turning to face Maggie. "Why'd they take off like that?" He had figured on an ass kicking for his boldness.

"The driver recognized you."

"Recognized me?"

"Yes! He knows who you are. They'll keep their distance."

"Why?"

"Because of who you are," she said, "because you're the grandson of Jacob Belle."

Adam got back into the car. He drove them to his parents' house, and when he parked in front, he did not get out. Instead he placed his arm on the back of the seat and half-turned to face Maggie. She did the same. Her skirt caught on the seat's material. It hiked up to expose most of her thigh. She either didn't notice or she didn't care. But now, as Adam drank in the view, he could no longer hold onto as much animosity towards the three pretend Mexicans as before. *Who could blame them? She was alluring.* The sight destroyed his train of thought. *My God! What was I going to say?* He breathed in deep.

"Maggie, those guys back at the market, you said it was because of my grandfather that they left us alone. Why?"

"He's powerful. Everyone knows him."

"What is he? The 'Al Capone of the north' or something?"

"Nothing like that. He's just respected."

"You mean, feared and respected?"

"Something like that." She thought for a moment. She decided he needed more—something positive. "His connections are why people fear him. They respect and love him for what he personally is, Adam. He's kind. He's just. And he's honest." She paused. "Like you—I see a lot of him in you."

Adam reached for his door handle. Her words had pleased him—comforted him. He opened her door. He held his hand out. She took it.

"Let's eat," he said. They gathered their groceries

and headed in.

~*~

Adam loved many things about Maggie Bartell: her looks, her deep concern towards others, her sense of responsibility towards her aging father and Adam's own grandfather, her delightful sense of humor —literally everything about her, but now, what he mostly appreciated was her skills in the kitchen. Dinner was delightful.

But when the couple retired to the living room to enjoy a movie together, well….. no video player.

"Shall we continue this at my place?" Maggie suggested.

"It's either that or we go buy a player."

"Let's go to my place. We'll fix this problem another time."

At Maggie's, the couple settled in together on her sofa. "Your place is so much more comfortable than mine," Adam told her. "I need to do something about that."

"Do what?"

"I don't know. Maybe it's the outdated furniture. It was old when I left here. It hasn't gotten any better in the last seventeen years. Has it?"

"No! I don't suppose it has. We'll shop—find you some things that make you more comfortable. Speaking of comfort, I think I'll change into something relaxing before we start our movie," Maggie said.

While he waited Adam paged through a photo album on Maggie's coffee table. It contained pictures of Maggie as a child, Maggie and her late husband, Maggie's parents, etc. And then he came across a picture of Maggie at about twelve years old, with his mother. He had forgotten that they lived only a couple doors up the street from him back then, and he forgot she and his mother had had a special relationship. Adam was an only child. His mother had always wanted more. She had wished for a daughter, but for medical reasons, couldn't have more children. She had taken Maggie under her wing after Vie Buckley, the mayor's wife, passed away—partially to compensate for herself not being able to have her own daughter, but mostly to help Maggie.

Adam turned the page. There—all alone in the center—was one five-by-seven black and white—one of those old photos with the rippled edges and the date stamped on the white border. The date was July 1931. The boy in the photo was his grandfather, he thought. Maggie came into the room as he studied the faces in the old photo.

"Who is this?" he asked pointing at the boy in the photo.

"That's your grandfather. That's Jacob Belle. It was taken at Cobb's Landing."

"Who's the girl with him?"

"Amelia Cobb."

"She sure looks a lot like you."

Maggie looked closely at the photo. "Yes. She does."

~*~

Morning came too quickly. The video had been an intense action, and neither Adam nor Maggie fell asleep during it, nor could they sleep afterwards for quite some time. Consequently, when they arrived to join Jacob Belle for breakfast they were scarcely functioning, but they could see that his table stood empty. When Tucci approached with a forlorn look on his face, Adam knew something was wrong.

"Where's my grandfather?" he asked.

Maggie moved close to his side and put an arm around his waist.

Tucci looked down at the floor.

"Where's Jacob Belle?" Adam demanded.

"We had to take him in this morning,"

"In?" In where?"

"Don't he know?" Tucci asked Maggie.

Maggie shook her head. Then she looked down at the floor.

"Don't he know what?" Adam turned to face Maggie. He grabbed her shoulders. He turned her to face him. She looked into his eyes. The time had come. The truth—the cold, hard truth—was needed. It was needed now.

"Grandfather Belle has cancer, Adam. It's terminal. Every once in a while he goes into a slump and has to be hospitalized and treated. Usually, a lot of rest and some increased medication brings him out of it."

"How often?"

"It started out being once a year or so. Then, every six months. Now, three. Less sometimes."

"Let's go," Adam ordered.

Tears formed in his eyes. *I don't know why I should cry. I don't even have the right. I hardly know him.* His thoughts turned to that night long ago when the news of his parents' deaths caught up to him. *Maybe I cry for me.*

At the car, Maggie opened the passenger's side door for him. Then she got behind the wheel.

"He's easy to love," she said.

Adam did not respond. He could think of nothing pertinent to say.

~*~

The apprehension Adam felt when he first passed through the old doors of the hospital panicked him. The place had not changed. Everything inside looked just as it did the night he was called in to identify his parents. The walls were the same cream-colored plaster and lath they were then, the same black rubber baseboard still lined their bottom edges, and the same drab checkerboard tile covered the floor. The odor, too, had not changed with the years. It smelled like death. It smelled like his last memory of his parents.

"I want him out of here."

"Come on," Maggie said softly as she locked her slender fingers through his and led him to the receptionist's desk. "Let's go find him."

She approached the girl at the desk.

"Jacob Belle?"

"Are you family?"

It was the same question, asked in the same, cool, professional tone that had been asked of Adam seventeen years before. He broke into a sweat.

"This is his grandson, Adam Belle," Maggie said.

"And you?" the girl asked.

"I'm his wife," Maggie said. She tightened her grip on his fingers. It made him feel safe. It gave him strength.

"He's in the new wing. Down this corridor until you come to a tee. Take a right and go up the ramp. His room is number 240, at the end—on the left."

She began writing in a ledger, her business with Adam and Maggie apparently over.

"My wife?" Adam asked as they started up ramp.

"Yeah. Hope you don't mind. Only relatives are allowed to visit cancer patients in this hospital—some sort of hospital rule. I thought you might want me with you."

"I do."

"Then I guess I'll have to be Maggie Belle for now."

Maggie Belle, she thought. *That's what it should have been when it became Maggie Bartell. It was supposed to be my fate. Even Adam's mother thought so.* Sadness began to close in on her. She pushed it away with a smile, a tighter grip on Adam's hand, and a silent vow that this time it would be the way it was meant to be.

They came to the end of the corridor. "This is his room," Maggie said.

Adam felt relief when he walked into his

grandfather's room and found him in a chair by the window.

"Are you alright?" *What a stupid question,* he thought. But it was too late. It had already been asked.

"You mean other than the fact that I'm dying?"

He did not turn to face his guests. "Listen, I probably should have told you before. I just never got up the courage to talk about it with you. I'm sorry."

"How long?" Adam asked. He really didn't want an answer. It was an automatic question, a programmed response from too many years of television. It doesn't matter what little piece of screenwriting you see, if someone is terminally ill, the question is always... 'How long'?

"They're not saying yet," he answered. "That probably means not long. It seems to me that when there's time left, they're not so skittish about telling you."

"That's not entirely true, Jacob." The voice came from behind them.

Adam turned to see who it was.

"You must be Adam Belle," the newcomer said as he extended a hand. "I'm Dan Brothers. I'm your grandfather's physician. Your grandfather is ill, and we need him to keep up a little better with his treatments so that he enjoys all of the life he has left."

"Just how much is that?" Adam asked.

"There are no guarantees. But let's get him to follow his doctor's orders a little better. That should help considerably. This episode was unnecessary and could have been easily prevented by your grandfather simply taking his medication as prescribed."

"That shit makes me stupid," Jacob Belle said. "Ever since you doubled it, I feel like a moron when I take it."

"Oh, come now, Jacob. It'll take more than a few drugs to make you stupid," Doc Brothers insisted. "And I didn't double the dosage. I only increased it a little."

"Ok, it doesn't make me stupid. It makes me dull. It

makes me forgetful."

"There are trade-offs, Jacob," Brothers said. "We all know that. But those trades are necessary. Drugs slow the mind a bit, but they also slow the progress of the disease. You know that, Jacob. Side affects can be unpleasant; it's true. But the benefits outweigh the problems. Your life may not be exactly what you expected or wanted, but it is life."

Doctor Brothers turned to face Adam. "Have a talk with your grandfather, Mr. Belle. He needs to stay on his medication or you won't have him around long," he said. Then he left the room.

"Dr. Brothers," Adam called after him, "how long will he have to stay here."

"Until we have his blood levels back where they belong," he said, without turning around. "Three or four days. He's skipped his meds for quite awhile."

"What exactly is wrong with him?" Adam asked Maggie.

"He has a form of leukemia," she said.

"You're talking about me as though I'm not in the room," Jacob objected.

"I didn't think you'd mind, Grandfather. Remember, you chose to keep me in the dark in the first place." Adam felt bad. What was he thinking? He should not have barked at a sick man like some insensitive old hound dog. "Look," he said, "I apologize. I was out of line."

"Me too," Jacob said, "I should have told you from the start. I didn't because I wanted you to stay because you wanted to, not because of my illness. Maybe I'm just being an old fool. Maybe I only think I have important things to say, things only I believe you might want to hear. Maybe what I have to say is all bullshit that had some meaning a lot of years ago and none now. Maybe I've just been wasting your time."

"I don't think that," Adam said. "And I want to hear what you have to say. You're the only connection I have to my parents, you know. I don't want to go through life without knowing what my family is about—what I am about—not when there's a better choice. Finish the story, Grandfather. Only take your medicine. Do as your doctor tells you."

"I hate to interrupt," Maggie said, "but I must be going. I have to run some errands for my father. Call my cell when you need me to pick you up, Adam." She left the room.

"Did you know Maggie well before I came home?" Adam asked.

"Yeah, I did," he said. "She's been looking in on me and your grandma for years. Her daddy made her do it. He and I go way back. We're the same age you know."

"No, I didn't know,"

"Seems odd, don't it?"

"What seems odd?"

"That her father and I would be the same age," he said. "And he would have a daughter who is younger than my grandson."

"That is a bit odd," Adam admitted. He began doing the math in his head. "The mayor must have been a virile old man."

"Maggie is adopted. She was only five when her parents were killed in a plane crash. Herb and Vie Buckley took her in immediately. They didn't have any special feelings for the girl or anything. I don't think they even knew her natural parents. They grabbed the girl so Herb could get further in politics. You see, Herb's father was the first mayor after the war at the Landing."

"The war at the Landing?" Adam asked.

"Didn't we get to the war yet?"

"No! No war yet."

"Well, that's this goddamn medication for you. Makes a man forget where in the story he is. Well, we'll get to the war a bit later. Anyway, Herb wasn't as well liked as his dad and his political clout had all the strength of a 'Save the Mosquito' drive. By taking the girl in, Herb figured that would all change. He was right."

"You know, I saw a picture of you last night at Maggie's. You and a young lady. Maggie told me it was Amelia Cobb. They look amazingly alike, her and Maggie."

"They should. Maggie's a Cobb. Do you remember me telling you about Jordan Cobb having a brother who went off to Oregon or Washington or some place out west, then got himself killed over gambling debts?"

"I remember."

"Well he didn't get killed, at least not out west, and not over gambling debts. He got himself killed at the Landing. I saw it happen. Him and a queer hit man named Tommy Delaney. But the night before he died, he took his pleasure from a young girl in the town. Cobb's brother—Jonah was his name—knocked the young girl up, and she had a daughter by him," he said. "That daughter was Maggie's paternal grandmother. Maggie Buckley may have been born with a different name, and may have spent most of her years as a Buckley, but truthfully... she is a Cobb."

"But she and her father, Mayor Buckley, seem close."

"Well, you know her," Jacob Belle said. "How could they not come to love her?"

"Is she much like her ancestors?" Adam asked.

"If Amelia Cobb weren't still alive, Maggie would be her reincarnation," he said.

"Amelia Cobb is still alive?" That surprised him, although he didn't know why. After all, his grandfather, one of the original Cobb's Landing gang, was still around. And he was about her age.

"Yeah!" he said. "She's still around. She lives at the family's old country estate near South Bend, Indiana. I haven't seen her for a few years now, but she writes now and then, just to let me know she's alright, and probably to see if I'm still around."

"How about Petruzzi?" Adam asked. "Is he still

alive?"

"No. He's been gone for years—died in prison. The Feds busted him shortly after prohibition—some kind of nasty drug business or something. An informant turned him over. He got twenty years but never lived to do them—got killed in a knife fight. The family thought it was a setup—probably was—and his position in the organization should have bought him plenty of protection, even in the joint. But it didn't"

"Did they ever figure out why he was killed, I mean, by whom?"

"Nah," he said, "they couldn't figure it out, so they just killed everyone they suspected. Twelve of them went down before it ended. Cleaned out the prison, it did."

"Are there any more of the original cast of this little drama around?" Adam asked.

"You wouldn't think of it as some little drama, or some little anything if you had lived it, smart ass!" His face turned red.

It made Adam feel small. He hadn't meant to hurt him. "I-I-ah-didn't mean to make light of it. I'm sorry."

He sat silent for a time. Then, about when Adam began to think their conversation for that day was over, Jacob spoke. "As far as I know, there's me and Amelia and one other guy who went by the name Beletucci, and the faggot who came to the Landing with Tommy Delaney. I can't remember his name anymore. He's the type of character a guy like me blocks out; I didn't have much time for queers then, and I don't now. That's what he was you know, a queer. Worse than a queer. He'd screw anything, man, woman or beast. I'm pretty sure he's still alive though. He was only about three years older than me; of course he seemed much older at the time. When you're seventeen, three years is a long span. I caught him and Delaney together on the evening of the day they arrived. Amelia was with me. There was a big party going on. The Landing was famous for their parties for which I always had to put up a huge canvas tent called a pavilion. It nearly filled the land between the cabins on the main level and the lake. Anyway, I was walking around the pavilion that night, carrying a large tray of drinks made from the latest batch of Canadian whiskey. It had been flown in sometime during that day. When I came by the large open fire pit that stood in the center of the pavilion, Amelia Cobb was seated on one of the concrete benches that surrounded it. I had thirsty guests to look after, so I tried to ignore her; but Amelia would not be ignored."

~*~

"Is this fire so bright that it's affecting your eyesight, Jake Belle?" she asked, in a smart-alecky but flirtatious way.

"No!" Jake said.

"Then mind your manners. You're supposed to say, 'Good evening Miss Cobb'. And it wouldn't hurt you a tiny bit to add something like, 'My, don't you look lovely this evening?' or the like, Mr. Belle."

"Good evening Miss Cobb. Aren't you looking lovely tonight Miss Cobb," he said.

"That's much better," Amelia said. "Now ask me to join you."

"I'm not sure I should do that. Your father might not like it."

"Daddy won't know the difference."

"He will too. He's standing right over there, talking to that woman in the tan dress and floppy hat."

"Yes. And in a moment he'll be dancing with the woman in the tan dress and floppy hat, and if I know my father, later he'll be bedding down with the woman without her tan dress and floppy hat. He not only imports that illegal booze for the guys in Chicago, he sometimes drinks it too. And about now, I can tell by the way he's leaning on her, he's had so much of it that the only thing he sees is that woman."

She hooked her arm through his and walked alongside, grabbing glass after glass from the large tray, and handing them to partiers along the way.

"Aren't they cute, Noah?" a woman said to her husband as she took a fresh glass from Amelia.

"Yeah! Yeah! Fucking cute, Clara," he slurred as he too reached for a glass. "Real fucking cute. Specially her," he added as he swung out to pat Amelia on the backside.

Jake saw the move coming. It was as though it came in slow motion. He gently pulled Amelia just out of the slobbering old man's reach and the drunken fool fell to the ground with a thud.

"Jees-crist, kid," he said.

"Get up, you idiot!" the woman said as she pulled on the uncooperative drunk's arm. "Do you know who that girl is?"

"Not a clue."

"She's Jordan Cobb's daughter," the woman said in a muffled voice. She did not want to draw any more attention to them than had already been drawn. She looked to see if Cobb had noticed the commotion. "Are you trying to get us killed, Noah?"

The man, having heard the name, Jordan Cobb, in the same sentence as the word daughter, was almost immediately sober and to his feet.

"My apologies, Miss, young fella. I had no idea."

The woman dragged the man off before anything else could happen. Jake and Amelia continued with their drink deliveries as if nothing had happened. When they passed the outdoor bar, the bartender told Jake that he need not make any more trips.

"Most of them have had enough," he said. "They'll soon be falling in the lake. Oh, by the way, cabin four rang for some service. Why don't the two of you go over there and see what they want."

The youngsters turned and walked away. They

headed towards cabin four.

"That's the cabin I put those two guys in this afternoon. The ones who came in on the plane. The ones whose luggage I dropped when you played that joke on me."

"What joke?" Amelia asked.

"You know what joke." He felt his face flush.

"No. I don't know. What joke are you talking about?"

"You remember." He looked at the ground. "You said you came out of the bath house naked."

"That was no joke, Jake Belle," she said. "I did come out naked, and you missed the whole thing." She smiled.

Jake Belle's knees weakened. He could feel his face getting hotter and hotter. He thanked God it was dark so Amelia Cobb could not see how red it was becoming. When he reached cabin four he grabbed the door handle and turned it without thinking to knock. It seemed to be stuck so he gave it a quick twist and pushed hard. It flung open. It bounced off of the wall inside the cabin. A mirror crashed to the floor. Broken glass arched out into the room like a wave. The two men inside, Tommy Delaney and his companion, jumped out of the bed and went for their guns. Both men were naked.

"OH MY GOD!" Jake yelled out.

Delaney grabbed a gun from the nightstand and started waving it around, not taking the time to cover himself.

"I ought to shoot you right here, right now, you little pervert," he shouted.

"OH MY GOD!" Jake yelled out again.

Amelia stared momentarily, and then averted her eyes. She turned and buried her face in Jake's chest.

"Put the gun away, Tommy," his friend said. "That's the daughter. You'll get us killed before we get to do the job we came here for."

Delaney studied the girl for a moment, then dropped the gun to his side.

"What the hell are you doing here?"

"Bartender said you needed something," Jake said.

"Well," Delaney said, "we do. Go and fetch us a new bottle of that Canadian whisky and two glasses, and be quick about it. And knock when you come back."

Neither Jake nor Amelia hesitated. They both turned at the same time, nearly knocking one another into the jambs of the door, then hurried from the gunmen's cabin without looking back.

When they were a safe distance away and Jake figured neither of the men could hear them, he spoke. "You don't have to come back with me when I bring them their bottle."

"I don't mind," Amelia said.

"I don't want you there," Jake insisted, "It's no sight a girl should see."

"How gallant of you, Jake Belle," Amelia said, "but no normal young man of your age should have to see such things either. You don't need to worry about me though. I'm a mob daughter. I've seen worse than that."

~*~

Anthony Russo, passing himself off on the locals as Father Gould, the parish priest at St. Michael's Catholic church, in nearby Cedar Ridge, heard confessions at five p.m. They would not last long. He would leave the confessional after forgiving the sins of only two of his congregation members.

The third to enter his confessional was a surprise—a shock, really.

"Bless me, Father, for I have sinned."

"When was your last confession, my son?"

"Well... gee. Let me think. It seems like a hundred fuckin' years ago, Anthony."

"Who the hell are you?"

"Take it easy. I'm a friend."

"And what do you want from me, friend?"

"I want to help you. And I want you to help me. I'm

with the Bartolli family."

A click of a pistol hammer being pulled back from inside the priest's side of the confessional stopped the conversation briefly.

"Easy. I'm not here to turn you in."

"Then, what are you here for?"

"Like I said. We can help each other."

"I can help myself. Right now. By blowin' your head off."

"Listen. Anthony. They know you're here. I can't fix that. But I can help you finish the job. The one you started for the Rosetti's when you pulled the trigger on Salvatore Bracco."

"And why is it you would want to help me?"

"Survival. I crashed one of their airplanes. Now they want to kill me. By the way, my name is Billy Brooks."

"Well... Billy Brooks. I should save them the trouble... shoot you myself. But I tell you what. I'm going to give you one chance. My sources tell me Tommy Delaney flew into the Landing. You go see him. Tell him to send a note with you saying you're alright. Go. Do that. Then we'll talk."

Billy Brooks left the confessional. He ran most of the way to the Landing. He looked for Delaney. This would be his revenge against Petruzzi and Cobb. This would even things.

Father Gould ran off the remainder of his congregation, giving them a sort of group forgiveness and blessing, and went to find Sheriff Morgan. *Now don't forget, Anthony,* he told himself, *act stupid and weak... like a priest.*

~*~

Across the bay from Cobb's Landing, two men sat in a small wooden rowboat. One of them looked through a pair of binoculars. He was watching the party at the Landing.

"What do you see, Sheriff?" asked the man without the glasses.

"Plenty, Father Gould," the policeman said.

John Morgan, the town's only peace officer, was a burley, uneducated, fifty-year-old tyrant who served his people through fear. He was not a model citizen. He was not an honest man. He was not even likeable. He was simply quite huge and tough and—the priest suspected—greedy. And that was exactly what was needed. A corruptible bully, who could be used for a price.

Sheriff John Morgan was just that. If pointed in the right direction, he would become the exact distraction that Father Gould, or Anthony Russo, or whatever he chose to call himself at that time, would need to finish the job he had began long ago, and that would put him right back where he belonged; in the good graces of his family's hierarchy.

"Is there drinking and lewd behavior going on over there?" the priest asked.

The sheriff studied the scene through the binoculars for a long time before answering, scanning from side to side until he settled on one spot. Focused there in the glasses were a man and a woman. She was sitting on a short, stone wall; her dress hiked up around her hips, legs spread wide apart. The man was facing her, his naked ass glowing from the light of the nearby bonfire. The couple was going at it like animals, rocking back and forth so violently that they knocked their half-empty whiskey glasses from the wall's concrete top.

"There surely is, Father," the sheriff finally said.

"Let me look," the priest said.

"Are you sure you want to?" the sheriff asked. "It ain't no sight for a man of God ta be lookin' at."

"I must see, Sheriff Morgan," the priest said. "It may not be the kind of sight for a shepherd to be viewing, but if I'm to tend my flock appropriately in the eyes of God, then I must see the wolves they need to be protected from."

Morgan lowered the binoculars from his eyes. The couple had finished anyway. He smiled. He handed the glasses to Father Gould. Then he spat into the lake's crystal-clear water. He sat on the boat's narrow seat, struck a match and lit his hand-rolled cigarette with it.

The pretend parish priest looked through the binoculars and focused on two men who were standing on the front porch of one of the cabins. They had apparently seen the flash of the sheriff's match, because they were looking directly at the boat, pointing and laughing. Both men were naked from the waist up. They grabbed themselves. They made a gesture imitating masturbation at the intruders in the boat. The priest dropped the glasses. The binoculars crashed to the floor of the wooden boat with a thud and broke in two.

"Seen enough, Priest?" the sheriff asked, as he grasped the handles of the oars and began bringing the boat about.

"Quite enough," Father Gould said.

The sheriff chuckled quietly and rowed off toward the end of the lake where his truck was parked.

~*~

"I hate to disturb the two of you," Doc Brothers said, as he entered the room. "But it's time for medication and, I think, a nap."

Adam looked at his grandfather. He appeared weak. Despite his objections, despite that he was insisting they weren't done with the day's story, Adam went for the telephone at the side of his bed. He called Maggie's cell number and asked her to come for him.

Then he helped the doctor get his tired grandfather into his hospital bed and assured him that he would be back first thing in the morning.

"Bring us some breakfast from Tucci's. The food here tastes like shit."

Adam looked at the doctor.

Brothers nodded his approval. "Nothing too spicy," he said.

"I'll do that, Grandfather," Adam said. "Have a good rest. I'll see you in the morning."

Chapter Nine

When Maggie pulled her car to the curb in front of the hospital's main entrance, she wore a larger-than-life smile. Tied to the car's roof was a shiny aluminum canoe. She leaned across the seat and opened the passenger's side door as Adam approached. Noon had not yet arrived.

"Jump in," she said. "We're going on an adventure."

"Where to?"

"We're going to the Landing," she said.

He glanced over his shoulder as Maggie pulled away from the curb: a picnic basket and a cooler. "Cobb's Landing?"

The sparkle in her eyes as she peered over the top of her sunglasses asked, "Is there another?"

Just moments from town, Maggie steered the car onto a narrow, grass-covered road. "Might be a little rough from here," she warned.

Rough, hell! Adam thought. *This isn't a road. It's two ruts in the grass. Shouldn't even need to steer. Ought to work like train tracks.*

"How far on this... ah...road?" he asked.

"About a mile or so."

It was obvious the trail had pre-dated heavy equipment. No leveling had been done, and it seemed to turn and drop sharply at times without reason, as though it followed an imaginary river bed. And the forest, even though only the poplars had gained their spring leaves so far, was thick enough to block the sun on occasion. *If it's this way now,* Adam thought, *what was it like in Jacob Belle's day? He must have been scared shitless walking*

112

the four miles to Cobb's Landing in 1931. Probably bears, and wolves, and God knows what else were after him—treacherous...but...strikingly beautiful.

"You alright?" Maggie asked. "You look a little pale."

"Yeah. I'm fine. Maybe a little queasy."

Maggie pulled the car to a stop at the top of a hill. "We'll portage from here."

She opened her door and stepped out. Adam followed.

Standing in from the front of the car, he could see that the road dropped into a deep ravine. In the small creek below, several posts stuck out of the water and the ground that bordered it. "What's that?" he asked, pointing out the decaying posts.

"Part of an old bridge," Maggie said. "Jordan Cobb built it. It was the only way into the place by land. After the bank robbery and the war with the town's people, it was Cobb and your grandfather who burned it down; or so the story goes." She pulled at the straps holding the canoe to the car's roof. "Come, help me," she said. "We have to carry our things to the lake from here."

"Can you fill me in on the war?" Adam asked as they pulled the canoe down.

"Well," she said, "if he's mentioned the robbery, he's about to fill you in on all of the details. He's systematic about things, your grandfather. I try to tell you and I'll have it all screwed up." She started loading the canoe with all they would take with them: picnic basket, cooler, sleeping bags, etc.

"Why the sleeping bags?" Adam asked.

"Just in case," she said. "Might rain."

"How far we gotta carry all this stuff?"

"It's not far," she said, as they rounded a curve in the path.

"I hope not. Can't see a damn thing with this canoe blocking me."

"It's only about another hundred yards."

"Say it like it is, girl. That's three hundred feet."

She paused for a moment before commenting, then, "Not any more. We're here. You've complained it away."

~*~

Adam couldn't see the water but he could feel its chill, cool from the winter's meltdown. He smelled the familiar faint odor; the sour scent of fish that had met their end and washed up on a nearby shore. All of his senses were awakened; those of a youth long ago spent in this country. He had loved this time of the year. He had loved the odors to which he was now being treated. Sour or not, they reminded him that this had been his favorite season as a child. It always signaled the end of another of his homeland's agonizingly long arctic winters. He felt joy, and he was surprised to find himself feeling it.

"Watch your step here," Maggie warned. "It gets pretty steep now, until we hit the water."

The incline seemed about forty-five degrees. The grass, sheltered from the sun by the tall poplars and huge weeping willows that filled the lake's shoreline, was still slippery from the morning's dew. They slid down most of the way. Had it not been for Adam's foot getting stuck beneath an exposed root, they would have slid all the way.

"You okay?" Maggie asked, one foot already in the water. "That was quite a ride."

"I'm fine!" Adam told her, but his ankle hurt.

"Ok, we're going to set the canoe down now," she explained.

Adam scrambled to set the load down as fast as he could. The canoe nearly slipped from his grip. They were not together in their effort. Maggie let the canoe slide down her right side while Adam slide it down his left. The ensuing juggling nearly ended in disaster. The basket went one direction and the cooler went the other. Maggie fell into the canoe—better than the icy water. Adam let the craft drop the last six inches, and reached to slap a mosquito that was voraciously feeding on the back of his neck.

"State bird?" Maggie asked.

"State bird," he said.

"Let's get this thing in the water. Where there's one of them there's always more coming. They won't bother us once we get out on the lake."

They loaded the basket and cooler in the canoe, and Adam shoved them off. They paddled west, the direction of Cobb's Landing. Adam felt excitement, anticipation.

~*~

"Can you feel the magic?" Maggie said.

"What?"

"The feeling," she said. "It's kind of an awe-inspiring sensation."

Adam felt something. But he wasn't given to admissions of feeling things beyond the norm. That was a girl thing, not a man thing.

Maggie studied his face. "Come on. It's ok. You can admit you feel something."

He smiled.

"Seriously. Everyone feels it as soon as they touch the surface of this lake. It's magic. It's mystery."

"It's probably just excitement from listening to all my grandfather's stories. That's all."

"That's all? Well… if that's all it is, explain how it is that everyone, even total strangers who come here, feels it? People who have never heard of Jordan Cobb or Cobb's Landing? Folks who have never laid eyes on Jacob Belle."

"I can't. Can you?" Adam said.

"I think I can. It's sort of like walking unexpectedly through Indian burial grounds, or visiting an early military post or something like that. It's atmosphere. History. It can be felt."

"I'm not sure I buy that," Adam said.

"Fine," Maggie said. "Just sit there and paddle. Pretend it isn't happening to you." She looked over her shoulder and smiled cynically.

~*~

After several minutes they came to a small bay-like indentation in the shoreline where a creek or small river once emptied into the lake.

"Is that the ravine we left the car near?"

"Yeah. See the log pillars that held the bridge?"

Adam squinted. In the distance, he could just make out the logs Maggie was pointing out.

The power of the water must have been furious at one time. At this end, where they sat now in their canoe, the floor of the lake fell off sharply. It went from rock-lined creek bottom to sandy lake floor far below in an instant, like a concealed waterfall. The sleek-shaped canoe seemed to rock from its influence. On the lakeside of the canoe, Adam caught a glimpse of something resting far beneath the water's surface.

"Hold it!" he said.

They stopped paddling. They held their paddles in the water, using them like a brake. "What's that?" he asked. He pointed out a large rust-colored object.

The ripples calmed. He could see its shape more clearly. It was a vehicle. A truck. It was old... older than any truck he had ever seen other than in the pages of some magazine. "How did that get there?"

"I don't know." Maggie said. "I just know it's there. It's always been there. At least as long as I can recall, it's been there. I heard once that it went off the bridge, up where we parked the car, and that there were three guys in it when it fell into the creek. Then the rapid current carried it to this drop off. The story goes that one of the guys had been shot dead before the truck got to the bridge, one fell out on the way down and was trapped beneath the truck and drowned, and a third guy swam back to shore. The sheriff shot him. The body of the dead guy drifted to the surface and washed to the shore a couple of days later. He had been plugged execution style, one shot, right behind the ear."

"What about the guy who got trapped?" Adam peered down at the old wreck in its watery grave. "How'd they get him out without pulling the wreaked vehicle out of the water?"

"They didn't," Maggie said. "The story goes that he was never found. Most believe he's still down there."

"Who were these guys?"

Adam studied the wreck. The sun had gone behind a small cloud. Without its glare on the water, he could see all the way to the bottom. The old truck was about half-buried in the soft sand that covered the lake's floor. He wanted to dive in. He wanted to swim down to the wreckage. He felt compelled to find the man trapped beneath.

"Gangsters," Maggie said. "Nobody seems to know for sure who they were or what this is all about, or, at least, nobody who's willing to tell. Rumor has it though, that the man down there," she pointed at the sunken truck, "the one who's trapped under the truck, is Jordan Cobb's own brother, Amelia Cobb's uncle."

"Who would know for sure?" Adam asked.

"Oh, the only one who will know for sure is Jacob Belle," Maggie said. She thought for a time. "Maybe Tucci."

"Tucci?" Adam asked. "Old man Tucci from the diner?"

"That's him."

"He was part of the Landing, too?" Adam asked. He knew Tucci was mob. He had said as much when Adam questioned him about whether he was at Grandma Belle's funeral, but he hadn't put two and two together, made the connection to Cobb's Landing, probably because his grandfather had never mentioned Tucci in his tales.

"He was there. He ran with Jacob and Amelia, but he didn't go by Tucci then. He had another name. I don't know what it was."

Adam took a long, last look at the wreckage and began paddling. He would bring the subject up with his grandfather the next chance he got. Right now though, he wanted to see Cobb's Landing.

~*~

The scraping of rocks on the bottom of the canoe as it floated into the shallows of Cobb's Landing didn't disturb Adam Belle. He did not even hear the sound. He was in awe. The sight he was seeing was not something he had expected.

"It's amazing, isn't it?" Maggie said.

"Wow!" It was all Adam could come up with. The picturesque view that stretched out before him was a vision from his grandfather's dreams. For an instant, he saw the cabins as they had been years ago, the lawn manicured. Adam's mind showed him oddly costumed guests milling about leisurely, and told him he knew how to dance the Charleston.

"What did you see?"

"You'll think I'm crazy."

"You saw it, didn't you?"

"Saw what?"

"The Cobb's Landing of your   grandfather's day."

"Is that what you see?"

"No, but the first time I came here I did. Mine lasted longer than yours though. Did you see the guests?"

"No!" he lied.

He did not want to admit to such things. Visions just weren't him, not his style. He was the logical—everything has an explanation—kind of guy.

"Did, too."

Adam had to admit, though, that there was a certain indefinable feeling, as he walked in his grandfather's footsteps.

He looked strait ahead of them. The lodge building. It was *The* lodge. It was the place where Amelia Cobb had first seduced his grandfather into a walk to the greenhouse for flowers for the tables. It was where their romance had started. It still stood. Perhaps it wasn't as proud as it had once been, but there it was: still standing. Remarkable! He stopped to study it.

"It's sad." Maggie stopped beside him and looked up at the building. "It's getting away. Deteriorating. Something has to be done or it'll be lost, like so many of the others."

"Does anyone look after this place?"

"Not in the past couple years. Your grandfather used to. Did all his life. But I guess he got too old."

Adam studied the lodge from where they stood. He had to agree; it was sad. The vision that his imagination had treated him to was indeed a far cry from the sight he was seeing now.

A small animal caught his attention, at the corner of the building. Too far away, he couldn't tell what it was. It went under in a spot where the buildings rock foundation had crumbled. Adam wondered if it lived there.

"Any plan for someone to take over?" he asked.

"Not that I know of."

"Maybe we should."

"I suspect that may be your grandfather's ulterior motive. Wouldn't surprise me anyway."

It set Adam to thinking. *Wouldn't be a bad life. Better than writing tech-shit for the rest of my life. I'd have to learn to deal with winter, though, the real challenge.*

As they moved closer to the lodge, Adam spotted another animal.

"There's a pair of them. You see them?"

"See what?"

"Raccoons. Two of them. Look! There goes another. Christ, there's a whole family of them living under there."

"That might be our first duty. Plug up the raccoon hole." Maggie said as she laced her fingers through his. The sensation felt good to him—natural, familiar—like she had always been a part of his life.

"Come," Maggie said. "I want to show you something. I want you to see the greenhouse."

"Where Amelia Cobb first took my grandfather."

"That's the one."

The path to the greenhouse was amazingly clear. It seemed traveled. Adam thought, at first, there must be more visitors than anyone had let on. Then he considered the season. *That was impossible. How would visitors get out here?* he told himself.

"Trail's kind of beaten down. Don't you think?" he said.

"Deer!"

"Yes?" He thought she had been addressing him, at first.

"No, dear. D E E R. The deer use this trail. They go to the lake for water and then to the old greenhouse where they nibble at the new growth of the plants."

"New growth?"

"Perennials."

"Of course." Adam said.

He was no botanist. That was for sure, but he did know what a perennial was. It did seem odd, however, that there would still be growth at a greenhouse so long neglected.

"Grandfather Belle used to keep it cleaned out. The greenhouse was among the fondest of his memories. He even grew plants here until a couple years ago. The last summer he worked the place, he planted things he knew the deer would go after. He figured the deer would keep the path clear for him if he did." Maggie tightened her grip on Adam's hand. "He told my father he'd be coming back out here this summer. Hoped to get some of the work done, stuff that's been neglected since your grandmother took sick and his health started deteriorating."

"How does he get out here?"

"Same way we just did."

"Seems like an awfully taxing trip for someone of my grandfathers age."

"Don't underestimate your grandfather. He's ill, that's all. You'll see when he recovers. He's been through this before. Plenty of times. He'll get well. He'll put twenty pounds on. And he'll seem twice as strong as he does now. You'll see." She turned to face Adam. "He won't give all of this up, until he's sure it's safe."

"Safe?"

"Yes. Safe. Safe from tourists tearing it apart hunting for treasures rumored to be here. Safe from teenagers wanting a place where they can party. Safe from hunters wanting it for a hunting camp. And safe from the law."

"From the law?"

"From the law," she repeated. "Cobb's Landing not only has a history. It also has secrets, secrets that need to be protected."

"Secrets? What kind of secrets?"

"The kind of secrets the mob usually needs kept," she said. "You know. Proof! Evidence! Where the bodies are hidden! Things like that. Mob things."

She tightened her grip on his hand and kept walking. The brush was closing in, narrowing the path. Apparently the deer weren't doing their job.

The conversation had sparked Adam's interest. He wasn't just curious. He was excited. He wanted more.

"Where the bodies are buried, eh?" He snickered a bit.

"Don't laugh. It's true. There're lots of bodies buried here. Some of them the government would love to know more about."

The couple walked on in silence for a moment. Adam began to think about what Maggie had been saying. Mob... secrets... buried bodies. *It's the hometown's legacy. It's my grandfather's history. It's my inheritance. You can tell me where the bodies are, who's they are. I'll never tell.*

"How much further?"

"Yards."

They rounded a bend. They cautiously sidestepped thorny raspberry bushes that the deer had left behind.

"Do you think deer don't like raspberries, or thorns?" Adam asked.

He looked ahead. There it stood, just past the raspberry bushes. The remains of the once-flourishing greenhouse.

"This is fascinating." he said.

~*~

To most, the old greenhouse might look like just that: an old greenhouse, rotted halfway to the ground and way past its usefulness. But Adam had knowledge of it, and a connection to it through his grandfather's tales. To him it was a work of art. It was beauty. And, to him it was a reminder of a simpler time, when youth and love collided within it's walls and created a lasting memory that remained as fresh as the flowers and plants that were once nurtured here.

"I can't wait to go inside." He took the lead. "Come on! Let's go!"

"Watch for snakes," Maggie warned.

"Snakes?"

He stopped dead. He could manage almost anything—anything but bats or snakes. Those were two of God's creations that scared the shit out of him.

"What kind of snakes? Poisonous?"

Maggie took the lead. "Oh, yeah! They're copper

bellies. Extremely poisonous." She took a few steps. Kicked some dead vines out of her way. Then she took a few more steps. "Watch for bats, too. The landing seems to be full of both. Probably won't see either though. It's a bit early."

"Why... you're every man's dream. A girl who knows bats and snakes."

"You aren't afraid of them. Are you?"

"Of course not," Adam said. He smiled. He hoped the paleness of his face would be overshadowed by the smile.

"What'd you do? Outgrow that?" *Oops! What're you doing, Maggie? You're supposed to let his memory come back on his own.* "Watch for them anyway. You never know."

"What do you mean, outgrow?"

"Oh, I just remembered your mother once saying you were afraid of snakes."

"How well did you know my folks, Maggie?"

"Your mom, I knew pretty well. We only lived two doors down. You remember?"

He did, but only vaguely.

"Your dad, I didn't know very well at all. He was always working."

Maggie was ten feet or so inside the greenhouse. Adam had stopped just inside the doorway. He had been checking the place out, and her as well.

"Maggie?"

"Yes?"

She turned to look back at him.

"This might seem like a strange question, but... what did my dad do for work? I don't remember."

"He sold insurance. That's why he was always working. He'd often have meetings at night, with clients. It was the only time he could get a husband and wife together."

She turned her attention back to the greenhouse. "Even early in the spring, before anything comes back to life, this place makes me feel good," she said. She stood still for a moment, looking over the damage the harsh winter had done to the plants. "Coming?"

Adam watched her struggle to clear dead vines from between a couple ancient, crudely erected planting tables.

"Need help?" He hoped she didn't. *Snakes!*

"I've got it."

She wore a pair of black denim jeans. Adam thought they fit like they had been assembled on her. She passed two more planting tables. One stood on three legs. Another leaned to the dirt floor, only two legs still attached. He watched her walk, captivated by her graceful movements. So captivated that he failed to grasp her disappearance around the corner.

"Maggie?" he called.

"Over here," she called back. "Come on. There's something I want you to see."

He moved towards the sound of her voice, kicking dead plant debris aside as he walked. He searched for snakes on the ground and bats that might be hanging overhead. His progress was slow, cumbersome, dangerous. Near the back wall of the building the path took a left. It passed through an eight-foot long arbor covered in dormant vines. *Grapes,* he figured. He bent a bit at the neck to pass under. Scouting for bats or snakes became impossible. *I wonder if my grandfather was shorter when he was a teen. Did he have to bend like this to get through here? Maybe the arbor wasn't even here when he and Amelia Cobb were kids. Maybe the years and the ground's moisture rotted the support posts and shrunk the thing.* He was deep in thought as he emerged through the far end of the arbor. He heard a noise. It came from behind him. It was a crackling sound. The sound of a large reptile slithering across dead leaves and branches. He was petrified. He could not move. He could not speak. Something touched him gently on the back of his neck. Something cool and smooth. It moved along the collar of his shirt, paused briefly at the lobe of his ear, and slowly moved to his chest. He caught a glimpse from the corner of his eye. The intruder was about two inches in diameter and orange in color.

He yelled.

Maggie began to laugh uncontrollably and squeezed his neck tightly.

"Very funny." Adam sighed in relief. "Now, what is it you wanted me to see?"

"Oh... just this," she said as she turned him to face her. "Thought it might be something you'd like."

She stepped back. Her shirt was unbuttoned down the front. Her bra was missing. The nipples of her round firm breasts were scarcely covered by the cloth of the shirt.

Adam stared. Slowly he searched the rest of her body. An unbuttoned shirt was her only article of clothing.

"Does it do anything for you?"

"Everything!" Adam felt himself breaking into a slight sweat. "It sure is warm in here." he said.

"Greenhouses are like that."

"I know. But this one's really warm."

"You ain't seen nothin' yet, Slick!"

She snatched him by the shirt collar. She forcefully put him to the ground and... hungrily... pulled at the buttons of his denim shirt. In moments she had him naked.

She kissed him passionately, her tongue diving deep into his mouth as she helped his penis into her. They rolled, twisted, yelled, screamed, and sweated in a passion like neither of them had ever before experienced. When they finished they lay there for a long time—silent—enjoying.

~*~

Adam watched, as the occasional cloud floated

effortlessly by in the clearest blue sky he had ever seen, and he was not concerned with snakes or bats.

"It'll be turning dark soon," Maggie said. She sat up and began feeling around for clothing. "We should pack up and start for the car," She handed Adam a shirt.

He looked it over. He handed it back. It was hers.

Soon they were dressed. They stood face to face in each other's arms. Adam took advantage of the moment. He kissed her, passionately, meaningfully. He slid his hands down her soft, smooth curves. Her hands traveled with ease down his sides and soon, almost automatically, their fingers were laced together. When Adam opened his eyes, all of the plants in the greenhouse had come to life and the structure appeared new, like it must have been when Jacob Belle and Amelia Cobb stood here, probably in this exact spot. Adam lost his balance. He stumbled.

"What the....?" he stammered. "Did you see it?"

"I did!" Maggie said. "Let's get out of here."

She dropped one of his hands and hung on to the other. They hurried through the arbor, then took the right towards the door. Neither of them looked back, until they were beyond the main complex and on the shore of Cobb's Landing. At the canoe, they stood and looked for a time. The beauty of this place, the magic here, overwhelmed them both. They drank it in. Then, knowing night would soon arrive; they got in the canoe and began paddling their way back down the shoreline.

As they passed over the sunken truck, they paused for one more look at the wreckage. Adam wondered if the man trapped there had Jacob Belle's bullet in him. He did not know why he thought that.

They arrived at Maggie's car just as darkness began to fall. They hurriedly packed and headed towards home.

"We forgot to eat," Maggie said.

Chapter Ten

"You're makin' less sense than ya did when we was kids, Jacob," Tucci said.

The medication Doc Brothers prescribed for Jacob Belle whenever he had an episode that required hospitalization almost always left him one step shy of comatose. It was unpleasant at best. A man like Belle, a quick-witted proud person, found this state intolerable.

Old man Tucci found it entertaining.

"Why the hell shouldn't I?" Jacob said. "You do! And you don't have to be under the influence of drugs to do so."

"Now don't go getting him too excited Mr. Tucci," Doc Brothers said as he entered the hospital room. "Next we'll have a heart attack to deal with."

Brothers moved to the side of Jacob's bed and grabbed his wrist. He placed his fingers over the artery, to check his pulse. He stretched out his left arm. The sleeve of his shirt slid up revealing a Rolex wristwatch. He began counting the heartbeats.

"I've got great news for you this morning, Jacob," he said. "We can take your medication down several notches. You're recovering nicely."

"How da fuck you do dat, Doc?" Tucci asked. "How da fuck you count and talk at the same time?"

"He's not really counting Tucci. He's just admiring that expensive new watch all my pain bought him."

~*~

Maggie and Adam had already made a morning visit to Tucci's Diner. They would have had breakfast at Adam's, but Adam wanted to see Tucci and catch up on any changes in his grandfather's condition. He knew Tucci would know what was going on. And he felt sure that he would also be honest with him.

Having missed Tucci, they ate a quick meal and went on to the hospital.

They walked into Jacob's room just in time to learn about Doc Brothers' new watch and where the funding for it had come from. Adam could see the thing gleaming on the doctor's wrist from the doorway. It was indeed impressive.

"You must be in a lot of pain, Grandfather," Adam said. "That's a big watch."

"It's expensive too," Doc Brothers said, his smile broadening.

"It must be," Jacob Belle said. "His rates have doubled since he got it."

"You've had your illness for, what, about eight years now, Jacob?" Brothers said. "I should have rushed out and bought myself one of these when you first came to see me with it. They were a lot cheaper then."

He started towards the door.

"I could have saved you a fortune, Jacob," he said as he passed by Maggie and Adam.

He nodded a good morning in their direction.

"I remember when your kind took chickens and pigs for your services," Jacob yelled after the doctor.

Doc Brothers poked his head back though the doorway and said, "Yeah, well, at least two things have changed since then. They're actually slicing bread before they put it in the bag now, and doctors no longer settle for livestock. They demand watches. Expensive watches."

Adam chuckled. He reached up to scratch an itch on his neck, just below the right ear.

Brothers noticed the scratching. He stopped to take a

look.

"Better get something on that. That's poison ivy."

Maggie rubbed a hand across her belly and squirmed a bit.

Doc Brothers glanced in her direction. Without hesitation, he lifted her sweater just enough to expose a little skin that had a bright red rash quickly developing on it.

"You too, Maggie? Where have the two of you been?"

"And just what have they been doing? Don't forget to ask them that, Doc," Jacob offered. "You don't get that by walking by it. Do you, Tucci?"

"No!" Tucci said. "I think you actually gotta touch the stuff."

He looked straight at Adam. Adam developed another itch. He began to scratch it.

"To get it there," Tucci said, "right on the ass like that, I think ya gotta almost sit in it, and I don't think it'll take unless you sit in it bare-assed. Will it, Jacob?"

"I think you're absolutely right, Tucci. You have to come into physical contact with the plant."

He glanced over at Maggie, who was now scratching at her backside. He smiled broadly.

"Isn't that about the way it is, Doc?"

"That's how it happens," Doc Brothers confirmed. "But, where do you suppose they came into contact with it? They've sprayed for poison ivy around here for years."

"About the only place that I can think of would be the Landing. Have the two of you been out to Cobb's Landing?" Jacob asked.

"I recall one time when we was kids, Jacob," Tucci said, "when both you and the Cobb girl came down with a case of poison ivy just about like that. I don't remember exactly where you got it, but it sure caused a stink."

"The greenhouse," Jacob Belle said. "We got it in the

woods out behind the greenhouse. Last time I was out there, I noticed that some of it had seeded itself inside the greenhouse. Have the two of you been in the greenhouse out at Cobb's Landing?" he asked.

The couple was now scratching vigorously.

"What were you doing in that old greenhouse?"

He glanced at Tucci.

"You'd better come with me, both of you," Doc Brothers insisted. "Let's get something on that rash."

Adam and Maggie were happy to follow. It would save them from further ridicule.

~*~

The journey from the hospital room to treatment room was a long one. Both cases of poison ivy were rapidly developing. Discomfort and anguish were the order of the day. Adam felt like he was walking the last walk of a condemned man. Maggie simply itched, and she itched in places she dared not scratch.

Adam had never before had poison ivy. Consequently he had no idea what the treatment might involve. Doctors and dentists he held in the same high regard as snakes and bats. They were the sort of people who had no problem dealing with torn skin, broken bones, and gallons of blood. He feared people like that.

Maggie, other than her occasional fit of agony over a newly developing itch, appeared tranquil.

"What is he going to do to us?" Adam asked her, recalling a case from his childhood. It was a kid who lived just up the block. Couldn't remember the name, but the circumstances came to him clearly. The poor kid was down with it most of the summer. Treatment was extensive. He had to have a whole series of shots. He wondered, *How many injections are there in a series?*

"We going to have to have a shot?" he asked.

"I don't think we'll need shots," Maggie whispered. She didn't sound very convincing.

"Here we are," Doc brothers announced. "You take this room. Mr. Belle," he pointed to the door on their right, "and you, young lady, can take the room across the hallway. Get undressed. You'll find gowns on the tables. I'll be in to see each of you shortly."

Adam shot Maggie a desperate look. She smiled sympathetically.

"You'll be fine," she said.

She opened the door to her assigned examination room.

It occurred to Adam that she would be alone with the doctor—naked—across the hall from him. "Why not share one room?" he suggested.

The doctor heard Adam. "That's how you acquired this condition. Being naked together." " Separate rooms, Mr. Belle."

As Adam got into the tissue-thin, open-down-the-back gown, he began to appreciate that his ass was hanging out in the air. That was precisely where most of the damage was. He looked at the red rash. *Never again,* he silently vowed. *If Maggie wants to play outside, she's not getting the top.*

Doc Brothers took his time, examining the rash with all the thoroughness of a pilot performing a pre-flight inspection on his aircraft. Adam thought he was there for the day. "How bad is it?" he finally asked.

"Oh... I've seen worse, but not by much. You'll recover though. It'll take a week or so, and you'll look like a leper and probably be treated like one, but you'll come around." Brothers started out of the room, then turned to add, "There's an upside. You get to smear ointment all over each other. That ought to be fun."

Brothers left the exam room.

Sure. We're allowed to smear ointment on each other, but we can't be examined together, Adam silently thought.

~*~

131

"How's it been for you, Maggie? I've been concerned," Doctor Brothers asked as he closed the door to her examination room.

"It's been hard."

"I can only imagine. You date a boy through high school. Plan to marry. His parents get killed in a car accident. And... just like that. Your world is torn apart at the seams."

"That pretty much sums it up."

"Is anything coming back to him?"

"His fear of snakes."

"Well... that's something. Not much, but something."

"Tell me something, Doc. Do you think his memory will ever fully return?"

"No way to tell. And I'm no psychologist. I'm just a family practitioner. But my colleague from the cities, Doctor Paulson, is a psychologist. And he thinks that full recovery is possible."

"What about you? What's your opinion."

"I guess, and I emphasize the word, guess, Maggie. I guess I question that possibility. I don't put much faith in it happening."

"Why?"

"Adam's loss of memory stemmed from the night his parents were killed. That was seventeen years ago. I would have expected his memory to return much sooner than this, if it were going to return at all. But, that's just me. Paulson's the expert. We're better off listening to him, for now."

"You know, there is one thing. He seems to be extremely at home with me, very open, like he was when we were kids... before the accident. Nothing at all like a new, awkward, budding relationship. Could that be something?"

"Could be. I'll run it by Paulson next time we talk. Anything else?"

"He definitely recognized this place when we came in. He pretty much freaked out. I think he remembered that night, at least the part of it when he came in here to identify his folks."

"You were with him that night, weren't you?"

"I was. It was prom night and he was my date. But I don't think he remembers that. Can't blame him, though. It's not exactly the way I like to look back on my prom."

"Well... you let me know immediately if there are changes. Will you?" Brothers took a long look at his Rolex. "Meanwhile, keep lotion on that poison ivy, and keep it away from water. Water will make it spread. And you might want to keep away from Cobb's Landing." He smiled.

"What can we do?" Maggie asked.

"Pretty much anything you want," he said. "Try to avoid anything too physical though. Bringing on a sweat will bring on itching, and I don't want you scratching. You'll scar."

Doctor Brothers moved to the door of the examination room, then turned to face Maggie. "Doctor Paulson might want to see Adam. He's mentioned it before. Would you be able to get him to cooperate if it becomes necessary?"

"I can try. But he's bound to ask why. What do I tell him?"

"I'll check with Paulson. I'll need to see how your rash is doing in a couple of days. I'll let you know what he says." He left the room.

~*~

Adam was in the hallway.

Dr. Brothers stopped to chat with him while Maggie dressed. He filled Adam in on how to care for the rash. He also went over his grandfather's condition with him briefly, filled him in on what he could expect in the future and what to watch for in his grandfather,

133

symptoms, etc.

"Most importantly, don't let him overdo. Fatigue is his worst enemy."

Then he left him to wait for Maggie.

~*~

"How long did he say it would take us to heal?" Maggie asked.

"About a week. Maybe a bit longer."

"What are we to do with ourselves for a week?"

Adam had been so engrossed in the story of Cobb's Landing, with his visit there, and with his new and unexplainably fast-developing love for Maggie, that he had forgotten he hadn't yet moved from Chicago. He still maintained an apartment and it was full of his personal things: furniture, clothing, everything he owned. And there was a girl. He hadn't even said goodbye.

"Where can I rent a truck?"

"Leonard Morgan. Why?"

"We've got some time to kill."

"Are we going to kill it in a truck?"

Adam thought for a time. *I hadn't planned on taking her with. Might be tricky breaking it off with Elaine having Maggie along. Ah! What the hell!* "I need to move my things from Chicago. I'm still paying rent on an apartment down there."

"So you've decided to make your move permanent?" She gleamed. It was her dream come true. That is, if she was reading him right.

"Thought I'd give it a shot, anyway. Try it on for a time."

"Don't you think the trip might irritate our rashes?' Maggie asked.

"We'll spring for a newer truck with air conditioning and comfortable seats. And we'll stop often so the trip won't be quite so demanding."

"What about Grandfather Belle? We don't want to leave him alone in a hospital bed, do we?"

"Doc told me he's going to be just fine. He should be getting out in a few days. Tucci will keep him company until we return," Adam promised her. "This is the perfect opportunity for this. I'd like to take advantage of it, get it behind me."

Maggie agreed. They rented a box truck. A large, comfortable one. And they left for Chicago that afternoon.

Their trip was to be short. Five miles. Neither of them could tolerate the itching. They decided to turn around and bring the truck back to Leonard Morgan and turn it in.

Morgan's burly frame nearly filled the front window of Cedar Ridge Ford as the truck he had rented to Adam Belle pulled into his parking lot and came to a jerky stop, just feet in front of him. *What the hell?* His expression echoed his thought.

Maggie and Adam looked at each other. They looked through the window at Morgan. They looked back at one another. They smiled with amusement. Then they got out of the truck and headed for the door.

Once inside Adam looked into Morgan's unfriendly eyes. This was the guy who had told him he wouldn't rent a bicycle to anyone from Illinois. Suddenly, the sight of Leonard Morgan became unendurable. "I'm returning your truck. I want a refund."

"Somethin' wrong wi' the truck?"

"No! We've changed our minds. We don't need it. We'll rent it later."

"O...kay!" Leonard said. He said it too slowly, questioningly. It really wasn't okay. "But I got to charge you anyhow."

Normally Adam would expect to pay a nominal fee for renting and returning something without actually using it. That was a reasonable request, and he was a reasonable man. "How much?" he asked.

"All of it," Leonard said.

"Really!" Adam said.

"Really!"

An itch developed in the middle of Adam's back, in the center where he could not reach. He became annoyed, confrontational. *This sour attitude, we're the only game in town, big balls no brain son-of-a-bitch is going down.*

"I ain't payin' for shit!" he shouted as he moved his face to within an inch of Leonard Morgan's.

Maggie grinned.

"You sure as hell are!" Leonard shouted.

"You do have a bit of your grandfather in you, Adam, now don't you?" Maggie said.

"Who the hell is his grandfather?" Leonard asked. Apparently he had forgotten their previous encounter at the pancake house.

"Jacob Belle!" Maggie and Adam said in unison.

"Oh, yeah?" Leonard yelled. "Well, mine was John Morgan!"

His chest puffed out like one of those Japanese beta fishes when it had caught a glimpse of itself in a mirror.

"John Morgan, the old sheriff?" Adam asked.

"That's right, smart ass. John Morgan the sheriff."

His chest seemed to puff even further.

"Well!" Adam said. "Well!" He repeated. He could not for the moment come up with an appropriate remark, so he stalled in silence for a few seconds. Then it came to him. A zinger. The perfect response for this bonehead. "Well! Your big hero is dead! At least mine is still alive."

That was all it took. The oaf took his first swing at Adam. Adam ducked. Leonard missed. He took a second shot. It brushed by Adam's left ear. Morgan crooked his arm around Adam's neck and they both went tumbling to the floor. They rolled around for what seemed a long time, kicking and swinging like a couple of school kids in a playground dispute, until Maggie shouted at them to stop.

"Get up!"

Both men obeyed.

"Shake hands!"

They did.

"Now, Leonard. Tell Adam how much you want for rent on the truck."

"All….."

"Don't say all of it or I'll tackle you myself."

"Okay! Okay! Forget it! I'll tear up the charge slip."

"I want to see you do it," Maggie insisted. Then she watched closely as Leonard walked to his desk, found the receipt, tore it up and handed the pieces to her.

"Thank you!" she said. She led Adam to her car in silence, and they were gone.

When they arrived back at Adam's house, Maggie made a few phone calls and arranged to hire a couple of locals to move all of Adam's things from his Chicago residence.

Adam called his former landlady. He wanted a clean break—no charges left unpaid.

"There are no bills to pay, Adam," his ex-landlady, Emma Pierson informed him. "Everything has been taken care of."

"By whom?"

"By something called The Cobb's Landing Foundation," she said. "The check came just this morning."

He hung up.

He didn't question it.

He had had enough for one day.

~*~

The couple spent the rest of the week at Adam's place, healing. Grandfather Belle spent his at the hospital, resting. The workers Maggie had hired spent theirs moving Adam's belongings. Adam wrote his ex-girlfriend and said goodbye. And Leonard Morgan, they found out several weeks later from Doc Brothers, came down with a severe case of poison ivy and spent his week—not knowing what had happened to him—scratching.

Chapter Eleven

Grandfather Belle did not answer the door when Maggie and Adam rang the following Monday morning. *Was something wrong?* Adam pounded. Still no answer. No sound. He panicked. He rattled the knob. The door opened. He went in slowly, afraid he might find Jacob lying on the floor. He didn't. Jacob was standing, back to them as they entered, in front of his bay window. He stared out at the intersection below, the one at the corner where the bank stood.

"Are you all right?" Adam asked.

"A little tired," he said. He wore a robe and slippers. Unusual.

It wasn't that he hadn't seen his grandfather in robe and slippers before. It was just that this time, given his recent hospital stay, his attire seemed to make a statement. It was as though it signaled the approaching end of an era. Adam wanted to do something. He wanted to help him dress. He wanted to prevent the era from coming to an end.

"I'm just tired," he said again. He stood silently for a time.

Adam stood behind him, helping him stare out the window like it was some activity he could actually help his grandfather with.

"It seems naked," Jacob said after a time.

"What seems naked?"

"The corner."

"What?" Adam asked.

"The corner," he repeated a little louder.

"Yeah! I heard that. But… just what is naked about

it?"

"The light," he said. "Didn't you notice? That goddamn flashing signal light! It's gone."

Maggie had, while Jacob Belle was in the hospital, pleaded with her father, the mayor, several of the city council members, and the city engineer's office, until she was successful in getting them to take the flashing light that blinked off and on, off and on, off and on, annoying the old gent until he could not think straight, and removing it forever.

"I thought you disliked the light," Adam said.

"I did!"

"Then what's the problem?" Adam asked. "Maggie had it taken down, just like you wanted her to."

"That doesn't mean I won't miss it."

"Excuse me?"

Adam was not getting it. Really. He glanced at Maggie for help. She threw her arms in the air. Then she smiled.

"It's kind of like me missing your grandmother," he started.

"You mean your 'living so many years with the devil' analogy?"

"Exactly! So you know what I'm going through."

Adam hung his head. He shook it back and forth. He did not want to get into it—to encourage him.

"Am I, ah, missing something?" Maggie asked.

"Believe me," Adam said. "You don't want to know."

"Really I do. But I don't have the time right now. You can fill me in this evening. Call me on my cell when you're ready to go."

Jacob Belle silently looked out at the empty electrical line that ran from corner to corner across the intersection, the one that used to support the light, and he sighed.

"I'll miss that light," he said.

He was a pitiful sight. Adam began to understand,

even agree with him. Then he began to feel sorry for him. He wanted Maggie put the damn light back. He looked helplessly over his shoulder at her. She was standing there, smiling from ear to ear. She shook her head, then shrugged her shoulders in a gesture that said, *I give up.* "You deal with this," she said. "He's all yours. I've got to check in with my father." Then she was gone.

~*~

"What were we talking about the last time we met?" Jacob asked. "I can't seem to recall just where we were. It's Doc Brothers' goddamn medicine. It's not fair. That son-of-a-bitch gets a Rolex, and I give up my memory. Great trade for him. Bad for me."

Adam had to think. His recent episode with Leonard Morgan seemed to tax his memory as much as Doc Brothers' prescriptions were taxing his grandfather's. "I believe the preacher and the sheriff were in the middle of the lake watching a couple of masturbating hit-men."

"That's right. Anthony Russo, alias Father Gould, had just finished hearing Billy Brooks' confession. And he had sent Billy to see Tommy Delaney. Then he went and enlisted Sheriff Morgan's help. And he was in the boat with Morgan, playing the timid priest, getting himself a first-hand look at the Landing and just whom he would be up against. He was a clever one, that Russo."

"How about the sheriff?" Adam asked.

"Morgan?" Jacob grinned broadly. "A far cry from clever."

"Kinda like Leonard?"

"That the grandson?"

"That's him."

"Well... I really don't know the grandson. But I've heard rumors. I'd say when people talk of the acorn not falling far away from the tree, they're describing Leonard Morgan."

"So, what was Brooks supposed to do when he found Delaney?"

"Well... I think the idea was that Tommy Delaney would shoot him. I think that's what Anthony Russo wanted to happen. Amelia and I arrived back at Delaney's cabin just ahead of Brooks. We had delivered a bottle of booze and had just left. When we heard someone rustling in the bushes, we ducked out of sight. We wanted to know what was up."

~*~

Brooks knocked softly on the two gunmen's door.

"Christ almighty, Brooks," Delaney said. "Knock like you got a set of balls."

Delaney pushed open the screen door and he and his partner walked onto the cabin's porch. The partner took a position in the corner, leaning against the wall in the shadows. He placed his hand behind his back, hiding the gun he held ready for whatever need might come.

"There's going to be a shooting," Amelia whispered.

"Think so?" Jake asked.

He crouched down further, pulling her with. "Keep down," he told her

"What are you doing here, Brooks?" Delaney demanded.

"Anthony Russo sent me." A silent moment passed between them. "He told me to get you to write him a note."

"A note?"

"Yeah!"

"What the fuck for?"

"Look, Mr. Delaney. Cobb run me off from here. Petruzzi wants me dead. Anthony just wants you to tell him I'm alright."

"Are you, Brooks? Are you alright?"

Billy Brooks carefully thought through his next move, what he would say next. Anything would be risky.

142

But what would be the least risky. Ah! What the hell. *This is my best shot,* he decided. *It's this or Petruzzi and Cobb will hunt me down and kill my ass.* "I know you've turned. I want to join up."

The gun slid silently from behind Delaney's partner's back. Click. The hammer went back.

Brooks closed his eyes.

Amelia Cobb cringed and pinched her eyes so tightly shut that her face took on the look of a rabbit.

Jake Belle, even in the dim light of the brush, found humor in her look. He chuckled out loud.

The pistol swung in their direction and fired. A branch from just above the two youngsters snapped and fell to the ground. They got to their feet and fled their hiding place before another shot could be fired.

"God... damn it, Brooks. Who the fuck followed you?"

Brooks said nothing. He waited for a bullet from Delaney's friend's revolver to find him.

"Get the fuck inside," Delaney ordered.

~*~

"What did he mean? Billy said he knew Tommy Delany had turned. What does turned mean?" Jake asked.

"I don't know," Amelia said. "I've never heard of that term before."

~*~

Anthony Russo had little trouble convincing Sheriff Morgan to help him investigate the Landing. Morgan had seen the steady increase of airplane traffic. He could smell money. He knew what those planes carried—whiskey, good old prohibited Canadian whiskey—and he wanted some for himself. And he wanted to profit.

Anthony Russo wanted the lay of the land. He had spied on Cobb's Landing one other time, when Cobb first came here, but had found it no threat to his hiding place. Now, though, considering its recent growth and Billy Brooks' ability to find him, the danger the Landing presented went from slightly possible to eminent. How long would it be? If Brooks found him, and Billy Brooks wasn't a mobster—Billy Brooks was a fuck-up—just how long would Russo be safe? He had to know. Spying was the answer. Morgan was along so Russo could put on a show. Morgan would be the witness to say to the town, "Nah! Father Gould is not one of them. Father Gould is a scared shitless priest, just like everyone thought." Then, as soon as this was over, Morgan would run to the landing in search of his slice of the pie. That's where Russo wanted him.

Just before the field glasses crashed to the floor and broke in two—another of Russo's staged incidents to keep Morgan thinking priest not gangster—Anthony Russo watched Delaney shove Billy Brooks into the cabin. And he watched the two hitters, as they picked up on the light from Morgan's cigarette and put on their obscene gesture aimed at whoever the intruder might be.

Secretly, Russo could not decide. Did he want Delaney to kill Brooks or not? But he doubted that he would. He knew Delaney. They had worked together a long time ago, and he knew how Delaney thought and he knew Delaney knew how he thought. Brooks had value. At least for now he did. He was the perfect fall-guy should something go wrong. He would be spared the bullet now, saved for when needed, but in the end, if it turned out he hadn't been needed; well… then they'd shoot him.

Russo found his view of the sheriff accurate. He had allowed Morgan to see enough. He was hooked. He would go for the money. Proof came as they arrived back at Morgan's truck.

"Where the fuck you think you're going, Priest?"

Morgan asked.

"Bring me back to the rectory," Father Gould said.

"Walk!"

"You're joking."

"No! I'm Not."

"I've got to get back. I've got to get started on this right now, Sheriff."

"Got to get started on what?" Morgan asked.

"On putting an end to that evil place. It needs to be closed down, for good. Now you're the only law around here and it's your duty to help me." He tried to sound commanding.

"To hell with you and to hell with your plans," Morgan said. "I got me some plans of my own. I only agreed to let you come out here with me. I never said I would back you in your move."

"Well, just why did you bring me out here if you had no intention of doing something about all that is going on at that place?"

Father Gould wiped a little imaginary sweat from his upper lip and looked down at the ground. It would give Morgan the idea that he was afraid of him. Scared shitless was the look he was going for, his priest act.

"To tell you the truth," the sheriff said, "I never thought we'd find nothin' out here anyway."

"Well, now that we did, don't you feel duty bound to take action, Sheriff?" He knew the peace officer would not back him. He counted on it. And he counted on this one last plea as punctuation to the sheriff's resolve to cash in on the Cobb operation. Morgan in the way was like a cloak for Russo and Delaney to hide under.

"Oh, I'm gonna to take action, Preacher," Morgan said, "only it ain't gonna to be the action you want."

"Wha-wha-what do you mean? What kind of action are you talking about?"

"The kind of action that gets me a lot of money, Priest. That's the only action that'll be taken, see, and you just go on about your business quiet-like, if you know what's good for ya."

"What kind of messenger of God would I be if I allowed this?" Father Gould asked. Once again he looked at the ground in front of him. Eye contact with the sheriff would not be advisable.

"The kind that's on foot," the sheriff shouted. "And the quiet kind. Now, get the fuck away from my truck. And, Priest," he paused for a moment to make sure he had Gould's full attention, "keep your goddamned lip buttoned about this. Get it?"

He slammed the truck's door and drove off, leaving the priest an hour into the dark of the night, alone and afoot.

Father Gould grinned. Then he began the long walk back to his church.

~*~

When Sheriff John Morgan pulled his truck into the Landing's main compound and brought it screeching to a halt in front of the lodge building, its engine let out a loud bang. It sounded like gunfire. It was not an accident. He had installed on the dashboard of the vehicle a lever that allowed him to retard the engine's magneto just enough to cause a backfire. He used this for effect when he wanted to intimidate. If he was not intending to intimidate, he was sneaking up on his pray like a timber wolf on a defenseless rabbit, and the loud bang would give him away, so the ability to make the adjustment from inside the cab was necessary.

Morgan was a bully, not a genius, and this one spark of intelligent thinking was considered his only spark of intelligent thinking. Truthfully, most felt that the idea had come from some mind that was superior to his, anyway.

It was nearly ten o'clock in the evening. The party had been going on since six and alcohol had taken its toll. Few of those who heard the bang reacted. Jordan

Cobb was the exception. He not only heard the bang, he
shot from his cabin, leaving a lady in a tan dress and
floppy hat standing on his front porch. He set out to
investigate, and he did so intelligently, with a gun in his
hand.

Morgan opened the door to his truck. He slipped a
big foot into the loose sand on the ground. Then, he felt
cold steel, just behind his left ear.

"Who the fuck are you, and what the fuck are you
doing at my Landing?" Cobb asked in a low, tough
growl that sent shivers down the neck of the county
bully.

"I...I'm County Sheriff John Morgan," he finally
said. He used a deep voice, deep enough, he thought, to
sound forceful. Tough. Like the man who just spoke to
him. "That's who the fuck I am. And I'm here on official
business. County business."

Cobb reached a hand around the sheriff, lifted the
front of his jacket slightly. He pulled Morgan's pistol
from its holster.

"Well, Sheriff," he said, "you won't be shooting
anybody on this official business of yours, now will
you."

"I'm an officer of the law, mister, and you can't......."

"Yeah! Yeah! Yeah! Sure! But I'm the guy holding
both guns." Cobb said. "Now, unless you can do
something to me with that pretty little badge of yours
like I can do with these guns, I would strongly
recommend that you accept the fact that I'm the one with
the power, not you. I'm sure we'll get on much better
that way. Don't you agree, Sheriff?"

Morgan paused. He did not want to admit that his
opponent in this standoff was right, but he knew full
well the one holding all the guns also held all the aces.
His position was precarious. Denying that would be
senseless. "What now?" he asked.

"Now, Mr. Sheriff, we go into my office and sort
things out in a civilized manner." Cobb emptied all of

the bullets from the sheriff's handgun. He handed the empty weapon back to Morgan.

"After you," he said.

He pointed at the front entrance to the lodge building.

Morgan walked ahead. He silently observed all that came within his vision on either side. He would try to remember everything he saw, store it in his head for future use. *Might come in handy. Never know.*

Once inside, the two men entered Cobb's private office. Cobb took a chair behind his desk, careful to position his loaded gun on the desk's top, barrel aimed menacingly in the direction of the guest chair. Morgan sat across from him.

"Now, what can we here at Cobb's Landing do for you, Sheriff Morgan?" Cobb asked. He spoke softly, politely, yet maintained an unmistakable tone of authority. He leaned back in his chair and awaited Morgan's answer.

"It's said there's been unlawful things goin' on out here, Mr. Cobb," Morgan began. His chest puffed up as he spoke, like some sort of blowfish trying to frighten off an intruder. He, too, leaned back in his chair. He pressed it until it creaked. "I'm out here to find out just what unlawful things are goin' on, and I'm fixin' to do somethin' about anythin' I find that's illegal."

"Is that a fact?" Cobb asked.

He leaned forward. The front legs of the chair crashed loudly on the hardwood floor. He peered into Morgan's eyes without blinking for a long moment. He did not speak. He waited. Morgan had the next move.

Morgan, unable to defeat Cobb in a stare off, finally looked down at his pants. He was surprised to see that his legs were jiggling up and down nervously. He tried to still them. He couldn't. He hoped Cobb had not noticed.

"That's a fact!" he said.

"I assure you, Sheriff Morgan, You'll find nothing going on here. Nothing illegal. Just a lot of folks having a good time."

Cobb had still not blinked.

"Is that a fact?"

"That's a fact." Cobb stood. "You're welcome to look around, Sheriff, but don't bother my guests. They came here to relax, not to be harassed by the cops."

"Is that a threat?"

"Not at all. I'm telling you this for your own good. Most of the folks you'll run into out here have little tolerance for the law. If you trouble them, especially when they've had too much to drink, I can't be responsible for your safety. That's all."

"Now that's what I'm talkin' 'bout, Cobb," Morgan said, "that drinkin'. That's the unlawful thing I come to stop."

"Drinking isn't illegal, Sheriff," Cobb said.

"Well it shor' is, Mr. Cobb. This is prohibition."

"Prohibition isn't about drinking, Sport, it's about selling alcohol. You can drink all you want, you just can't buy it legally," Cobb told Morgan.

He knew he was incorrectly interpreting the law. He didn't care. Hell, he doubted that this miserable excuse for a lawman would know the difference anyway.

He was right.

"I know that, Cobb. But I intend to catch one of 'em payin' for booze. That's how I'll get 'em."

Cobb smiled. He was aware of the town's sheriff's contemptible reputation and he knew what this scheming parasite wanted. He wanted money. He wanted to capitalize. He saw himself as entitled to what they call a piece of the action. Cobb's first instinct was to place a bullet neatly between the sheriff's eyes. They were too far apart to please Cobb anyway. That's not what he did. It's only what he wanted to do. After all, he wasn't uncivilized. He was mob. And as mob, he recognized something in Morgan—corruptibility. The seedier the character, the more corruptible he would be, and Morgan was seedy indeed. He could be useful. Cobb would let him live for now.

As Cobb escorted Morgan outside, he decided that the present was as good a time as any to make an alliance with this, the area's only law. He stopped just short of stepping off of the front porch into the sand. "Tell me Sheriff Morgan," he started, "just what is it that you want?"

Morgan had already stepped down. When he turned to face Cobb, he found himself looking up at him. Cobb had planned it that way. It was one of his most adhered to rules. Gain the advantage. Be the greater presence. Never negotiate until that has been accomplished. He blocked Morgan from coming back up to his level.

"What is it that you want from us here at the Landing?" he asked again.

"I just want to enforce the law, Mr. Cobb," Morgan said. "That's all."

"Bullshit, my friend," Cobb snapped.

He moved himself menacingly close to Morgan, into his space. "You came here to gain from this place, to profit. It's money that you want from us."

Morgan was not used to anyone seeing through his strategy. This man, Cobb, was different, clever, foxy; not to be bullied like most folks. He could not intimidate Cobb. Just the opposite was true. Cobb intimidated him.

Cobb, on the other hand, found humor in Morgan's lack of intelligence. It made a small, but noticeable, smile appear on his face.

"What's so funny?" Morgan asked.

"Nothing, Sheriff. Now, let's get down to it. You seem like a reasonable man, Mr. Morgan, and you happen to be in a position to be of some value to me and my organization."

"How's that?" Morgan asked.

Cobb thought he could actually see the man's ears perk up, like those of a wild animal when it hears the snapping of a dry twig off in the distance.

He smiled once again, hoping that the smile didn't

dampen his negotiations. He hoped the sheriff would see it as a sign of politeness rather than an insult. "I think, Sheriff Morgan, that your position as head of the area's chief law enforcement agency should give you, I mean us," Cobb quickly inserted the 'us' with purpose, as a first subtle step of bringing the lawman into the organization, "an advantage that has been long needed here at the Landing."

"What advantage would ya be thinkin' of, Mr. Cobb?"

Morgan surprised himself. He rarely called anyone mister. He didn't know why he did it. It made him feel weak—embarrassed. Did Cobb deserve it? Or, did he demand it? Either way, Morgan was uncomfortable. He wasn't the one in control. "I mean, Cobb," he corrected.

"Mr. Cobb. You'll be working for me, and you'll be paid handsomely for it. Everyone who works for me is paid handsomely and addresses me as Mr. Cobb."

"I'll be working for you?" Morgan asked. Hostility dissipated. Loyalty and respect emerged. The thought of being handsomely paid was a powerful thought indeed. He wondered what handsomely converted to in dollars and cents. But he was sure it was more than sheriff wages. "What is it I'll be doin' for you?"

"You'll be here when we have parties. You'll keep things peaceful. You'll also be running intervention services with the town's people for us," Cobb told him.

"Intervention?" Morgan asked.

"Yes, talk to people for us, get them to feel we're not their enemy. Make them see there's no cause for alarm. We're simply what we are, a private place for big executives from the big city to come to unwind when things get a bit too tough on them. You can do that. Can't you?"

"Just how much is handsomely?"

Cobb wondered how long it would take Morgan to ask that.

"Well, let me see. How much do you get for being a

peace officer?"

Morgan told him. As soon as the figure had slipped out he began mentally kicking himself. He knew that Cobb's offer would be based on what he had just blurted out. He knew he should have lied. He should have told Cobb his wages were higher than they actually were.

"I will pay you twice that amount," Cobb told him, "and you can keep your present position so you'll still have your wages from that job."

He watched as the wheels slowly turned in Morgan's mind. *This is taking entirely too long*, Cobb thought. *This idiot can't add. It'll take him until morning to calculate his new wages in his head.* Finally, Cobb told him what it came to.

"That's a lot of money Mr. Cobb," he said. "All I have to do is keep the town folk off your back and knock a few drunks around out here?"

"No!" Cobb said. "You won't touch the guests. All that will be required of you in so far as the Landing's guests are concerned is that you keep an eye on things. I want this clearly understood. I do not want you to do anything but have a word with an out-of-hand guest. If that doesn't do the trick, then you are to find me. I'll see to any head knockings that need doing."

Cobb started down the steps. That was enough of Morgan for one night. He supposed he could stand the man in small doses. For now, though, the dose was reaching a toxic level. Any more and he would succumb to his desire to shoot the oaf. Things would come to that soon enough. He knew it. He swung a muscular arm over the sheriff's shoulder. "Do we have a deal, Sheriff Morgan?" he asked.

"Deal!" Morgan said.

"Good. You'll start out here on Friday night about seven. Plan on spending both Friday and Saturday nights out here from now on. Until then, do what you can to convince the people in your town that we're not a bunch of dark creatures, will you?"

"I can do that, Mr. Cobb," Morgan said.

Cobb reached out a hand and opened the door to the sheriff's truck for him.

"See you Friday."

"Friday," the sheriff said.

He started the engine of his truck. It let out a loud backfire that made both men jump. He had forgotten to place the engine's timing back to its normal position.

"Oh! Sheriff!" Cobb yelled over the noise of the loud motor. "When you see the priest again, tell him I need to see him. Tell him that most of our guests are Catholic and could really use his guidance on Sunday mornings. Tell him I'll even build him a chapel."

The time had come. Russo, sooner or later, needed to know Cobb wasn't stupid. Besides, hunting is more fun if the prey knows you're coming.

Chapter Twelve

"Tomorrow I'll dress," Grandfather Belle promised, recalling Adam's look earlier that morning when he showed up to find Jacob in pajamas. "I'll feel more up to it. I'm sure."

"I really don't mind," Adam said. "You've been through a lot."

"Maybe you don't, but I do. I despise being sick, feeling weak. I always knew that the day would come when I'd end up this way. I knew someday I would be charged for my past sins. It surprises me that I'm so unprepared."

"What do you mean... be charged for your past sins?"

Adam thought of his grandfather as a genuine man, one with a big heart and a good soul, not as someone who had sins to pay for—at least none severe enough to merit cancer. "What sins are you talking about?"

"I have many. But the greatest is Amelia Cobb."

"A schoolboy romance isn't exactly sin," Adam said. "At least in this day and age it isn't. Maybe back at Cobb's Landing it was. Maybe to the mob it was. But that's old-fashioned thinking. You don't subscribe to that, do you?"

"Of course not! My time with her at the Landing was nothing. It was everything to me in those days, but it was, as you call it, a schoolboy romance. Those have gone on for centuries, and, I hope to God, they go on for centuries more." He moved to the front window as he spoke.

"What then? What's the big sin with Amelia Cobb?"

Jacob Belle stared out at the street below for a moment. "Come over here," he said. "Take a look at these fools."

Adam heard the crash and the long blasts of car horns before he could get to his grandfather's side.

"Programmed idiots," he snickered. "They can't navigate the intersection without the light. I knew this would be trouble, I just knew it. Should have left the light there."

"Back to this big sin of yours, Grandfather. I really want to hear this."

"I'm not entirely sure that you do," he said.

"Oh, I do."

"It's the reason you and I were kept apart all of those years," Jacob started. "I would have thought that would be payment enough for the size of the sin, but apparently it wasn't."

He coughed a few times and seemed to use up the air in his lungs far too rapidly.

"Our relationship went on a lot longer than anyone knew. When they shut down the Landing, after the war out there, I stayed on with the mob to look after the place. Amelia Cobb, I had been told, had been badly injured in the gunfight and later died of her wounds. Maybe I told you this. Maybe not. Anyway, she didn't die. But it did take more than two years for her to heal."

In the mean time, thinking Amelia dead, I met your grandmother and married her. Had I known Amelia was still alive, I would never have married. I would have waited for her, maybe even moved to Chicago to be at her side. That wasn't the case though. The organization needed me to watch over the Landing. It had to be kept in good repair, because the mob still used it as a hideout for it's members who needed a place to go until this situation or that situation cooled off. They let me think she had been killed, I suppose, so I wouldn't leave.

Anyway, when I found out the truth I was devastated. I had married. And instead of being married to the love of my life, I was married to your grandmother. I should have accepted the way things were, but I didn't have the strength for that. I had an affair with Amelia Cobb, one that lasted for a very long time. I hated myself for it, but I could not bring myself to end it."

"Did my grandmother know about Amelia?"

"She knew of her. She knew Amelia had been my first love. But she always thought Amelia had died."

"Why didn't you just leave Grandma and hook up with Amelia when you learned she was still alive? That's what most folks do."

"That was then, not now," he said, "and then, in those days, leaving one's spouse for another wasn't done. Commitment was stronger than love. It was a rule of society that everyone lived by. Especially Catholics. The married would stay married no matter what. The only viable way out of that kind of commitment was death. I understood that. Your grandmother understood that. Even Amelia Cobb understood that."

"So you chose to have an affair?"

"I did," he said.

"How did you pull that off with you way up here and her in Chicago?"

"That was easy," he said. "You see, my job with the Landing grew. After two years, considering the place was still active... not the parties, just the occasional gangster on the lam... I was promoted to manager for the Landing, a fill-in for Jordan Cobb."

"Did you travel between here and Chicago?"

"Not for at least a couple of years. All communications came in with guests. Even my paydays came that way. God, how your grandmother hated that."

"Why?"

"Sporadic! Never knew when payday would come."

"I can see where that might piss a woman off."

"Anyway," Jacob went on, "when Cobb died, I went

to Chicago for the funeral and to meet my new boss. That's when I came back in contact with Amelia. She took over as administrator of Cobb's Landing when her daddy died. Then she started spending summers here. And I spent a lot of time in the winter in Chicago. If I wasn't with her, she was with me at the Landing. Your grandmother hated the Landing. She never wanted to be with me when I was out there. My summers, for the most, were consumed by my job, twenty-four hours a day, seven days a week. Amelia and I were young. Opportunity was abundant. It seemed the natural course to take."

"Didn't you feel guilty? I mean, most guys that I know couldn't pull that sort of thing off without getting caught. Their own conscience, sooner or later, would trip them up."

"Oh... it was a battle alright. But love won; guilt came in second. It wasn't conscience that tripped us, but we did get caught."

"I thought you said Grandma never knew."

"She didn't," he said. "At least, to my knowledge she didn't."

"Then who caught you?"

"Your father. Actually he didn't exactly catch us. I, in a moment of weakness, kind of told on myself."

"Why would you do that?"

"Amelia and I had been involved for many years. Out of the blue, something happened that should not have happened. Her wounds from the Cobb's Landing war had left her unable to bear children. Consequently we did not concern ourselves with prevention. The doctors had been mistaken. Amelia got pregnant. There was a little girl born, our little girl. We named her Elizabeth. And she was an angel; she never fussed like other children. She always obeyed her mother and me. She was perfect and beautiful. Then she died."

A tear slid gracefully down his cheek as he related his sad tale. Several moments went by in painful silence.

Then he brushed the tear aside and continued. "I was devastated. I had only two close friends, Amelia and Tucci. Amelia couldn't comfort me. She hurt too badly. And Tucci was never much comfort, too tough, been through too much, having watched his own dad get gunned down and all that. I turned to your father. The shock was too much. He wasn't able to handle finding out I had a secret life. And finding out he had a little sister, well... that didn't settle at all. He turned on me. He took you away. And he never again had anything to do with me. But, at least he didn't tell your grandmother."

"That's the whole reason that my father stopped seeing you and Grandma? There had to be more than that. Are you sure it didn't have something to do with your working for the mob?"

"I told you before, the fact that I worked for the mob never bothered your father. He loved his mother very much. He always protected her. I had the whole second life going with Amelia Cobb. It took my summers. The time your father was not in school, I spent at the Landing and away from him. So he grew close to his mother and distant from me. I suppose when he learned of my affair, and the fact that I had another family on the side, he may even have felt cheated. I guess he thought Amelia got my valuable time and he and your grandmother got what was left. I never thought of it that way, back when this was all taking place. Otherwise I would have tried to fix it. God knows! I wish I had."

"I always hated my parents for keeping us apart. When they died, and left me on my own like that, I hated them even more."

"It might be me that you should hate. It was my indiscretion, my sin, my fault that all of it happened the way it did. You should blame me, not your parents."

~*~

Adam thought for a time. He did not want his grandfather to talk. He wanted to catch up on his history in silence. He could not side with Jacob Belle. Jacob Belle had been wrong—wrong to keep so much from his family—wrong to have a life apart from them—wrong to have two families. Adam's mother and father, on the other hand, had been equally as wrong. They should never have stopped a grandfather and grandson from seeing each other, especially as close as the relationship between the two of them had become.

Adam had only been six, but still he remembered. To him it had been a great loss, one that he did not understand. *Maybe love was the culprit*, he thought. *Maybe my father loved his mother too much and his father too little. Maybe my grandfather loved Amelia Cobb and their daughter more than he loved his son and grandson. Maybe...! Maybe... Maybe love can do more damage that good.*

"I think I'll take a walk."

"Do you want to know who paid your rent?"

"Something called The Cobb's Landing Foundation, according to Emma Pierson, my ex-landlady," Adam said. "Exactly what is that?"

"Mostly, it's Amelia. It started out as an organization that looked after Petruzzi's money for him. When he went to prison, you see, he didn't know or trust the family anymore, too many personal enemies, so he left his old friend, Jordan Cobb, to watch over things for him. Well...when he died in prison, the Cobb's kinda secretly inherited. Then when Jordan died, he used Petruzzi's money to support the Landing while he was alive, but when he was gone, Amelia took over. Now, Amelia, by then anyway, had had it with the mob, so, since nobody knew she even had the money, or that it had started out to be mob money, she decided to use it to do good. She still does it. She's the one who took care of your expenses."

He struggled to get to his feet. Adam moved quickly

to help him.

"Goddamned medication. It makes me weak as a mouse." He began shuffling off towards the bathroom. "That doctor and his drugs will have me pissing my pants before it's all over." He shuffled into the bathroom and grasped the doorknob to close the door. Just before it completely closed he said, "She's been looking after you for years. She and I." Then he shut the door.

"I know you don't know this, Adam, but her and me have been watching over you all along," he shouted through the closed door.

"Couldn't it wait until you're done in there?" The sound of his grandfather pissing in the commode seemed to detour Adam's ability to concentrate on the conversation.

Jacob Belle quieted. Soon the door opened.

"Amelia... rather, The Cobb's Landing Foundation, the organization Amelia has directed since her father passed away, owns the company you worked with. The same foundation gave you the scholarships for college."

"Maggie mentioned that organization. She calls it mob money. That true?"

"True, I guess, but before you go gettin' your underwear in a wad, remember what I said. Amelia puts a lot of it, like the money for your college, care on your folks' home so you'd always have a place to come back to, parks for the town and many other improvements, to great use."

"But it's still mob money! Now, I realize it's quite noble to provide parks and things like that for folks, but what about money for one individual like me. That's not a noble effort. That's charity. That's being supported by the mob."

"Ah, Adam. Don't look at it that way. Me and Amelia meant no harm. We were just helping, after all, you are family; and family takes care of their own."

"By that do you mean family, or FAMILY?"

"Mob isn't as dirty a word as you might be thinking.

We're your people. We are your family. And like any other family, we take care of our own. And you are ours. You were born into it. You're the grandson of a gangster. Like it or not, it's the truth."

"What about my father? Was he mob?"

"Not actively like me, but he was mob. Like I said, born into it."

He studied Adam for a long moment. *Perhaps,* he thought, *the time had come—time for some truth.* "How much do you recall of your parents and the night they died?"

"Not much. I remember them bringing me to the hospital. I remember looking at their bodies. I remember… and this makes no sense at all, but I think I was dressed in a tuxedo."

"You were. Do you recall who found them?"

"No." Adam thought for a moment. This conversation was upsetting. It was one he wished to end. "Can we change the subject?"

"We could. But we shouldn't."

The ring of the doorbell ended their talk abruptly. *A blessing,* Adam thought. *Who knows what turn this might take next?* He went to answer the door. Before he opened it, he turned to face his grandfather.

"Did I know Maggie before?"

"Why? Do you remember her?"

"It's just the way I feel around her. Comfortable. Like we had been together forever. Strange."

"Not so strange. Answer the door, Adam."

It was Maggie coming for him. Adam was pleased. He had missed her today.

Jacob, too, was pleased to see her. He wanted to talk to her. He wanted her to fill Adam in. He wanted his grandson to remember his childhood and he did not have faith in doctors. Jacob Belle was always a doer—never one to wait around and see what happens. And it made sense to him that his grandson could be recalling his past as easily, possibly even more easily, if only he were told what to remember. This waiting game was a game Jacob Belle never did do well. He wanted it to stop.

"Did I hear there was an accident in front of the bank this afternoon?" Maggie asked.

She knew what Grandfather Belle was about to say. The tail end of his and Adam's conversation had been louder than either of them thought. She picked up on it in the moments before she rang—not that she was one to eavesdrop, she just hadn't wanted to intrude. So she waited for them to finish before she rang. But she did believe in leaving Adam's recovery to doctors, so by changing the subject before the subject could surface, she could give the doctors time, something that Jacob Belle would not give.

"Was it a bad one?" she asked.

"Not bad enough. Those fools deserve to kill each other if they can't read a simple stop sign." Jake said.

"Ah! The compassion of a true gangster." Adam said.

"He filled you in on the mob, did he?" Maggie said.

"He sure did."

"How'd it sit with you? I remember when my dad gave me the talk. I was stunned. You learn anything else?"

"I learned all about the priest and Leonard's grandfather."

"I'll bet that was a treat. Leonard's grandfather anything like Leonard?"

"Identical!" Grandfather Belle said. "Now, why don't the two of you get the hell out of here? Let an old man get some rest."

"What about tomorrow? Adam asked.

"Tucci's! For breakfast. Don't be late."

"One last question?" Adam asked.

"Go ahead." Jacob said.

"How old was Elizabeth?"

"She was your age. A couple of months older."

Chapter Thirteen

"Rough night?" Maggie smilingly asked, when morning came. She handed Adam a steaming mug of freshly brewed coffee.

"A little rough."

"Where were you?" she asked.

"Right here."

"No. I mean, in your dreams. Where were you in your dreams?"

"How many buildings were there at Cobb's Landing?"

"I'm not positive, but I think there were about thirty," Maggie said after searching her mind for a moment. "Why?"

Adam took a long sip from his coffee before answering. "There were thirty-four," he said.

"How do you know that?"

"I dreamed it. I spent most of the night at Cobb's Landing. It was strange. I must have woke up six times, but when I fell back asleep, I always ended up back at the Landing, and it would be in the same moment I had been in before I awoke. I've never experienced anything like that before."

"I wouldn't imagine you would have," Maggie said. "It wasn't until recently that you even heard of Cobb's Landing."

"I don't mean that. I mean the part about waking up and going right back into the same dream when I fell back asleep. With my grandfather filling my head with information about the place on a daily basis, I can

163

certainly understand some of it resurfacing in dreams. But a dream that can't be broken by waking up... well, now that's... that's different. That scares the shit out of me."

The phone rang. Maggie rose to answer it.

Just as she placed her hand on the receiver a thought entered Adam's mind. "Maggie," he said.

The phone was half way to her ear. She stopped to listen.

"I know where the bodies are buried."

"How do you know that?"

She moved the phone's receiver close to her ear.

"I saw it in my dream."

Maggie stared at him for a moment, phone's receiver held tight to her ear.

"Hello?" the caller said.

"Hello," Maggie answered. It was Grandfather Belle. He had awakened early. He was impatiently waiting at Tucci's Diner.

Maggie and Adam hurried. They showered and dressed in only moments, or so it seemed to them. Then they made their way across town to join Jacob Belle for breakfast.

Tucci was standing in the doorway as they approached.

"I see you two recovered without scars," he said, referring to their recent bout with poison ivy. He had seen neither of them since the incident.

Adam and Maggie ignored his comment and followed him to Jacob's table. On the way Adam began to think, *It's always the same table. It never changes. Why don't these two old gangsters follow the rules? They should alter their habits: like television gangsters. Repetition is dangerous. That's how hits are made.* Tucci snaked his way around tables filled with guests in the front of the restaurant. *Christ, Adam!* He told himself. *Get a grip. You're letting them get to you.*

"You should be more careful," he said as they arrived

at the table. "You shouldn't sit in the same place all the time."

He seated himself in the chair opposite his grandfather, and next to Maggie.

"Good morning to you, too!" Grandfather Belle said. "You look like someone beat the shit out of you with a rubber hose; no marks, but beaten just the same. Maggie, Darlin', you do this to him?"

"No Grandfather Belle. I think you did," she said. "It seems he spent most of his night at the Landing. In his dreams."

"Oh, that explains it. I remember when we first started talking about all of this. It was right after Grandma's funeral. I spent several nights at the place myself. That can sure wear a person down."

"How many buildings were there at the Landing?" Maggie asked.

"Thirty-five," Grandfather Belle answered, without hesitation.

Maggie glanced at Adam.

He began to search his mind. *What did I miss? I counted thirty-four.* Adam stirred his potatoes with a fork. *Where's the missing structure?*

"You gonna eat those spuds or just stab at 'em some more?" Tucci asked.

Adam forked a big portion into his mouth. As he chewed the answer came to him. "The bath house!" he said excitedly.

Tiny chunks of his breakfast escaped.

"Sorry," he said.

"What?" Jacob asked.

"I said, sorry," Adam repeated.

"No, not that. I mean before that."

"Oh, I said the bath house."

Jacob Belle picked up his napkin. He brushed at food particles on the front of his shirt.

"Actually, if you count the storehouse, there were thirty-six. Nobody ever considered it a building though.

It was more of a dug-out."

He brushed a few more specs away, then laid his napkin back on the table.

"So... what about the bath house?" he asked.

Adam looked puzzled.

Maggie intervened.

"He dreamed last night that there were thirty-four buildings in all at the landing. The bath house must be the one he missed."

"The bath house was my favorite of all," Grandfather Belle said.

Then he went back to his breakfast. He scraped the last of his scrambled eggs into a neat little pile and pushed them onto his toast with his fork.

"Eat up," he ordered. We'll go back to my place and I'll tell you why."

Adam picked at his food.

"Something troubling you this morning?" Jacob asked.

"No. Not really. Just dreams."

"Dreams. Dreams will do it. Especially those about the Landing."

"It wasn't the ones about the Landing that trouble me. They tire me, but not trouble me."

"What then?"

Adam looked into Maggie's eyes. He wondered, *Should I just let it pass? No!*

"I saw Maggie and I as teenagers. We went to the prom."

"And that troubles you because...?" Grandfather Belle questioned.

"Because I never went to a prom."

He looked again to Maggie. "Did I?"

"Adam," Maggie did not know which direction to take. Should she let the doctors deal with this? Should she follow the turn things had just taken? Was there a way to do both. She didn't want to lie to him... tell him they had never dated... and have him find out later on his own. That approach might cause mistrust. "Adam, you did go to your prom. I was your date."

Tears formed in Adam's eyes.

"Was it on the night my folks died?"

"Yes." Maggie grabbed his hand and squeezed. She turned to Jacob.

"Maybe we should change course today. I could take him home and he can get together with you tomorrow or the next day."

"No!" Adam said. "I want to keep going." He looked at Maggie, then at his grandfather. "I'm alright. Really."

Jacob put the last bite of his breakfast into his mouth, took one final gulp coffee. Cold! His lips curled in disgust. "You sure?" he asked.

"Yeah."

"Well... come on then. Let's get to my place. I'll tell you what was best about that bath house."

Adam deserted what was left of his breakfast. He rose to follow his grandfather. "I can hardly wait," he said.

"I have a doctor's appointment. After that, I'll be at the house," Maggie said. "I'll be by to get you at five."

"At the house?" Tucci asked. "You two shackin' up now?"

"What a disgusting term," Adam said, disapprovingly.

"What!" Tucci defended. "That's what we called it when me and your grandpa was young."

"Yup, Mr. Tucci, I'm Adam's shack job," Maggie said. She smiled broadly at the old gangster. She rose and kissed Grandfather Belle on the cheek. Then Adam.

"I can hardly wait for tonight, Stud." Then she walked proudly from the restaurant into the street.

~*~

Jacob Belle wasted no time getting to his apartment. His brisk walk, a contrast from the day before when he would not dress, was a mystery to Adam.

"You're in an awful hurry this morning," Adam commented.

"I got to get to the can."

"Something not setting well with you? Your medicine?"

"Tucci's coffee. It tasted like shit this morning. And it's about to run right through me."

"What was wrong with the coffee?" Adam asked. He had barely touched his.

"He's getting old and forgetful. Every once in awhile he forgets that he's been soaking the pots in some kind of cleaning solution overnight. He makes coffee with the chemical rather than with water. I think he might have done it this morning."

"Well I'm glad I didn't drink it."

"You didn't drink it because you were late," Jacob said, as they climbed the stairs to his apartment.

"We weren't late. You were early. Why do you live here?"

"I like it here," he said. "Why shouldn't I live here?"

"No reason, really. I just thought that you would prefer a house, that's all."

"Isn't this a house?"

"This is an apartment."

"It is," Jacob said. "But, it's still home. Same as a house but I don't have to shovel snow in the winter or mow lawn in the summer."

He fumbled with his keys. Adam took them and opened the door.

"Thanks. We would have been here all day."

He went straight to the bathroom. Then through the closed door, "The mob bought the bank out just after the robbery. A few years later, when it had been decided that I would stay on and take care of the Landing forever, or at least for as long as I could, they put the building in my name and set up a fair price for the bank to pay me for their rent. That would be my pay for my job at the

Landing. It was also a good way for them to launder some of their money."

Do all old people insist on talking through a closed bathroom door? I wonder if I will, Adam thought. "I'm not sure I want to know all of this."

"Sure you do. " After all, it'll be yours when I'm gone." he said, coming out of the bathroom.

They settled quickly into chairs in the living room.

"Tell me about the bank robbery," Adam said.

"I thought you wanted to know about the bathhouse."

"I do. I want to know why it was your favorite of the buildings."

"Because that was where I got my first piece of ass," he said. "It was mid summer of thirty-one, July fifteenth, as I recall. I had been awakened early by the sound of an incoming airplane, one that arrived from Canada with a fresh load of Canadian whiskey. I knew that it was due in. I also knew that it would have no passengers on board and none of the cargo was for the Landing. So I wasn't required to meet it. But I was only half asleep, so I got up and dressed in a hurry. It wasn't until I arrived at the landing strip half beaten to death by thick underbrush that I realized I didn't need to be there. But since I already was there, I decided to watch the landing. I stood in the brush at the edge of the woods. I watched Billy Brooks come out of the woods from the other side of the runway and run up to the plane's door. He ducked in the shadows as the door opened. Someone got off. Not the pilot. It was too quick. The plane had barely come to a stop. There had to be a passenger on this whiskey plane. Anyway, whoever it was disappeared into the darkness before the planes engines were shut down. Then Billy came out of the shadows. He watched the guy who got off the plane until he was out of sight. Then he ran to the plane and handed the pilot something."

"I felt a shiver down my spine, like someone, or something had been watching me."

~*~

"It's mighty early to be out, isn't it, Jacob Belle?"

The voice came from the darkness. It was Amelia Cobb.

"You scared the snot out of me, Amelia," Jake said in all too high a voice for a young man of his age.

She giggled.

"That's real funny, isn't it?" he said.

"Come on, Jake," Amelia said. "Walk me to the bathhouse."

"Who was that?" Jake asked. "I saw somebody get off the plane and disappear into the woods, just before the pilot got out."

"I'm not sure," Amelia said. "It could have been Daddy's brother, I guess. I heard he was coming to the Landing."

"Which brother?"

"What do you mean, which brother?" she said. "He only has one brother, my uncle Jonah."

"The dead brother?" Jake asked.

"Excuse me?" Amelia said.

"The brother from out west; Oregon or someplace?"

"That's the brother, but he's certainly not dead," Amelia said. "He just got off the plane, silly. Did he look dead to you, Jake Belle?"

"Well, I don't know," Jake answered. "It was pretty dark, and I was pretty far away."

"Oh! Jacob Belle! I swear! Sometimes you can be so...so...so agitating. Come. Walk me to the bathhouse before I just go off into the woods alone and get myself lost or something." *Boys! Mother was right. They understand very little.*

Jake's mind drifted back to the time when the two hit men arrived and he had left Amelia standing outside the bathhouse stark naked while he ran through the brush to do his job at the airstrip. He hadn't so much as turned around to get a glimpse. And it was a sight he had longed see. He thought for a moment. *No way*, he thought. *No way am I going to miss an opportunity like that again.* Of course he would walk her to the bathhouse.

~*~

Meanwhile, Jonah Cobb made his way to his brother's quarters. The pilot had given vivid directions. Even in the dark... even in strange territory... he was able to make his way easily. He knocked on Jordan's door for several moments. He felt for the knob. It seemed to turn of its own accord. He let go as though it was electrified. The door swung open. On the other side stood Jordan Cobb, his handgun aimed at Jonah's face.

"Don't shoot! It's me! It's Jonah!"

The two brothers just stood there, face to face, looking at one another for a long moment.

Time seemed frozen. *Is it really Jonah? Is it really my brother? Or am I looking at a ghost?* "I got a telegram saying you might be on your way, but I didn't believe it," he finally said. "I'm still not convinced."

"Well... here I am. In the flesh."

He held his arms out wide.

Jordan grabbed him, pulled him close, and held him tight.

"I heard that you had been killed."

"I thought I was going to be for a while myself," Jonah Cobb admitted. "They chased me half-way down the west coast."

"Who?" Jordan asked.

"The Palanos," Jonah answered.

"Why were they after you? What did you do to them?"

Jordan Cobb could not imagine the Palano brothers having anything to do with any of his people. True, they had been long time rivals of the crime family to which the Cobb's belonged, but a peace existed; a truce that had been negotiated twenty years earlier, and had shown no indication that it would be broken since. The Palanos operated in the west these days. The Bartolli family, the family that the Cobbs belonged to, the family that was now led by Petruzzi, worked the north-central region, from the city of Chicago—where the family was headquartered—south to the Indianapolis area, and north to the Canadian border. Their chief enemy was Rosetti, not the Palanos. The Palanos had no overlap to fight about. Unless one of the Palano brothers, Jimmy, most likely if it was anyone, had decided to renew the old war. That was a possibility that always existed in the business. And it was the possibility each family guarded against at all times. Greed sometimes changed things without giving notice.

"I got caught screwing Jimmy Palano's wife," Jonah answered, with a small grin on his face. "I got some buckshot in my ass to prove it."

"I told you years ago, Jonah, when we were just kids, that if you didn't stop thinking with your pecker, you'd one day get yourself killed. Didn't I?"

Jordan loosened his grip on his brother and pushed him far enough back so he could look into his eyes. Jonah was known for his exaggerations. Only his brother could see a lie in his eyes. This time there wasn't one. But something was wrong. The Palano's didn't miss. Nobody got by them with a little buckshot in their ass—nobody! With them, it was enough buckshot to finish the job or none at all.

"Yeah. You told me," the younger Cobb admitted, "but I ain't dead."

"Is there anything else that you need to tell me about your trouble with the Palanos?" Jordan Cobb asked.

He knew his brother. Jonah had a habit of making things appear smaller than they really were. Especially if the situation was sticky.

"What do you mean?"

"I mean... are you certain there isn't more to your

problem with Jimmy Palano than getting caught in his old lady's bed? Because, long as I've known Jimmy, I've never known him to miss."

"He didn't miss. Want to see the buckshot?"

Jordan hoped he was not getting one of his brother's snow-jobs... enough truth to sound real... not enough to be accurate. This whole thing wasn't about a piece of ass. Hell! He didn't care who was nailing who. What he cared about was what trouble might follow, what repercussion might hit at Cobb's Landing, or on the front door-step of the Bartolli Family. That was his worry. And to the Bartollis, the Palanos were always a concern.

"Jonah, if you can think of anything I might need to know, you best tell me."

"There's nothing, Jordan. I swear. It was just about getting caught in bed with Jimmy's old lady. That's all."

"Come," Cobb pulled his brother through the open door. "Come in here. I'll make us some coffee."

~*~

This kiss was not the first that the young couple had shared, but it was the most passionate. Amelia, her sensual tongue searching deep into Jacob's mouth, began to slide the suspenders of his bib overalls down over his bare, muscular shoulders. Once the front of his pants had slid to reveal his deeply tanned and rock hard stomach, and while their tongues were still probing deeply into each other's soft, wet mouths, she began to unbutton her dress.

"What are you doing?" Jake asked, in a voice that showed both excitement and fear.

"I want to feel you against me, our skins touching. I want to feel your warm body against mine," she said.

He wanted to object. He was afraid that this would go too far. Then he was afraid it wouldn't. He pulled her tight for a moment. Her gentle hands that were working steadfastly on the buttons whose holes seemed too small at the moment were now trapped between them. He thought he could feel a breast, soft yet firm, press around the hands and brush lightly against his hot, naked skin. It was too late. The unbuttoning had reached that point—irrevocability. The squeeze that was meant to stop things before they went too far had instead, aided things. It had served to free the hot, round breasts that he had been watching grow into reality throughout the short time they had been together. He loosened his grip. Then they were pressed tightly together. They were one. He could think of nothing in life that might feel better.

~*~

The coffee on Jordan Cobb's wood-burning stove began to boil over. Jonah jumped from his seat to rescue the pot while Jordan dashed across the room to a small cupboard where several mugs hung from shiny brass hooks. He freed two of the large cups. Then he returned to the table just as his brother arrived with the pot of steaming coffee.

"I built a golf course," Jordan said, as Jonah poured their coffee. "Just this spring."

"Did you?"

"I did," he said. "I thought just in case you weren't dead that you might somehow show up. And I thought you might want to play."

"Do you play?" Jonah asked.

Jordan Cobb had always been a worker, not a player. He rarely chased women. He seldom drank or partied excessively. He never gambled. And learning the game of golf?…well…work had always taken precedence over such things.

That, however, was not the case with his younger brother Jonah. Jonah did all of those things, and he did them as often as he could.

"No. I never learned," Jordan said.

"Then I shall teach you. We'll begin as soon as it's

light out."

"I can't today," Jordan said. "Petruzzi's here. We've got business to see to."

At the sheer mention of the name, Petruzzi, Jonah Cobb's face began to pale. The two of them had a history. Jimmy Palano's wife was not the only mob boss' wife who Jonah Cobb bedded in his many madcap escapades. Mrs. Petruzzi had been one of his early conquests. Petruzzi had sworn vengeance at the very next sight of this young scoundrel, and all knew that not only he had meant it, but what he had meant when he said it.

"Is he staying long?" Jonah asked.

"Don't worry, little brother," Cobb said. "I will hide you from the big, bad mob boss. He'll be going back to Chicago in a day or two. Until then, we'll put you in with one of the other's until they've gone. You just stay out of sight."

"What do you mean, they?" Jonah asked.

"I don't understand," Jordan Cobb said.

"They! You said in a day or two 'they' will be gone. Who are 'they'? Who does Angelo have with him?"

"Don't you even think about it, Jonah Cobb! You know very well who 'they' are. Petruzzi has his wife with him on this trip, and you are to stay away from her. Now, don't you go fuckin' around with this. Even I won't be able to save you this time." Jordan Cobb was angered. He rose to his full height and peered down at his younger brother. "I mean it, Jonah. I don't want any trouble here. And if you have some notion in your head that'll bring me trouble, you just get your ass back on that plane and disappear. Do you understand?"

"I'll behave myself, Jordan," Jonah said, holding his hands slightly over his head in a sign of surrender. "I promise."

~*~

Jake Belle found himself shocked at the fact that he had become the aggressor when Amelia Cobb's dress slid gently, like a floating feather in the breeze, to the bathhouse floor and gathered itself like the pedals of a fragile flower at her bare feet. He hadn't meant for things to go this far. But here they were, both of them, naked and trembling, full of passion and desire for their first taste of the full meaning, of the final commitment of their love for one another. Her young flawless nipples stood out like sweet, ripe cherries as he held her back at arm's length to look at her magnificent young body. A few short weeks ago it was that of a girl. Now it had become that of a young woman. He felt his erection grow as he studied her. He thought it impossible. It seemed to swell until it hurt. He welcomed the pain. He knew that it was the pain of anticipation.

"I want you, Jacob," Amelia said, as she took a long up and down search of his firm, muscular frame. "I want you to make love to me."

"Are you sure that we should be doing this?" Jacob asked her. He wanted her, too. More than he thought possible. But he also wanted to give her the opportunity of backing away from what they were about to do. He knew that once they went past this place in their relationship, they could never take it back. It could never be undone.

She moved closer to him; close enough so that even the most minuscule breath of air could not come between them. She kissed him, long and hard. It was a kiss that replaced words. It was a kiss that told Jake Belle that she did not want to turn away from the moment. It was the kiss that made all of what was happening to this young couple alright, acceptable, even necessary. They simultaneously bent at the knees, sunk to the floor; and laid in a bed of their own clothing, where they made love. Clumsily at first, but more gracefully and more satisfying as they continued; until they had reached the climaxes of their young lives. It would be an experience that neither would ever forget. And one that neither of them would ever regret.

~*~

On his way to showing his brother to a cabin that he would temporally share with two of the mob's protectors, Jordan Cobb took a detour to show the younger Cobb the golf course that he and Jake Belle had built, and he was so proud of. Their journey took them close by the bathhouse. It was only luck that the two men were occupied with conversation and did not hear the youngsters within, the two who were nervously peering out a small, high-up window at them.

"By the way," Jonah Cobb said, "where's that pretty young daughter of yours?"

"I would imagine she's still in bed," Jordan answered. "You know how much sleep these youngsters require. It takes a lot to wake them."

As soon as the two men had passed, and were out of sight, Amelia and Jacob both grabbed for their clothing. She placed hers on a bench so that she could shower, and he pulled his on so that he could get back to his cabin, where he would pretend he had been all night. He would shower later.

~*~

It was the shrill sound of the telephone's ring that plucked Jacob Belle and his grandson, Adam, from Cobb's Landing and threw them back into the modern day. It was Maggie.

"I'm running late. I have a few quick errands to run for my father. Then I'll be there. You boys alright with that?"

"We're good," Jacob said. "It's your girl. She's late. Probably out with another man."

He hung up the receiver.

Adam smiled. He had no idea how late it was getting anyway—too into his grandfather's tales.

"Did Jordan Cobb ever find out about you and Amelia in the shower?"

"Not that summer," Jacob Belle said. "He did find out some time later, but that was long after all of this took place."

"What do you suppose would have happened if he had found out? I mean, at the time?"

"He probably would have had one of the gay hit-men kill me."

"Speaking of the gay hit-men," Adam said, "was that the two mob protectors that Jordan Cobb made his brother, Jonah, bunk with?"

"It was. I suppose he thought the brother would be less apt to get into trouble that way."

"I'll bet old Jonah really appreciated that one."

"Probably right. Can you imagine? The woman chaser of the century, bunking with two queers." He started to laugh at the thought. "I never thought much about it. But that's really funny."

"Can I ask you something? It's not about Cobb's Landing."

"Anything."

"How close were Maggie and I? I mean when we were young—before my parents died."

"Well… I'm probably not the one to ask. You remember. We weren't allowed to see each other in those days. But from what little I did know of what went on, I'd say pretty close."

He got up from his chair and walked to a roll-top desk in the corner of his living room. "I have a picture here someplace." He dug around. "Here it is. It was taken at Tucci's the night of your big dance. What'd they call it? A prom?"

He handed it to Adam. It was of Adam and Maggie, in formal dress. He was pinning a corsage on her. The soda counter at Tucci's Diner was in the background.

"Your folks were at the mayor's party. I guess everyone was too busy to be there."

"Who took the photo?"

"I did. From my table in the back. The one you ate breakfast at this morning. Used a telephoto lens."

Adam could see exhaustion in his grandfather's eyes. He chose to ask no more questions. In fact, he welcomed Maggie's knock on the door. He, too, was tired, and wanted the day to be over, just as much as he assumed his grandfather did. The long night's dream of Cobb's Landing had taken its toll.

Plans were made for all of them to meet up as usual in the morning, at Tucci's. Maggie and Adam bid Jacob a goodnight, and walked out the door.

"Adam," Grandfather Belle called to him from his apartment doorway. "I was to all your things. Your first communion. Your confirmation. The night at Tucci's Diner when I took that picture. I stood with you at the hospital when your folks died. I watched you graduate from high school. And I was there when you graduated from college. And, Adam, I stood beside you at the funeral. Me and your grandmother, and Maggie."

They stared at each other for a time.

" I thought you might want to know."

Then he closed his door.

Adam and Maggie walked silently down the flight of stairs, and to the car.

"Good day?" Maggie asked.

"Great day," Adam said.

Chapter Fourteen

Horns blew from both sides. Maggie's car had just cleared the intersection in front of the bank. The two cars, one from the left and one from the right, could not have missed her back bumper by more than inches. Now they sat nose-to-nose, grills pushed through their radiators, fluids pouring out on the pavement. Only the drivers occupied the cars—one woman, the other a man—both of them looking stunned, as they crawled from behind deployed airbags. Neither of them bled. And when Maggie and Adam got out of the car, they saw Grandfather Belle hanging out his upstairs window.

"WHAT'D I TELL YA?" he yelled.

Sirens grew louder. Help was on its way.

The episode took less than a half-hour to clear up. What Maggie did see, she saw in her mirror. It wasn't much. Adam, lacking eyes on the back of his head, saw even less. They were not good witnesses, so they were quickly sent on their way.

Adam's house was in a state of mass confusion when he and Maggie walked in the front door. There were items strewn everywhere—things from his apartment in Chicago. They were in every corner of the living room.

"I see the movers arrived."

"They sure did," Maggie said.

"Let's get out of here," Adam suggested. His day had been long. He did not wish to deal with this.

"That might not be such a bad idea. Where?"

"Well, let me think. Either we go to your house and pretend that this disgusting mess doesn't exist, or we go out to dinner and deal with it later this evening. I'll leave it to you."

"Dinner," she said. "I bet we can deal with this better on a full stomach."

"Ok, but I don't understand why we'd want to."

"Want to what? Deal? Or go to dinner?" Maggie asked.

"Want to deal with this."

"Oh, come on. It'll be fun," she said. "At least it will for me. I get to learn a lot about the man I've grown to know and love just by looking through the things from his former life."

"Is that something I want?"

"Maybe not. But that is something you're going to get. I do have my standards when it comes to being the quintessential nosey woman and I've always said—give me an apartment full of a man's belongings and I'll tell you all about that man."

"What if that man isn't the same man?"

"What ever do you mean by that?"

"Nothing really," Adam said. *Maybe best to keep quiet. Wouldn't want to be misunderstood by the quintessential woman. The quintessential man knows there are things in his past that should be hidden from the future.*

"I lived the quiet life. Not much of interest. That's all." He put his arms around her and pulled her in. Their morning had come too quickly and Adam hadn't had time to shave. Maggie pulled back a bit when she touched his face with her palm. It reminded him. "I'll shave before we take off."

"Good plan," she said. She watched him from the open door of the bathroom, silently for a time, then, "You, know, you might have a point. The man from Chicago who showed up for his grandmother's funeral after a long absence, that man was reserved. Mild. He would never have gotten into a wrestling match with Leonard Morgan. I don't even think he would have gotten into bed with me. He was a bit timid. At least I thought so."

"Is that right?"

Adam glanced at her reflection in the mirror.

"That's right."

"Then how did all of this happen? How did we get together? I wasn't timid, sweetheart." He used his Cagney imitation. " I was just detached."

"You were timid. And if I hadn't taken things in hand, you'd be sleeping alone these days."

"Is that so?"

Adam toweled the excess shaving cream from his face. He pulled a fresh shirt over his head without unbuttoning it. He unzipped his jeans and tucked in the shirt.

"That's so."

She watched him dress.

"You always do that? You always pull your shirts over your head without unbuttoning them?"

He slid by her in the doorway.

"Shall we go?"

"Where will we go?"

"How about that quiet place on the water? What did you call that little settlement?"

"You mean Morgan's Junction?"

"Yeah. That's it. Let's go there."

"Sounds good to me."

They stepped onto the front porch. Adam pulled the door closed behind him and inserted his key into the deadbolt lock.

"Yes. Lock it up." Maggie said. The practice was foreign to the area. This was a small town, a safe town. Folks rarely locked up. "Wouldn't want someone to get your fine Chicago belongings. Would we?"

She walked to the car and got in. Adam followed.

~*~

After Maggie turned onto the highway towards

Morgan's Junction, Adam picked up their conversation where they had left off earlier.

"Well, now. About my go-round with Morgan? I suppose you think you had something to do with that, as well."

"No. That would be a direct result of all the time you've spent with your grandfather." She looked at him. She smiled. Her eyes took on a sparkle. "You see," she began to explain, "you are Jacob Belle's grandson. Hell, Adam, you are Jacob Belle, all over again. You just don't know it yet. But you know, the more time you spend with him, the more like him you become. Knocking the crap out of Leonard Morgan? Well... that would be something your grandfather would have done with glee when he was younger. My dad used to tell me stories. Jacob Belle was quite the character in his day."

"He still is."

"Yes he is. He's just slowed a bit. Slightly more mellow."

"Maggie, do you really think I'm like him?"

"Yes," she said. Her smile faded. "I think you're a lot like him."

"Is that a good thing or a bad thing?"

"It's a good thing."

~*~

It was not until they had eaten, and were enjoying a glass of wine that Maggie resumed their conversation.

"Want to know what I like best of all the traits you share with your grandfather?"

"Yes."

"That Belle assertiveness," she said. "I like it. It fits you"

"Really?"

"Really."

"Then you're going to love this. At least I hope you will."

Then Adam began to think. *Am I about to screw things up? Am I moving too fast?* He looked across the table into her eyes. He reached out and took both of her hands in his. *Here goes!*

"Maggie Bartell. Will you marry me?" he asked, his voice trembling. Then he began to fear that the answer would not be the one he wanted.

Maggie stared.

He knew he had just made a dreadful error. He was devastated. He froze. He couldn't breathe. He looked to the floor and waited for the axe to fall, the axe that would sever their budding relationship.

"When you asked me in high school, I said yes. Then when your folks got killed, you forgot me, and I was devastated. When Billy Bartell asked for my hand I almost said no, because of you. It was a struggle—a real conflict. I loved you. Billy was a replacement. But I finally married him and it was good. We could have had a life together. But you know the story." She fell silent. She looked at the floor. "Adam? Promise me you won't die on me like Billy did. Can you promise?"

"I will sure try."

"I guess that'll have to do. My answer is ... YES!"

She got to her feet. She moved around the table. Then she threw her arms around Adam's neck and pulled him close. She kissed him, a long and passionate kiss.

"We'll have the ceremony at Cobb's Landing," she announced.

"We can get married anywhere that you choose. I only care that we do. I want to spend all the rest of my days with you."

She held him tight for a moment. Then broke the embrace. They finished their wine, paid the bill, tipped the waiter, and then they drove back to Adam's house.

~*~

Once inside, Maggie looked at the mountain of things

from Adam's Chicago existence. They all but filled the living room. "Shall we put some of this stuff away?" she asked

Adam studied the heap. He picked up a small leather case. "Let's dance," he said.

He opened the case and thumbed through until he found the perfect CD. Slow songs by artists of the sixties. He put the CD in the player and they danced, silently and closely, to several of the selections.

"Adam?" she asked, breaking the hold the moment and the music had on them.

"Yes?"

"Where are the bodies?"

"What?"

"The bodies," she said. "When we woke up this morning, you told me that you knew where the bodies are buried. Where are they?"

She pushed back far enough to look into his eyes.

"Not far from the old greenhouse," he said. "It was so clear in my dream. I felt like I could reach out and touch them. There are no headstones. Just markers buried in the dirt, flat rocks with letters, probably initials. They were crudely gouged. Like they had been done without proper tools—by the untrained. And each marker had a number. There's a map too, telling who belongs to each set of initials."

"Where's the map?"

"I'm not sure," Adam said. "It's close to the main lodge. My dream is kind of blurry here, but I think the map is underground."

"Underground?"

"Yeah. A cellar. Maybe there's a cellar under the lodge. I'll ask my grandfather."

"So! Just when did you want to do this thing?"

"Which thing is that?" Adam asked.

"This getting married thing," Maggie said.

She waited.

No response.

"Well?"

"When would you like to?" Adam finally asked.

"Soon," she said.

"Then soon it is."

Adam surveyed the heap of articles the movers had piled in the living room.

"What are we going to do with all of this junk?" he asked.

The clutter seemed to have grown while they were dancing. He studied it. *These are my belongings? These are what I called possessions back in Chicago? What was I? Hard up?*

"Take them to a landfill?" Maggie jokingly suggested.

A couple of prints. A box of photos. The rest is shit. Could have hauled it all in the trunk of Maggie's car.

"What do you want to do with it?" she asked, a frown that mirrored his developing on her face. "Do you really want any of it?"

The landfill might well be the answer, Adam thought. "Very little of it. I can't believe I was this poor."

He pushed on the arm of a rocker that he had spent many hours sitting in, while reading or watching television. The damn thing fell off.

"Maybe the moving guys broke it," Maggie offered sympathetically.

"I don't think so. I think it's been broken for a long time. I think most of my stuff is in this condition." He gave the pitiful mass another hard look. "You know, I've never cared much about possessions. Not until recently. Not until I came back home and got close to you and my grandfather, and listened to his tales about the Landing. Now I care. And most of this stuff isn't possessions. It's shit."

Adam kicked at an old vinyl covered ottoman whose top had a long crack in it, revealing its cotton stuffing.

"I guess all of this is changing me more than I thought. I tell you what. Let's get some sleep. Tomorrow we'll burn most of this." He gave the room one more look. "I can't believe I actually lived this way."

~*~

When morning came, Adam couldn't wait. He dug in. He dragged things from the living room as fast as he could, and piled them in his back yard. Most of it was out of the house before the coffee was done.

Soon, Maggie was at the door. "Before coffee?" she asked.

"Get 'er done," he said. "That's my motto."

"Call grandfather?"

"Not yet."

"I'll pour us coffee. Then I'll call him," Maggie offered.

Adam studied the growing pile. He laughed.

"What's so funny?" Maggie asked.

"Oh. I was just thinking. It might be fun to set fire to my past, watch it go up in smoke. How many guys get to do that?"

"Very few, I would imagine. You want me to cancel today with your grandfather?"

"I guess. This'll probably take all day and some of the night. Not the hauling, that's almost done, but the burning."

Maggie dialed Jacob Belle's phone. No answer. She called Tucci's. He was there.

"Where are you?" Jacob asked.

"We can't make it today, Grandfather."

"Why not?"

"Adam's things arrived from Chicago."

"So?"

"Today we cremate them."

"Cremate them?"

"Yes. We're going to set fire to them... in the backyard... put them out of their misery."

"That bad, eh?"

"That bad," Maggie admitted.

"Well… just don't set fire to each other. We'll meet up here tomorrow morning. Any change, call me. Ok?"

"We will."

She hung up the phone. Then she poured them each a cup of coffee.

~*~

It was almost ten when the fire department came. It took until eleven-thirty to put out the flames. The siding on the south end of the garage would need replacing. And the citation for burning without a permit would have to be paid.

"How do I get a permit?" Adam asked the fireman who seemed to be in charge.

"Stop at the station. You can get one there."

"How much?"

"How much for what? The permit? Or the fine?"

"Both."

"Permit's free," the fireman told him. "The fine's one-fifty."

"One-fifty?"

"Hay! Don't blame me. I don't set the prices."

"Sorry. I don't mean to… it's just that… well… the fine's pretty steep. How come the permit doesn't cost?"

"We're not after money. Just warning."

"Warning?"

"Yeah! Warning. For guys like you. We'd like to know in advance so we can be ready for ya."

The fireman grinned. Then he left.

~*~

Maggie drove Adam to the fire station .

"One of these days," he told her, "I'll have to buy myself a car."

After the third inoperable rental from Leonard

Morgan, Adam and Maggie decided to share her car rather than suffer the likelihood of being stranded somewhere... nowhere.

"You can't afford one," she said. "You spent most of your money getting your things moved here, and the rest of it will go to paying that new fine you just earned."

"Well, at least the permit's free."

Adam paid the fine. He applied for a permit. There was still much to burn.

"Wait a minute," he said. "This permit says I can't burn until between the hours of 8 P.M. and 6 A.M."

"That's so we can see the flames should things get out of hand," the girl at the desk told him.

It made sense. He supposed if they had been able to see the fire from a distance this morning, he might not have to replace the siding on his garage.

He asked Maggie to take him to his grandfather's. There was still much of the day left—time for Cobb's Landing.

~*~

"It's about time you got over here," Grandfather Belle scolded. "I heard the alarm. Thought you'd be along. Come in. Let's get started. We have a lot of ground to cover today."

"You look good," Adam said. "You look well-rested."

"Where did I leave off yesterday?" He ignored the comment.

"I believe you just got laid." Adam smiled.

"That's right," he said. "You know, that first piece of ass, that's the best one. You never forget it. It's usually unexpected... spontaneous... develops from the heat of the moment. And you remember it for the rest of your life."

Adam could relate. He may not remember his first time, but he could remember his first time with Maggie.

I'll bet it was because Amelia Cobb was the love of his life, he thought. *I know Maggie's mine.*

"What about Grandma? Do you remember your first time with her?"

"Vaguely."

"Today," he started, "I'll tell you about the bank robbery." Adam's curiosity peaked. "But first, we need to go into a little more detail about the good sheriff."

He was silent for a moment, gathering his thoughts. Then he continued.

~*~

Morgan had been keeping the peace, or he thought he had been keeping the peace, at the Landing's parties for weeks. Jordan Cobb kept a distance. It was either that or do what he had wanted to do the first time he saw Morgan: kill him. But this weekend Cobb had to get close. He was tired of playing the game and so was Petruzzi. And it was time for Morgan's real use.

Morgan was never going to get the priest to visit the Landing. Father Gould, or Anthony Russo the hit-man hiding out as a priest, knew what fate awaited him at Cobb's Landing. This whole thing with Cobb sending the sheriff to speak to Russo was just to let Russo know his cover had been penetrated. Cobb and Petruzzi wanted him to know they were coming for him. They figured he'd be too busy covering his own ass to be a danger to the organization. But now, the time had come. They were both at the Landing. Their soldiers were in place. The war that had been erupting in Chicago with the Rosettis was well under control and for the head of the Bartolli Family, Angelo Petruzzi, to deliver to the head of the Rosetti Family the corpse of their chief henchman, the hitter who took Salvatore Bracco, would be a blow they would never recover from.

"I have something for you." Cobb said, as he approached Morgan from out of the darkness behind him. "Something I need you to do."

Morgan was startled. He nearly drew his gun. He did not speak. He just stared at Cobb, awaiting his instructions.

"There's going to be a robbery, Sheriff."

Cobb looked down at the dark ground between them. He waited a moment.

"The bank in town."

He looked up. He made eye contact with Morgan. He needed to be sure Morgan was understanding him

"I want you to see to it that it goes down exactly as planned. I don't want anyone hurt. I want you to see to it."

"You want me to just let somebody rob the bank?" the sheriff asked.

"That's exactly what I want you to do," Cobb said.

He pulled a cigar from his vest pocket, pushed it towards the sheriff's red face. Morgan took it and placed it between his lips. Cobb dug back into his pocket for a match. *Expensive cigar. My favorite. Oh well. If it'll keep me from hearing his voice it'll be worth the price.*

"I can't just let somebody rob the bank," Morgan objected. The cigar filled most of Morgan's mouth, making his words barely recognizable. "What kind of sheriff would I be if I did that?"

"The kind that works for me," Cobb said.

He placed a hand on Morgan's muscular shoulder and turned him towards the path that led back to the lodge. They began to walk.

"Don't worry though, Sheriff. Your position in the town won't be hurt by any of this. Just do everything like I tell you and you'll come away looking like a hero to the rest of the town."

Morgan's ears perked, like a dog's would when it heard its master calling him to dinner. He always wanted the town to look upon him as some sort of hero, but could never find a way to make it happen.

One question came to Morgan's mind and he decided

to ask it.

"Does this place need the money?"

"No!"

"Just when is this bank job to take place?"

"Monday," Cobb answered. "Nine o-clock sharp."

"Why nine o-clock?" the sheriff asked.

"Because that's when the man we want will be there."

"Who's the man you want?" Morgan asked, as the two of them reached the front steps of the lodge.

Cobb stepped up onto the porch of the building, but blocked the sheriff's attempt to follow him.

"Gould," Cobb said. "The priest. Father Gould. That's who we want."

"I told you," Morgan said, "that I would have him come out here. I've even talked to him about it, told him you would build him a church and everything. He just hasn't had the time yet. There's no need to rob the bank to get him. He'll show up."

"Too late for that," Cobb said. "You had your chance. Now we do it our way." Cobb stared down on the sheriff. *Did Morgan actually believe that the landing had need of a church and a priest? What a moron.* "Good night, Sheriff. Monday morning, the bank will be robbed. See to it that none of the town folk try to be heroes. I wouldn't want anyone hurt. I'm making it your responsibility to see to it. Oh... and... don't alert the priest, Sheriff." Then Cobb turned and disappeared through the entrance to the lodge.

~*~

In one of the cabins at Cobb's Landing, two men were sitting silently at a small table. Parts of pistols were spread out on white cloths in front of them. They cleaned each piece and meticulously placed it back in the exact position it had been taken from. These were professionals. They were serious about the task at hand.

The silence would not be broken until the guns were once again fully assembled and ready to do the job they were intended to do—flawlessly.

Outside the cabin, three youngsters, Jacob Belle, Amelia Cobb and a fifteen year old boy named Frank Beletucci, who had recently showed up at the landing, looked in through a badly soiled window. The men inside had not allowed anyone in to clean since their arrival a couple weeks earlier. Seeing was difficult at best. But see, they did.

"Look," Amelia Cobb whispered to the two boys, "I told you they were up to something. They're here to do a job."

"A job?" Jake Belle asked.

"Yeah," Beletucci said. "A job." His speech was foreign. Italian. "I seen it lots of times before."

Frank Beletucci was the son of one of the guests, a man who had recently arrived and who was spending most of his time with Cobb and Petruzzi.

"I seen it a bunch of times back in Chicago. My father done some jobs."

"What the hell are you kids doing?" A gruff voice yelled from the darkness behind them.

It was Amelia's Uncle Jonah.

"Why... you little spies." The two men from inside the cabin jumped to their feet. "It's alright, Delaney. It's just Jordan's daughter and a couple of kids. I'll run them off," Jonah Cobb said. "Amelia," he said turning his attention toward his niece and her two companions, "these two men, they're the kind who could kill you without blinking an eye. Now you get out of here and you stay out of here. Forget this cabin even exists. Do you understand?"

The three youngsters turned without a word and disappeared into the darkness.

"Coming in," Jonah Cobb yelled out, prior to entering the cabin of the two hitters. He opened the screen door and entered cautiously. He did not wish to be gunned down.

"Them little fuckers gone?" one of the gunmen asked.

"They're gone," Cobb answered.

"You sure?" the other gunman asked.

"I said they're gone," Jonah Cobb answered, his impatience growing like a weed. He did not like men like these. He never had and he never would. He and his brother had always been on the management side of the family's activities and, although it did become necessary to deal with the likes of these two on occasion, he had always found it distasteful. Jordan never seemed to mind doing it, but Jonah hated it. "Let's just get on with this," he said.

Why didn't Jordan take this part of the job. He does it well, and he knows I hate it. I bet he thinks this'll buy me favor with Petruzzi. Well... I don't care if it does. I will still screw that fat bastard's wife if I get the chance, Jonah was thinking.

Jonah was right. Jordan had put him in charge, hoping a successful conclusion in dealing with all of this would show Petruzzi that there was value in his younger brother. And he hoped it might buy a small portion of forgiveness for Jonah, or at least, bring a peaceful hatred toward him. The incident with Jonah Cobb and Mrs. Petruzzi was mostly her fault, after all. He had been drunk as a skunk and she had been the seductress. And Jonah Cobb hadn't been the only man she had planted her hooks into, just the only one still alive. Besides, Jordan thought it possible that his brother might even gain a new sense of responsibility from having this task thrown in his lap. Maybe Jonah might grow past his irresponsible womanizer stage... become a real asset to the operation.

"Now let's get down to business. You two know your jobs?"

"Yeah. We know our job," Tommy Delaney insisted. "What do you think we are? A couple of amateurs?"

"Don't get wise with me," Jonah Cobb said.

"You don't like us, do you Cobb?" Delaney's partner asked.

"No. I don't," Cobb answered. "There are two types of men in this world that I can't stand. There are hit-men and there are fags, and the two of you fit on both counts. Now let's go over Monday's plan, so I can get the hell out of here."

"When all of this is over, Cobb, when we've finished this job and your big brother isn't watching your back like a she-bear guarding her cub, I swear I will get you," Delaney said. Then the three of them got down to business. They went over the plan like professionals, until there could be no room for failure. Then Jonah left the cabin. He went to the greenhouse where he had made himself a comfortable little place to sleep. He had originally been put in with these two, but that first morning, when he woke up before them and discovered them sleeping together, naked, he deserted the cabin and went out looking for other quarters. He was a ladies' man. He could have no one knowing that he had shared quarters with queers. He'd never again get laid by one of the wives of the wealthy gangsters who had sought his services on occasion. And he simply couldn't allow that to happen.

~*~

Billy Brooks had held a grudge. He had not been responsible for the crash of the company's airplane and he knew it. He did not deserve to have been threatened with a gun, then run off like that. And he certainly didn't deserve to be killed. And for that injustice, he had turned the tables. He had joined the other side, a side the Cobb's and Petruzzi were not even aware existed. And it was now coming together.

Delaney and his friend belonged to the Rosettis. The Cobb brothers had been too tough on the two of them, too strong against their sexual orientation. On the other hand, the Rosetti gang didn't care. They had welcomed the gays with open arms, and then they sent them to the Landing to save Anthony Russo, not to kill him.

Jonah Cobb was there at the mercy of yet another gang gunning for the Cobbs and Petruzzi. Jimmy Palano had spared Jonah's miserable life for a single purpose, so his people could follow him to Cobb's Landing; a place they knew existed and figured was much less secure than the Bartolli headquarters. Their aim? Kill Angelo Petruzzi and the Cobbs.

That done, and there would be no more Bartolli Family, and the territory—and all the money to be made there—would belong to them. Jimmy Palano chose to join with the Rosettis, not really an ally, but usable. Jimmy's plan was to use them. Then destroy them. Jimmy would let the Rosettis do all that they could, hoping for Russo to die in the action since the Palanos had no real use for him. Hell, maybe they'd get lucky and the Rosettis would do all of the killing for them.

But just in case, their man, Paulo Beletucci was there. He'd take up the slack. In the end, no mater what, the Palanos would rule the empire the Cobbs and Petruzzi had built; and the world would just have to do without Jordan and Jonah Cobb, and without Angelo Petruzzi.

~*~

To Billy Brooks, all of this was opportunity. He believed in the Rosettis and he believed that Jimmy Palano's people were there to help because they wanted to settle the old score with the Bartolli Family. And he thought his future secure. He saw himself as on the ground floor of a whole new organization, one where he would not be judged for something as little as crashing a plane in a storm. He would be one of the Cobb's Landing heroes.

He walked slowly up to the little cabin's door.

"Delaney," he called in a loud whisper. "Delaney," he repeated a little louder. "You in there?"

"That you, Brooks?" Delaney asked.

"Yeah."

"Well get your ass in here."

"I gave the message to the pilot like ya told me to," Brooks said.

He let the screen door slam shut behind him. Delaney's partner jumped. He cursed. He pointed his gun at Brooks. Delaney's hand pushed the gun downward, so it aimed at the floor.

"I know you got the message to the pilot. Beletucci's here, ain't he?"

Paulo Beletucci was an enforcer for the family, just like Tommy Delaney—or so Delaney thought. He had no idea Paulo actually belonged to the Palanos. His unique talent as a hitter who never left a trace behind him when he worked made him sought after, and made him look like an independent. Few new he was well planted within the Palano outfit.

The Palanos thought it a stroke of luck when Tommy Delaney requested Paulo Beletucci join him on this one.

~*~

On his way to the greenhouse, Jonah Cobb spotted the sheriff. He was just getting into his truck.

"Where you headed?" Jonah yelled over the trucks loud engine.

"Into town," Morgan answered. He threw what was left of Cobb's cigar onto the ground at Jonah's feet.

Jonah stomped it out.

The night was yet young. The strength of the bootleg whiskey had put an early end to the evening festivities. Almost all had drunk their fill. Now they were back in their cabins, sleeping it off, looking forward to the monstrous headache they would awaken with.

Jonah Cobb enjoyed these little parties. He would

generally end up getting laid by some intoxicated woman, that is when the Petruzzis did not attend. Jordan did not allow him to attend if Angelo and Ellen were there. Jonah preferred gatherings where Canadian liquor was on the menu. People didn't get smashed quite as quickly, and these things went long into the early morning hours. It was unfortunate that the good stuff had run out on the same night he had to deal with the gay hitters. He had completely missed the short party. Jonah Cobb hadn't yet had a drink, and he wasn't ready for the party to be over.

"Mind if I ride into town with you?"

"Jump in," Morgan said. "Can't get you back here, though."

Jonah Cobb went around the sheriff's truck and got in. "I'll find my own way back," he said as he closed the door.

He, like his brother, didn't care for the sheriff, so the lengthy ride into the town went by without conversation. Even when Morgan brought the vehicle to a stop in front of his office, neither man spoke.

Jonah Cobb just got out of the truck and headed up the street. When he walked past the drug store, he saw that there was still a young lady behind the counter, cleaning up the soda fountain. He spotted no other patrons inside. He pulled a flask of whiskey from his jacket pocket and took a long pull on it. He screwed the cap back on it and reached for the handle of the store's front door. He looked again at the girl. She was a real dish. He entered. He walked up to the counter.

"We're closed," the girl said, smiling pleasantly at the handsome stranger who had just appeared. "I'm sorry, but we're closed, Sir."

"What's your name?" Jordan asked.

"Cynthia. Cynthia Lindgren."

"Well, Cynthia Lindgren, You sure are a pretty girl. How old are you?"

"Seventeen, Sir."

Seventeen wasn't very old, but, on a night like this one, one where all the seasoned women he was used to had retired for the evening, seventeen would have to do.

"Tell me, Cynthia Lindgren, have you ever had a drink of good Canadian whiskey?" He put on the most charming of his smiles.

"No, Sir."

"Would you like to try one?"

"I don't know, Sir. I mean... I always thought I might like to taste it once, but, no....I don't think I'd better."

"Oh, come on, Darlin'." He pulled the flask from his jacket. "Pour about half a glass of that soda for us. We'll top it off with this." He raised the container. "You'll love it. I promise you that." He smiled broadly.

"But, it's sinful." She giggled a little.

"Sinful is usually the most fun." He winked at her.

"What if someone comes by?"

Cynthia nervously peered towards the little drug store's entrance.

"I thought you were closing," Cobb said. "Just lock the door and turn down some of these lights. We'll have a drink and just talk. Come on."

Cynthia Lindgren walked over to the door and locked it, just as the handsome stranger had suggested. She then turned off almost all of the lights.

"What's your name?" she asked as she slid her slender body behind the fountain counter and began pouring soda into two glasses.

"Jonah Cobb," he said. He wished he hadn't. It was too late. Why hadn't he given the girl a different name? Stupid!

"It's nice to meet you, Jonah Cobb," Cynthia said, as she held out her hand to touch his. "Where did you come from?"

Jonah took the hand into his. It was soft and warm, softer than any other he could remember touching. This would be his sweetest conquest. "I'm from Chicago. I'm just visiting around here. This sure is a pretty little town you have."

The girl came around to his side of the counter and took the stool beside him. She felt older. Grown-up. Here she was, sitting in the almost dark, having a real drink with a handsome stranger. This was alright. This was what she wanted, and he was a nice man. No harm could come.

Jonah Cobb poured them a second drink. They engaged in long conversations while they sipped away at their whiskey. They began to slur their words. He poured them a third. *What do you think, Jonah? A Virgin?* When he thought she had had enough, he leaned in and kissed her. She did nothing to discourage it. He poured another. When they were half way through this one he slid a hand around her young breast. When she did not pull away, he slid a hand up under her dress. He kissed her hard on the mouth, probing with his tongue. She breathed in and out deeply. She seemed to enjoy. *Foreplay. What a waste of time.* He slid a finger under her panties and began stroking lightly at her pubic hair. She tried to stop him. He was too strong. Soon they were on the floor, her dress pushed up around her waste; her panties torn from her young and tender body.

He had had his way with her. Now he was gone. She lay there, crying, for most of the night. Then, just before dawn, she gained control of herself and left the little store for her home.

~*~

Jonah Cobb walked back to the Landing. He did not look back. As he entered the main compound, he saw two sedans, their motors idling, aimed towards town. It was Monday morning.

~*~

200

"You hungry?" Grandfather Belle asked. "I can fix us a sandwich."

"How about we go down to Tucci's," Adam suggested. "I'll buy."

"You can't afford it."

"How would you know that?"

"I heard you got a fine this morning." He grinned. "Something about burning without a permit, I hear."

"How the hell did you find that out already?"

"Adam," he slid his chair back and rose to his feet. "Come with me."

He walked toward his front window and drew back the curtain. "What do you see?"

"Don't tell me they flash fire calls on the bank clock along with the time, and the temperature in Fahrenheit and Celsius."

"Look past the clock, at the other corner," he said, as he slapped Adam softly on the back of the head.

There stood, big as life, the fire station.

"See it?"

Adam nodded.

"And Tucci has one of those scanners," he added.

"Come on," Adam insisted. "I can still afford a sandwich."

Adam grabbed his grandfather's jacket off the hall-tree. He held the door open.

"I don't need that," Jacob said. "It's fifty-eight degrees. I just saw it, on the sign."

"Well, that's not quite warm enough for no jacket. Put this on."

He did.

They went to Tucci's—an enjoyable lunch, and a pleasant visit with the old gangster, during which, it was suggested that they could have the ticket fixed, if Adam wanted them to.

He declined.

~*~

"Was there a cellar under the lodge?" Adam asked when he and Jacob were once again alone.

"Nope," he said.

His answer surprised Adam. He was sure there was. His dream told him as much.

"Is there a cemetery out there?"

"Of sorts."

"Of sorts?"

"Yeah. It's really not much of a cemetery. It's just a spot in the woods where the bodies are buried."

"Is it near the greenhouse?"

"It's up behind it. Not very far from the greenhouse, probably fifty paces or so," he said.

Tucci approached the table with a fresh coffee pot.

"What are the two of you talking about now?" Tucci asked.

"The cemetery," Jacob Belle offered without hesitation.

"Did you tell him about the cellar?" Tucci asked.

"You told me there was no cellar," Adam said.

"No. I told you there was no cellar under the lodge building," he corrected. "The cellar is behind the lodge, dug into the bank, near the steps that lead to the upper cabins."

"Is there a map in this cellar, a detail of who was buried where?"

Adam was too loud. The two old gangsters looked around the café. Then Tucci spoke.

"Keep your voice down. Your grandpa could get into a lot of trouble if word of all this gets to the wrong people. Best you save talk of all of this until it's more private."

"Why?" Adam whispered. "Did he do some of the killing?"

The two old men looked at each other for a long time, then Jacob spoke.

"I buried them. That's just as bad."

~*~

The two Belles returned to Jacob's apartment. The walk there took them past the bank. The sign informed them that the temperature had gone up to sixty-two degrees.

"The radio said this morning, that tomorrow will be even warmer," Jacob said. "Perhaps this weekend it will be warm enough to visit the Landing, if you'd like."

"I'd like. Are you feeling well enough to go out there?" Adam asked.

"I think so," he said. "I recover from these things rather quickly. I think it pisses that young doctor off sometimes. He probably feels it's cutting into his income. Come to think of it, it probably pisses off old Schultz too."

"Who's old Schultz?"

They began to climb the steps. Adam wanted to keep him talking. He wanted to see if his grandfather would make the climb without running out of breath.

"The undertaker," he said. "He's nearly as old as I am. I think he wants to bury me before he goes." He climbed some more. "If he dies before me, I'll bet the son-of-a-bitch comes back to haunt me, just for spite."

They reached the top step. Jacob reached into his pants pocket for his key. He had not run out of breath.

"Is this my test?"

"Test?"

"You know what I mean," he said. "You kept me talking all the way up those stairs. Was that my test? Did I pass?"

"Yes, Sir."

"Good. Then we can go to the Landing. By the way, thanks for looking out for me." He opened the door. They went inside. They took up their same chairs as before. "Where were we," he asked.

"Jonah Cobb had just returned to the Landing after

203

his night in the drug store with the seventeen year old girl."

"Do you know who that girl was?"

"Cynthia Lindgren."

"More than that, Adam," he said. "You ought to know. You're about to become her relative."

"Her relative?"

"Aren't you going to marry that lovely young lady?"

"Yes, but-- *How the hell did he know already?*

"Then she'll be one of your ancestors, or at least one of your children's ancestors. She's Maggie's grandmother," he said.

"The one who committed suicide?" Maggie had told him in conversation that she had a grandmother who had killed herself at a young age.

"That's her."

"Why did she do it, I mean, why did she take her own life?"

"Shame," he said. "You see, most of the town never bought her story about the handsome stranger getting her drunk and taking advantage of her. Almost everyone in those days figured that a girl who was foolish enough to get drunk with a strange man, all alone like that, well... that girl kind of deserved what she got. They weren't at all nice to her after that. Finally, she just couldn't take it. She killed herself, and left Maggie's mother an orphan. She probably would have ended up in an orphanage had it not been for the mob. They all figured that the child was one of theirs, and they saw to it that she got a good life despite her undesirable beginning."

"The cars that Jonah Cobb met as he arrived back at the Landing, were they the crew that was headed to rob the bank?" Adam asked.

"That's exactly who they were. Jonah Cobb looked into the first car. He spotted Delaney and his queer roommate in the back seat. He walked on. There was no way he'd ride with them. The night before, he had had to suffer through a trip into the town with the annoying

Sheriff Morgan. That was enough. In the second car was a driver, all alone. He was a young fellow Jonah had seen around the Landing a few times. He didn't know his name. I don't remember it either. Anyway... the back seat was empty, so Jonah opened the door and slid in. Me and Amelia and Frankie Beletucci watched from the thick brush about twenty feet away. None of them saw us."

~*~

The telephone's ring interrupted his story. It was Maggie. She was parked out in front of Grandfather Belle's building, calling from a cell phone. The fire that was supposed to have been extinguished by the fire department earlier that day had caught hold once more and was now slowly working its way towards Adam's back door. *One-fifty. And the fire's not out. I should let the gangsters fix the ticket.* He was only annoyed because all of this was putting an end to the story of Cobb's Landing for the day—probably not cause enough to turn two old gangsters loose on anyone.

The siren at the fire hall began to sound as Adam hung up the phone. He looked at his grandfather. He shrugged his shoulders and threw up his arms.

"I take it that's for you," Grandfather Belle said. "Go! I'll see you in the morning."

Chapter Fifteen

It was well past seven in the evening. The firemen had all left. Maggie and Adam worked the ashes with a couple of old garden rakes they had found hanging from nails in the garage.

"Well... something good comes out of most disasters. I never used to believe that, but... I guess I have to now," Maggie said.

"I wonder why I hadn't looked in there before?" Adam was referring to his father's old garage. When they opened its service door to look for rakes they discovered it—his mother's car.

"Weren't you saying you had to get yourself a car?"

"Yep!"

"Well, now you don't."

"That is, if it still runs. Been sitting for an awful long time."

"You know anything about cars?" Maggie asked.

"I know how to drive them."

"I mean, do you know anything about fixing them?"

"Fixing? No. When I was in Chicago, I knew where to take one to get it fixed. Around here, I'm afraid I don't know even that much."

"Leonard Morgan," Maggie said.

"You've got to be kidding. That guy's a Bozo. Hell, his rentals won't even make muster."

"He's a Bozo. That's for sure. But he's a Bozo who knows a lot about cars—old cars. Like your mother's. He's said to be a genius with them."

"Maybe it still runs."

Adam stirred the ashes with the rake. A tiny spark leaped up, trying to escape the tool. He studied its slow drift back to the ground. It floated hypnotically from side to side as it fell. Adam watched it land. He took aim and stomped it with his foot, snuffing it out forever. He thought about the car in the garage. It would have gone up in smoke that morning when the siding burned, if the fire department hadn't showed up when it did. That would have saddened him. Suddenly the one-fifty for the fine didn't seem so bad. He would consider it the cost of the car.

"Is the car going to bother you?"

"Why would it?"

"Because it was your mother's?"

"Are you kidding? It's a sixty-one Chevy Impala two-door hard top. And it still looks new. I loved that car the day my father bought it. I always loved that car."

That's odd, he thought. *I remember the car.*

"Didn't you and I take it on dates?"

Maggie blushed. Then Adam remembered. They had. And then he recalled his grandfather's words, the ones he used to describe his first time with Amelia Cobb in the bathhouse at Cobb's Landing. Adam's own first time with a woman came into focus. It had happened in the back seat of his mother's sixty-one Chevy. And the girl was looking at him at that very minute—blushing.

"Shall we see if it still works?" Maggie asked.

"The back seat?" Adam asked.

~*~

Lightning flashed off in the west. A few drops of rain hit.

"We should go inside," Maggie suggested.

They dropped the rakes in the grass and headed to the back door. Inside, in the light, she turned to look at Adam.

"Oh! My God!"

"What?"

"Your face."

"What's wrong with my face?"

"It's black. It's covered with soot."

Adam looked at her.

"You're not little Miss Clean, yourself." He placed a hand on each side of her face and turned her head. First left. Then right. "Perhaps we should shower before we eat."

"Come on," she said. "I'll do my best to clean you up."

"Are we going to shower together?" Adam asked. They had never done that.

"Why not?" she said. "If it was good enough for Jacob Belle and Amelia Cobb, it ought to be good enough for us."

"Yes, but, you know what happened to them when they showered together."

She smiled. "Like I said, if it was good enough for Jacob Belle and Amelia Cobb, it ought to be good enough for you and me."

Their shower had taken more time than usual, and when they shut the water off, they heard two things. The sprinkle had turned to a downpour, and the phone was ringing persistently. Someone was determined.

Maggie ran, naked, to see who it was. It was Jacob Belle.

"Where have you two been? I've been ringing forever."

"In the shower," Maggie said, without thinking.

"Both of you? At the same time?" *Busted!*

"What is it?" Maggie asked.

"Tell Adam we won't be able to get together in the morning."

"Something wrong? You alright?"

"I'm fine. Brothers wants me to go see some other quack again. I'll be gone all day."

"Who is it?" Adam asked. He stood beside her, with

one towel wrapped around himself and one in his hand for her.

"It's your grandfather."

"Is he alright?"

"Here. You talk. I'll dry." She snatched the towel and snapped him on the back-side with it.

"Ouch!" he said into the receiver.

"What's going on over there?" Jacob Belle asked.

"Oh... nothing. What's up?"

"Brothers just called. I have to go see some old doctor, a specialist. It's over sixty miles away and, like I said, he's old, and he's slow. I imagine it'll take all day."

"Is it serious?"

"Routine. I get to go after each episode. Just a check-up. I think it's got more to do with insurance money than my health. Anyway, I called to tell you I won't be home tomorrow. We'll get together the next day."

"How will you get there?" Adam asked. "Do you need me and Maggie to drive you?"

"No," he said. "Tucci will take me. He always takes me to these things. Then we stop at a pub on the way home and kick the shit out of some youngsters, just to keep in shape."

Adam did not react. He said goodnight and hung up.

"I hope they don't come home all bruised like they did last time," Maggie said.

Adam shot her a curious look. He reached for the phone.

"You can't control those two Adam," she said, "Give it up."

~*~

Morning came late. The back yard battle with the fire caused Adam to oversleep.

Maggie handed him a cup of coffee as soon as his eyes opened. "I need to tell you something," she said.

Adam took the coffee. He blew on it, then sipped. He

leaned against his pillow.

"Something serious?"

"Not too."

He looked toward the window. He saw his mother's Chevy hooked to a wrecker, going down the alley behind his house.

"Is it about my car?"

"How did you know?"

"Psychic," he said. He took another sip of coffee. "This coffee is great."

"I called Morgan. He's coming for your car."

"He's already got it. I just saw it going down the alley. He won't do something bad to it just because it's mine, will he?"

"No. He may not like you, but he loves old cars. And he likes me. He'll fix it right."

Adam got out of bed. He went to the window and watched Morgan go down the alley with his car in tow. He felt Maggie's arms around his neck. He felt her firm breasts pushing into his back. He felt a gentle kiss on the back of his neck.

"How long you been up?" he asked.

"About an hour."

"Why didn't you wake me?"

"Because I wanted to call Morgan and I thought you might object. Besides, you were so cute sleeping there."

Adam smiled. He probably would have objected. "So when did you call Leonard Morgan?" he asked.

"As soon as I got up," she said.

Adam stared out the window at the empty alley long after his car had disappeared around the corner. "It looks like it's going to be a nice day. What'll we do with ourselves?" He would miss his grandfather's Cobb's Landing stories.

"Well," Maggie began, "let's start with a nice home-cooked breakfast. Then we'll have choices to make."

"What kind of choices?"

"Let me see." Maggie pulled away from his back and

slid around to his front side, wedging herself between him and the window. "We could go spy on your grandpa and Tucci. Or, maybe we could go down and watch them work on your car, but we might want to rethink that one. I wouldn't want to spend the day watching you and Morgan rolling around on a greasy concrete floor. I know. We'll picnic at the Landing. You can show me the cemetery."

Adam was immediately excited—raring to go—no longer hungry.

"Let's pack the cooler," he said.

"Hold your horses there, Stud. We'll be eating before we go." She slid from between him and the window. "You dress. I'll cook."

~*~

The last time they had visited the Landing, they had left the picnic basket, and most everything else that they would need at Adam's house. The canoe they had deposited in Maggie's father's garage.

When they went to get it the Mayor's Cadillac blocked the garage. He was nowhere to be found, nor were his car keys. Retrieval of the canoe from where it hung from the rafters, above the car, went poorly. Adam, after all was said and done, would be paying to have the top of the mayor's Cadillac repainted.

"Leonard Morgan?" he asked.

"He can fix it."

"You call him."

~*~

Soon they were launching the canoe in the still waters of Jesse Lake. Things were looking up. *Stay away from the poison ivy,* Adam silently warned himself.

As they paddled over the ancient truck that was reputed to have carried Jonah Cobb, Maggie's great-grandfather, to his death, they stopped. The sun had gone behind a small cloud, so they could see all the way to the bottom.

"Look at it," Adam said. "It stands there, nose held high, back-end buried in the sand, looking like it's there to guard the entrance to the Landing—like a sentry."

He studied the old truck. He found it captivating. *A man's grave. That's what it is. That's... all it is.* He wondered if Jonah Cobb had struggled long before he drowned. He wondered if anyone had tried to help.

"Someday, we should try to get that out of the water," Maggie suggested. "You know, it's only theory that Jonah is my great-grandfather. I wouldn't mind proving it."

"How would we do that?" Adam asked.

"If we can find him, even a bit of him, they can run tests and tell if I'm related."

"Really?"

"Really. So someday, let's see if we can find him down there," Maggie said.

"Someday we will. Know anyone with a barge?"

"Leonard Morgan."

"That figures. Why is it he keeps popping up in my life. I can hardly tolerate him...yet..."

"I told you, Adam, the two of you are linked by Cobb's Landing. Might as well get used to him."

Adam looked up the ravine where the truck had initially come from. Two things seemed different. For a moment he could not place them. Then it dawned on him. He could see parts of the old bridge that had once spanned the chasm. And flowing water had replaced the snow covering he had seen the last time he looked up the gully. "It's easier to see," he said.

"The old log pillars?"

"Yeah," he said. "Must be the water flowing through the creek. I think last time I might have been blinded by the white snow and ice."

"Even when the water flows, it gets harder to see

every year," Maggie said. "The old log pillars must rot a bit each winter, and the water gets less and less every year. This creek runs between two lakes, and the one it flows from... well... it's the water level. It drops a little more every year. The first time I came out here, it was just a year after graduation, my father took me out here, this little creek was a river."

"What happened?"

"Father says it's the lack of snow. He says we only get a fraction of the snowfall these days that we did in the days of Cobb's Landing. I guess, one day, this will dry up completely."

Adam sunk into deep thought as he stared up-river at what remained of the old bridge. *That must have been one hell of an explosion. Look at the size of those pillars. And the width of that ravine! I can't imagine. If Jonah Cobb was on that thing, in a truck when it blew, he must have been dead before he ever hit the water.* He looked back down at the truck. *Funny. No burn marks. Maybe the bridge blew just as he got there. Maybe he was going too fast to stop. Maybe he drove over the bank and washed down here. What ever happened, it had to be horror.*

"You alright?" Maggie asked.

"Fine."

He looked again up-river. Then, down into the water. He hoped that the bullet that was supposedly in Cobb had numbed him. *What the hell! He was a criminal. A rapist. He took advantage of a young girl. A child, for Christ's sake! He deserved pain.* He stopped feeling sorry for the man and began paddling.

He looked into Maggie's eyes. Jonah Cobb's indiscretion was likely her origin. For that...he was grateful.

~*~

"How much farther to the Landing?"

"It's not far now," Maggie said. "Just around that little peninsula." She pointed ahead

"It looks like a finger, pointing out the direction." he said.

"It does, doesn't it? It was a sand bar when the water was higher."

Only moments later it seemed, they were pulling the canoe onto the grassy shore of Cobb's Landing. Adam looked with awe at the lodge building. *Magnificent!*

"That roof needs repair," he said. *What a shame,* he thought. "Seems winter has taken its toll."

"Maybe we could do something about it this summer, before it goes any further." Maggie suggested.

Adam did not want to disappoint Maggie. But a handyman, he was not. "We could certainly try. Maybe when we pull Jonah's truck out of the water." He sized up the old building. *I hope Jacob Belle passed down something more than looks and attitude. Skill, for instance. Skill would be nice.*

"Lets take a walk through, see for ourselves what the damage is, see if it's something we can handle on our own."

Adam pulled at the main entry door and its handle came off in his hand. He stuck a finger through the hole left behind and pulled again. It began to move. The old hinges screeched in protest. Finally they gave up. The door flew open. It slammed hard against a log hand railing, breaking it in two. A large raccoon rushed out of the building through the open door, brushing against the leg of Adam's trousers and hitting Maggie square on the shin. The coon tumbled to the ground. It stared up at Adam and Maggie for a moment, and then went running into the deep woods.

"I bet he thinks you knocked him down on purpose." Adam said.

"Did I see right?" Maggie asked. "Did that critter actually shake his head at me in disgust?"

Adam thought it had, but he didn't admit it.

"Shall we?" He held a hand out in the direction of the opening to the lodge's lobby.

"Think it's safe? Think there's more of those critters?"

"Only one way to find out," he said.

They entered and had a quick look around. The damage done by the harsh winter had not penetrated to the interior of the building. The work that needed doing seemed limited to the roof.

"It doesn't look too bad," Adam said. "I bet we can patch it up before it gets any worse, but I think we'd better find out how that raccoon got in and put a stop to that before there's a whole family of them living in here. I've heard they can do a lot of damage in a short time."

They looked the lodge over, finding only minor flaws they felt capable of dealing with, and then set out in search of the cemetery.

"Where to from here?" Maggie asked as they approached the greenhouse.

"Not inside!" Adam said. "I've had enough poison ivy for this year."

"I agree. One more trip to Doc Brothers and he'll think we're slow learners."

~*~

Adam sized up the area. "The cemetery is about fifty yards beyond the greenhouse. In a little clearing." They squeezed around the greenhouse, carefully to avoid any kind of ivy...or snakes.

"We should clean out a trail through here," Maggie suggested.

"Maybe not. Wouldn't want it too open. Anyone could come up here."

"I suppose you're right."

Behind the greenhouse, the going got easier. Another fifty yards, just as Jacob had said, brought them into a clearing.

215

"Jesus, Adam!" Maggie said, as she looked up a small incline where the first of the Indian style mounds appeared. She rarely cussed. "Jesus!" she said again. She walked up the incline. She brushed the sole of her shoe over a flat rock. The number fourteen and the letters A. C. appeared. "What does this mean?"

Adam was busy uncovering another of the markers, then yet another. He did not answer her. They went on searching for more than an hour. They found all of the numbers, one through fourteen, each with two letters that they believed were initials of the occupants.

"That's it. All fourteen." Adam said.

"That's enough," Maggie said. She studied the area for a moment, and then began backing away. She stopped. "Adam," she said.

"What?"

"Come here. Have a look at this."

Adam walked to her. His eyes followed the direction she was looking. From where they stood another slight rise appeared some distance from the others—on a taller hill. That made fifteen—not fourteen.

"We missed one." Adam said.

He started to move towards it. At the site, he bent down and pushed the brush aside. Then he swept around with his hand until a flat stone appeared. *A.R.* "Anthony Russo," he said.

"Who?" Maggie asked.

"Anthony Russo. My grandfather told me about him. He was the priest back in the thirties, except…he wasn't a priest. He was a rival gang member, a hit-man, hiding out as a priest. A. R. stands for Anthony Russo. I'm sure it does"

"How do we find out?" Maggie asked.

"The map! My grandfather told me where to find the map. Come on. Let's go." He grabbed Maggie's hand. They ran back to the lodge, to the door that led to the kitchen. That would be their starting place. They stood with their backs to it.

"Grandfather said look right—by the stairs." He scanned the bank. "There," he said. "Right there." He pointed. "The map is in a root cellar carved into the bank over by those stairs."

"I don't see anything," Maggie said.

"Come on. I'll show you." He took her hand and began pulling her in the general direction of the steps. Once there he let go of her hand and started tugging at the brush covering the bank. A few armloads and there it was—an old wooden door that had faded from age and was now the color of the bank itself. It had become invisible with age. Adam pulled on it, half-expecting the handle to come off in his hand like the one on the lodge door had done earlier. The door opened surprisingly easy. He looked for a raccoon to jump out at him. None did.

"After you," he said.

"Not a chance," Maggie said. "Not until you've searched the place over and can tell me without a doubt that there's nobody or no animals, snakes, corpses, or anything else in there to get me."

He started into the darkness, the only light being that which shone in through the open door, most of which was being blocked by his own body. "A flashlight would be nice," he said.

"I might have one in my backpack. You wait here. I'll look." Maggie returned just moments later with her backpack. She dug around in and finally came up with a flashlight. Its batteries were all but dead, yet it would do. It provided enough light to see inside the cellar. The map, or more correctly, the list of names along with the grave number for each name had been chiseled into the stone wall at the back of the room. Adam began reading. Maggie pawed through her bag. She found a scrap of paper and a pencil. Adam looked for number fifteen. There beside the number was the name A. Russo. He looked at the others, and read out loud. Maggie listed all of the names. Then the two of them gazed at the wall in silent respect. It was a memorial—a monument to those who died in the Cobb's Landing war. It captivated them, until a deafening crash of thunder sounded. Lightning had struck, close to the opening.

They looked toward the cellar's exit. It was as if the sky was on fire—blinding orange.

"What now?" Adam asked.

"Let's go!" Maggie shouted.

Adam looked at the lake. The once still water now sported huge waves. "Go where? A small man could surf on that."

"Let's get to the canoe. We have camping gear in it, and food," Maggie said. "We'll hide out in the lodge until this blows over."

She started to run towards the canoe. Adam followed.

~*~

Within a short time, they were inside. Adam busied himself trying to get a fire going in the ancient stone fireplace that nearly filled one wall of the main lobby. Maggie sorted all of their stuff. They had food. They had sleeping bags. They were out of the weather—safe—comfortable.

The storm worsened. Soon, the lake became invisible through the dense rain, and the canoe they had dragged close to the lodge—but for the occasional bolt of lightning—could not be seen. The thick storm clouds blocked the afternoon light, and inside the building what little light they had came from the fire—romantic, yet frightening.

"I'll have to gather some wood. This little bit isn't going to last," Adam said.

"It's a downpour out there. You'll catch pneumonia," Maggie objected.

"We'll both catch it if I don't, especially if this storm goes on long." Adam looked over the things they had brought in from the canoe. "Zip together sleeping bags?"

"They sure are." Maggie smiled, then turned her attention to the food she had brought along.

Adam opened the door. "Doesn't look good. Could be an all-nighter."

Maggie looked outside. She had to agree. Even if the storm were to let up, it was getting late. They'd end up portaging in the dark. "Oh, well," she said. "I wanted to camp here with you once, anyway."

"You planned this—storm and all?"

"Plan it? No," she said. "Like it? Yes."

"You Cobb girls are all alike," he said. "My grandfather warned me about you."

He went through the door to find firewood.

"And you Belle boys are all easy," she shouted after him.

~*~

Adam hauled armload after armload of broken tree branches into the lodge. His last trip, Maggie thought to be too long. She went looking. She found him struggling with a large root. It was sticking out of the ground, begging to be burned. She grabbed on and helped him pull. When it came loose, they both sailed to the ground, landing on their backsides in a deep, cold puddle of rainwater. Maggie screamed. Adam laughed out loud. He got to his feet and held a hand out to her. She grasped it. He did not pull. He stared off into the distance. He squinted—another grave—a small one. "It has to be the little girl." he said.

"What little girl?" Maggie asked.

"The daughter."

"Whose daughter?"

"The daughter of Amelia Cobb and Jacob Belle," Adam said.

He pulled Maggie to her feet. They walked towards the lodge. They looked back at the grave several times as they walked. They looked until they could see it no more through the rain. Then they went back inside.

"We forgot the root."

"C-c-c-cold!" Maggie said. She was soaked to the bone—shivering violently.

They peeled off their wet clothing and hung them on the backs of the only two chairs in the lodge that still had four legs. They pushed them close to the fire to dry. Maggie spread out one of the sleeping bags on the floor for them to sit on. They pulled the other one around their shoulders to channel as much of the fireplace's heat to them as possible. They soaked it in until they began to feel comfortable.

"We need to eat something." Maggie said. She rose, letting her share of the sleeping bag float to the floor.

Adam watch as her naked body passed in front of him on the way to the picnic basket. He wanted to take her right then, but she was right. They needed food. "What we got in there?" he asked, referring to the picnic basket.

"Chicken." She dug a bit more in the basket. "Potato salad. And there're chips and some bread and butter for morning. Just in case it might still be raining."

She pulled out two plates and two forks.

"Adam."

"Yes?"

"I never knew. I had no idea they had a child."

"I don't think anybody did."

"When was she born?"

"She would be my age."

"When did she die?"

"I'm not sure. I think she only lived to be about six. At least I was six when my parents backed away from my grandfather. I guess... NO... I know... she was the reason for that parting. My grandfather told me that much."

"Do you know how she died?"

"No. He didn't tell me that."

"That's terrible." She thought for a time. Then,

"Maybe we shouldn't get married at the Landing."

"Why not?" he asked.

"Bad luck?"

"I think we're supposed to be the first."

"The first to what?" Maggie asked.

"The first to have good luck... change the trend. Break the spell."

Maggie filled their plates and placed them on the floor between them and the heat. Then she sat beside Adam and pulled the sleeping bag back over her shoulders.

After they ate, they made love by the light of the fire, while the storm went on and on. Whenever they made love, to Adam Belle it was special. But the two times at Cobb's Landing seemed more—like the place brought out a passion in them far beyond the norm, and a satisfaction that exceeded most other things in life. Both Adam and Maggie knew that night, when they both lay there exhausted, that they would spend as much of their lives as they could at Cobb's Landing, and they would always take the time to make love while they were there. Adam could see his grandfather's and Amelia Cobb's enchantment with this place, and he knew why they could share it with no one. If they hadn't kept it all to themselves, they would have spent their life without this feeling. It was not him. It was not Amelia Cobb. It was this place and its magic that controlled. Now it was going to take its time to control him and Maggie.

Maggie had been looking at her penciled list of names and numbers when she fell fast asleep. The paper fell to her chest. Adam picked it up. There was just enough light from the fire to barely make out the writing. Most of the names he did not recognize. Morgan's name was there, in space number four, and Tommy Delaney in ten, and when he came to space fourteen the fire was either dimming or his tired eyes were giving out. He squinted. He read. He squinted harder. He read again.

Number fourteen. A. Cobb.

Chapter Sixteen

Morning at Cobb's Landing came with an unimaginable brilliance. *The sun never shone like this over Chicago,* Adam Belle thought, *unless it did before there was a Chicago.* The hard rain had lasted almost all night and the few remaining storm clouds on the eastern horizon, sun shining through and around them, gave off a pinkish cast that might cause the prettiest orchid to wilt in shame. *Red sky at night, sailors delight. Red sky at morn, sailors be warned.* His grandmother's old saying came to mind. *Funny. How do I remember that? I was only six when I last saw her.*

He went out the front door of the lodge, onto a covered porch. Naked or not, he wanted a better view of the morning sun. He did not see Maggie as she walked up behind him. He felt her.

"Good morning," he said. "Sleep well?"

"I did. Better than I ever have."

"Even with the storm?"

"Even with the storm. Hardly heard it."

She pushed her warm, smooth breasts into his back, put her arms around him, and kissed him softly on the back of the neck. "We'd better get moving," she said. "It's going to storm again. Look at that sky."

Adam wanted to spend the day. He wanted to explore. "Are you sure it's going to storm again?"

"Positive," she said. "I've never seen it fail. When the sky gets like that in the morning, all bright red, it's going to brew up a giant of a storm. I thought everyone knew that."

"Oh, I've heard that," he admitted, "but I'm not so

sure I believe it."

"Believe it," she insisted. "It's going to storm. Let's get dressed. Then you can help me get the canoe in the water so I can pack it."

After dressing, Adam dragged the canoe to the shore. Maggie packed. Then they made toast over the fire in the lodge... savored one last, brief moment at the Landing before packing all of their gear into the canoe. They knew they would be back. And they knew it would not be long. But... still. They did not want this visit to end. Maggie was right, however. Clouds rolled in and sprinkles of rain showed, before they saw them coming.

"We'd better get moving," Adam said. He would rather have stayed, rain or no rain. But they had no food left to hold out against another storm.

They looked back at Cobb's Landing, as they paddled off towards home. It would be their last glimpse for this trip. Adam sighted down the lodge's roofline—sway-backed. *It'll take more than shingles,* he thought. Then his eyes were drawn to the back corner. Something moved. He squinted. A raccoon. It was squeezing its way under the building. *Bring mortar and bricks,* he told himself. The crumpling foundation was letting them in. "Did you see him?"

"I sure did."

"He's probably been out in the brush all night, waiting for us to leave. Getting soaked to the bone."

"You think?"

"Yep! And you know what else I think?" he asked.

"What?"

"I think you'd best be cautious."

"Me? Why?" Maggie asked.

"Just in case he holds a grudge, takes it out on you."

"Why me?"

"Well you're the one who knocked him down. At least that's what he thought. Better be careful."

He watched the shoreline, as the canoe floated over the quiet water of Jesse Lake. The sprinkling had turned to a soft drizzle, but the wind remained calm. Visibility was the best it would be. The snow was all but gone, and although some of the trees had fresh new growth popping out on their branches, many were still barren. Another week, maybe two, and he would see nothing from the seat of the canoe. He searched the underbrush near the landing as he paddled, spotting many things, scraps of rusted metals that looked like ancient car parts, pieces of concrete and rock... possibly old foundations, steel barrels, and many other things he could not put a name to. He vowed that he would explore. Soon.

"Turn. We're here," Maggie said.

"Did we have a tail wind or something?" Adam asked.

"Welcome back. I thought you might have left me for good; it's been so long since you spoke. Where have you been?"

"Exploring," he said. "I've been scouting the shoreline, looking for interesting things we can check out."

"See anything?" she asked.

"Plenty."

"What?"

"Rust colored... well... junk really, I suppose. Stuff that might be fun to look at. That's all."

"We can walk in next time, if you'd like. It's a long way, down a crooked path. The brush will be thick. And the only way in was the bridge, so...since it's no longer there, we'll have to cross the ravine. That'll be tricky."

She steered the front of the canoe into their landing. The rain began to pour almost as hard as it had the afternoon before. Thunder sounded off in the distance.

"We'd better get going, get all this stuff and the canoe up that bank before it washes out on us. There's no place for us to duck out of the weather here," she warned.

Adam began grabbing things from the canoe and setting them on the shore as fast as he could. Once the craft was empty he dragged it from the water. He picked it up. He ran up the hill with it. He was back on the shoreline before Maggie could get a good grip on the cooler.

"I'll run that up to the top. You get the sleeping bags. Throw them up the bank as far as you can. I'll get them from there."

Her strength amazed him. The bags landed over the crest. Teamwork had them and all of their belongings at the car in minutes. Soon the canoe was tied down and all of their other things were in the back seat. They headed for home.

~*~

When Maggie pulled to the curb in front of Adam's house she nearly rear-ended Adam's mother's old Chevy. Apparently Leonard Morgan had some success with it, or maybe he didn't, and simply gave up and had the thing dragged home. Adam wondered; W*here did my father get the car?* He tried to remember. Nothing. *I wonder when he got it. It had to have come from some other town. All that this town ever had, far as I know, is a Ford dealer. This is a Chevy. Maybe he bought it used. Maybe it had been someone else's trade-in. Cheap bastard!*

"Look!" Maggie said excitedly. "There's your car."

My car. Now there's something I hadn't given much thought to. He opened the door and stepped into the rain. He walked to the driver's door of the Chevy and opened it. *Battery's good. Interior light's on.* He sat behind the wheel. *No keys!*

"I wonder where the keys are," he yelled beck to Maggie.

"Try above the visor." she suggested.

"Nothing."

"On the floor?"

"Nope."

"Ashtray?" By then she was at the door beside him.

Adam shook his head—no.

"Let's go inside. Maybe he left a message on the answering machine," Maggie said.

When Adam opened the storm door, a large brown envelope fell out onto the water-soaked front steps. Maggie quickly picked it up, and pressed it between the palms of her hands.

"Keys!" she said. She handed the package to Adam.

Adam slapped the envelope down on a small table just inside the door.

"First thing we better do is to get out of these wet clothes. And a hot shower might help take the chill out of our bones. Don't you think?" He smiled at Maggie.

~*~

After they had scrubbed Cobb's Landing off their bodies, they dressed in fresh clothing. Maggie was getting quite the wardrobe stockpiled in Adam's closet. They both decided they were starving.

"I'll cook," Maggie suggested.

Adam sat at the bar in the kitchen and watched her. He opened the envelope that Leonard Morgan had left inside his storm door. He found the keys to the Chevy and a short note.

He read it.

"Well I'll be damned," he said.

"What?"

"Check this out," he said as he handed her the note. Maggie read it.

Nothing much wrong with her. I had Murphy's gas station give her new tires and a battery. He'll bill you The tow and the labor is on me.

L. M.

227

"That Leonard is a tough one to figure out," Maggie said.

"Scary. Isn't it?"

The phone began to ring.

"Want to guess who that is?" Maggie asked.

"I don't think I have to guess. What are we thinking, anyway? It's nearly nine-thirty."

"Sarcasm will get you nowhere," Maggie said as she picked up the phone. It was Grandfather Belle. He was wondering what was keeping them. He had been waiting for hours.

"Of course he has," Adam said.

~*~

They quickly devoured their breakfast and headed out. Soon. Adam was knocking on his grandfather's door.

"You look pooped."

"I am a little tired this morning," Adam admitted. "Storm kicked my ass, I guess." He took off his jacket and hung it on the hall tree "How did your testing go yesterday?"

"Just like the last time and the time before that, and the one before that," he said. "Not much change in my condition. The only thing that really changed is his fees. The old bastard raised them again. I think next time, if there even is a next time, I'll pass. I won't waste the money."

"You can't do that," Adam said.

"Sure I can," he insisted. "He doesn't do anything anyway, except make sure Brothers is doing things right. And Brothers always is. Now, where did we leave off last time."

"I believe Jonah Cobb just got back to the landing after his night in town, and the cars with the bank robbers were lined up and ready to go."

"That's right," he said. "The crew was ready and

waiting for Jonah and he had just returned and gotten into the back seat of the tail car. Alone. The two queers were in the lead car. Now Delaney... he had a real dilemma on his hands. You see, he had to find a way to stage some sort of ambush on the way back. Jonah Cobb needed to die and the priest needed be saved from the bullet. And it couldn't look planned, at least not to Petruzzi and his bunch. The problem was, if it looked planned, they would know it had been Delaney who did the planning. He was the only one with enough brains. So... he had to make the whole thing look like someone else had ambushed them and he and Russo had made it through the ambush without being hurt.

Now, an ambush couldn't just take place. It needed the right spot. Otherwise it had no chance of success. He scoped out the whole rough trail between the Landing and town. He chose the bridge. That done, he needed a fall guy. Would it be Brooks who took the blame? Or would it be Sheriff Morgan?"

"Wait a minute," Adam said. "I thought Billy Brooks had been run out of Cobb's Landing."

"He was. But... Billy Brooks was very much around. And he was very much a part of this. He may not have been at the Landing, but he was there for the robbery. He got in Jonah Cobb's car at the bridge."

"How come Jonah didn't just shoot him? I mean... he was an enemy of the Landing, wasn't he?"

"He was. But Jonah didn't know it. Jonah Cobb had never laid eyes on Billy Brooks before the moment when he got into the car with him. And he didn't question it, because Tommy Delaney had told him they were to pick a guy up at the bridge. A guy who was there checking things out ahead of time."

"So did Delaney push the blame off on Brooks?"

"No. He went with the sheriff. He figured Petruzzi and the bunch would buy it. Hell, they'd like to believe that Morgan did it. They all hated him anyway. Hated him and mistrusted him."

"So, how was Delaney figuring to get the sheriff to cooperate with this ambush plan?" Adam asked.

"Tommy Delaney was smart, way smarter than the simple minded Morgan. And he was cunning and real likable. He could talk the shoes off of a bum. And he never gave failure a thought. He knew the sheriff would do what he was told. Mention money and Morgan would always be onboard. Better yet! Mention Jordan Cobb."

~*~

As the car in which Tommy Delaney was riding turned from the bouncy trail onto the smoother gravel road outside town, he pulled a piece of paper and a pencil from his pocket. He began to write.

Morgan, when the crew leaves the bank, I want you to get a couple of your deputies and I want you to beat the crew back to the bridge. I want you to ambush the two cars and I want nobody but Delaney and the priest to be alive when you get done with them. They will be in the lead car. Shoot the driver and only the driver, then, Delaney will take over and drive the car back to the lodge. Kill everyone in the second car, and then report to me—you and your men. Tommy Delaney signed the note, Jordan Cobb. He folded it neatly and put it in his pocket.

As they pulled up in front of the bank, Delaney jumped from the still-moving car. He rushed to the other driver. "Go south when we leave here," he ordered. He wanted to give Morgan time to set up his ambush.

"But the Landing's north," the driver objected.

"I know the Landing's north," Delaney said. "Do you want everyone in the bank to know where we came from?"

He looked at the driver for a moment and when he did not respond, Delaney continued.

"Go south. We can loose any tail we might have before we go back home."

"I get it," the driver said.

"Good," Delaney said. "Now, let's get in there and get on with it." He turned and started towards the entrance of the bank. The others got out of the cars and followed.

Jonah Cobb looked down at the boardwalk that ran in front of the bank. He thought that these things, these wooden sidewalks, had gone the way of the hitching rail years ago, and that all sidewalks were made from cement these days. It was, after all, nineteen thirty-one. He remembered back to last night's visit here and to his pleasant episode at the drug store. He tried to recall the walk in front of that establishment. *Had it too been wood? No!* He didn't think so. He pulled a bandana from his jacket pocket and tied it around his mouth covering much of his face. Then he reached into his other pocket for his pistol. He found the pocket empty.

"Jesus Christ!" he said.

"What's the trouble, Cobb?" Delaney asked, as he pulled his bandana up to cover his face.

"My gun is missing," Jonah Cobb told him. "My goddamn piece is not in my pocket where I keep it. It's gone."

Delaney grinned. An omen. A piece of good luck. Something fell into place. Billy Brooks was supposed to plug Cobb, if he got the chance. Now, with Cobb unarmed, even Billy Brooks should be able to handle the job. Then, all Delaney would have to do is kill Billy Brooks. Not that he wanted to. Actually, he was starting to like Brooks. Too bad. Fact was, Brooks couldn't be trusted. He was too stupid... too weak. Petruzzi would get the truth out of Billy Brooks inside of ten minutes.

"Just stay behind me, Cobb. You and Brooks grab the priest and hold on to him. You don't need a gun for that. Billy, you got your piece?" Delaney asked.

"Sure do," Billy said as he pulled the revolver from his jacket.

"There you go, Cobb," Delaney said, as he pulled the

bank's door open. "Billy's got a gun."

He walked into the bank and fired three rounds into its ceiling. He gave no thought to the quarters above the bank. The bullets were followed by a scream. Then a thud—a body hitting the floor. This was not going well.

"This is a stick-up!" Delaney shouted. "Nobody move!"

Everyone in the lobby stood still, like statues. Delaney looked them over one by one, stopping at the priest. After a moment he gave the priest a barely discernable nod, then swung his head in Jonah Cobb's direction. He whipped his head towards the priest to let Cobb know that he was to guard him. Jonah Cobb moved closer and held a hand in his jacket pocket like he had a hidden gun there. Delaney then searched the bank's lobby for the sheriff.

"You there! Lawman!" Delaney shouted once he had spotted Morgan. "Come here," he ordered.

When Morgan approached he continued. "Take your gun out, real careful like, and lay it on the floor."

Morgan followed the instruction. Delaney handed him the note he had written in the car. When Morgan started to read it Delaney stopped him by placing a hand over the paper.

"Now, don't you do anything brave, Lawman. Just get all these people over by the wall, and keep them there and keep them quiet. After we're gone you read that note and you follow the instructions, and nobody here has to die. Get it, Lawman?"

Morgan nodded and began moving all of the bank's patrons to the wall. Delaney sent the two drivers behind the counter to empty the cash drawers into canvas bags they had been carrying. The whole thing was smoothing, going as planned.

Jonah Cobb looked in Billy Brooks' direction. Something struck him as odd. Billy wasn't paying any attention to the priest they were supposed to be guarding, and the priest, during the commotion with Delaney giving orders to and disarming the sheriff, had missed the only opportunity he would have to try an escape. Cobb knew that the priest wasn't a priest, that he was Anthony Russo, that he was a member of the Rosetti gang, and he also knew that Russo was no dummy. Russo knew this all added up to a death sentence for him. Why wouldn't he take his only opportunity to escape? Why, when everyone was busily paying attention to Delaney ordering the sheriff around, didn't Russo just shove Brooks out of his way and make a run for it? Hell, Brooks wasn't paying attention. He was even looking the wrong way. It would have been easy. It didn't add up. Then Jonah Cobb took a good look at Brooks. He was holding his pistol out in front of him, yet there was a bulge in his jacket pocket. He stared at the bulge. Then he saw it. The sparkle of steel. Brooks had another gun in his jacket. Jonah Cobb knew that it was his gun. Billy Brooks had picked his pocket. He carefully moved around the priest and up close behind Billy. In one swift move, he snatched his gun out of Brooks' pocket and placed the other hand around the pistol Billy was holding. He hadn't been quick enough. The gun fired. The bullet ricocheted around the bank's lobby. It lodged itself in the back of the head of one of the bank's patrons; a young woman in her mid thirties who had been holding the hand of a child, a five year old blond-haired girl with ringlets that fell around her tiny shoulders. Blood exploded from the woman's head and splattered into the child's ringlets, turning them to a ghastly wet red. The dead woman's hand did not let go of the little girl's. She was dragged to the ground with her mother's corpse.

Sheriff Morgan was powerless to act. His gun was still lying on the floor where Delaney had made him drop it. Delaney, both hands gripping his revolver tightly as if he thought the thing might jump from his grasp, began waving it menacingly back and forth between Morgan and Cobb, wondering to himself which one would react. Both of them remained still—statue-like. Both knew that the slightest movement on their part was likely to bring on gunfire, probably from all directions. Delaney quieted.

The sheriff reached cautiously out to help the little girl with the blood-soaked ringlets get free of the dead woman's grasp. He tucked the child behind him. The rest of the people who were in the bank when this all began gathered close to Morgan. He reached out his arms to shelter them. For the first time in Morgan's career, folks were treating him like a hero. He silently treasured the moment. He had no idea it would be the last time.

Tommy Delaney was growing tired of trying to make this abduction take on the guise of a bank robbery. Every possible thing had gone wrong and it was time to end it. He commanded the two drivers to finish getting the loot into the bags and head for the getaway cars. They did as they were told.

The bank job crew, Russo in tow, left the bank and Sheriff Morgan pulled out the note. He read it. He was purposely slow about it. Delaney and the others needed time to escape. As soon as he was sure enough time had gone by, Morgan walked over to his gun and picked it up. He headed for the door. They weren't gone yet. There was a commotion at the rear car. The priest was being shoved into the back seat. Brooks and Cobb were arguing. Cobb shot Brooks and shoved him into the car, then ran to the other side and got in beside the priest. The lead car, Delaney's car, had already turned around. It stopped when the shot from Cobb's gun rang out.

Morgan had to do something, anything, to make things appear that he was still on the job and still on the side of the people he had sworn to protect and serve. He shot into the air. Delaney's car, once the driver heard the sheriff's gun fire, was rapidly back in motion. A return shot planted lead in the doorframe just above Morgan's head.

He fell to the boardwalk. He stayed still until the second car sped off into the distance. Then he got up. He delegated the watch over the bank to one of its officers, instructing him to send for the undertaker, and called on a deputy who had been in the bank, all along. The two of them left the bank. Morgan was about to carry out the job Delaney had outlined in the note.

When the car carrying Jonah Cobb, Anthony Russo and the corpse of Billy Brooks pulled away from the bank, its driver attempted to turn around to follow Delaney's car as ordered. Cobb jammed the barrel of his gun hard into the back of the driver's neck. He ordered him to go north. The driver obeyed.

Morgan ran across the street. He climbed into his truck He cranked the engine over as his deputy slid in on the passenger's side. The engine did not fire. He released the starter button for a moment to let the starter motor rest. He watched the undertaker and one of his helpers carry a large woman on a small stretcher down the outside stairway that came from the apartment above the bank while he waited. Then he tried the truck's engine again. It still did not fire. The deputy pointed to the lever on the dash—his intimidation lever—the one he would use to make the truck backfire. Morgan had forgotten to place the lever back where it belonged, back to where the engine would fire and start. With the motor finally running, Morgan picked up two more men from his office, and started for the Landing. He needed to get to the bridge, to the ambush site, and he needed to get there fast. He sped off leaving a cloud of dust from the town's unpaved main street in his wake.

~*~

"Adam, I don't feel very well," Jacob Belle said.

Adam looked at his grandfather's face. Tiny beads of sweat were forming on his upper lip and on his forehead. Adam slid his chair back from the table and went to the kitchen sink. He filled a glass of water and began looking around for a cloth that he could wet to cool his grandfather down with.

"I think, maybe, it might not be such a bad idea to call Brothers," Jacob said.

Chapter Seventeen

Maggie and Adam sat in the car in front of Grandfather Belle's apartment for a long time. Dr. Brothers had called for an ambulance. They had already hauled their patient off. As they sat there on the street in front of the bank, Adam could not help but wonder, *Was this the spot where Delaney's car had been parked during the bank robbery? Or, was it Jonah Cobb's spot?*

Tears began to well up in his eyes. The end was coming... and it was coming too fast. He began to cry.

Maggie pulled him close. She held him tight.

They sat there for nearly an hour. Maggie finally convinced him they needed to be at the hospital. "But let's go by your place and shower. Our eyes are red. That won't do," she suggested.

Adam agreed.

Maggie drove. As she swung her car in front of Adam's house her front bumper and the rear bumper of Adam's mother's Impala touched.

"I really need to move that thing before one of these cars is completely ruined," Adam said. "I'll pull it around back after I clean up."

"Don't do that Adam. Let's drive it. Let's take it when we go over to the hospital. It'll help take our minds off of the situation."

After a quick shower and a reminder of just how unpalatable food could be from those machines at the hospital, Adam agreed to a sandwich, after which, felt more able to cope.

The old Chevy started and ran smoothly. Its dual exhaust with glass pack mufflers gave a nice mellow tone that pleased. It reminded Adam of a youth before the death of his parents, a time when kids road the streets of the town in cars that sounded as good as this one. Maybe it was this car he was remembering—maybe not. But there was something familiar about its handling, and it brought on a fondness. He embraced it. He began to appreciate and enjoy driving the car. "This is alright," he said.

"Kind of makes you feel like a teen doesn't it?" Maggie said. She slid close to him on the bench seat.

He pulled the car to the curb in front of the hospital. He opened his door and got out. Maggie slid under the steering wheel and got out behind him. At the top of the steps of the hospital stood two glass doors that opened automatically whenever anyone walked up to them. They took forever.

"Are these things always this slow?"

"Long as I can remember," Maggie said. "There they go," she added as the doors began to move, grinding metal on metal, and then stopping completely, about halfway open. "How would you ever get a wheelchair through here?" she asked.

Adam smiled. He held his head high. *Can't go on getting weak kneed every time I come here. Not with my grandfather in and out so often,* he told himself. They passed through the doors and walked directly to the nurse's station.

"Jacob Belle?" he asked the nurse.

"Are you relatives?"

"We were a few days ago. I guess we still are."

She was the same nurse who had been at the desk every time they came here. *What is she? Programmed to ask that? A robot?*

She looked at him over the top of her glasses.

"I'm his grandson, Adam. And this is my wife, Maggie."

"He's in room 212," the nurse said.

"Thank you," Maggie whispered to the nurse, as

Adam began walking rapidly down the hall.

"Why don't they build these places a bit more pedestrian friendly?" Adam asked when he took the fourth turn. "Is this a stress test or something? Is it meant to give the visitor a heart attack? Is this to drum up more business?"

"No. It's just been added on to one too many times," Doc Brother's voice came from one of the rooms. "I need to see you, Adam. In my office. It's two doors down on the left. I'll be in there in a few minutes."

Adam and Maggie entered Brothers' office a few seconds later. On an overstuffed vinyl chair sat an older man, dressed in a white doctor's jacket. In his lap laid a clipboard. He did not look up. He did not acknowledge their arrival. But when Brothers came in, the man rose.

"Adam," Brothers said, "Maggie, I'd like to introduce you to Dr. Mathews." Mathews nodded, but didn't offer his hand.

"Mathews, here, is your grandfather's heart specialist."

"Heart specialist?" Adam asked.

"Yes. You see, in addition to his other ailments, Jacob has a heart condition. It's really quite serious. It's more of a threat to his life than anything else. I'm afraid, and I understand that I'm not sounding too optimistic at this point, but I'm afraid this will get him long before the cancer does, if we don't do something immediately. You see, today's episode wasn't cancer related. It was a heart attack. A serious heart attack."

"Can I see him?" Adam asked.

"You can look in on him, but he's pretty well under at the moment. I don't think he'll even know you're here. We've had to put him on some pretty heavy medication so he can rest and heal a bit, before we take any further action."

Brother's looked at his colleague for a long moment, as though he were looking to the older doctor for support of some sort.

The old doctor nodded his head.

"Adam, we need you to sign a release so we can treat your grandfather. You're his closest living relative."

Adam looked at Maggie.

Maggie looked at Brothers.

Brothers looked Mathews.

Then Mathews turned towards Adam. It had gone around the horn and was back in Adam's lap.

"I don't think so. Not right now anyway."

Disappointment filled the two doctors faces. Pride filled Maggie's.

"I want to see him," Adam said.

The old doctor threw his hands in the air. "Young man," he said, "you have no idea what a delay will do to your grandfather."

"Sir," Adam said, "I have no idea about any of this, and until I do, you'll not get my signature on anything that gives you, or anyone but my grandfather, the right to decide for him."

Maggie nodded her approval.

"Just this afternoon, my grandfather told me that he was done seeing you. Now I have no explanation as to why he felt that way, but I do know that he was adamant about it. So... I shall have to consider that, until such time he is able to speak for himself, as his last word on the subject. I suggest, Doctors, that you do all that you can to help my grandfather regain full consciousness so that he can sign his own release. Once you've been able to do that, I will ask him for his permission to make future decisions for him. Now, if you don't mind, I'd like you to point me in the direction of my grandfather's room."

"Young man," the old doctor started.

"Don't young man me, Sir. And, Dr. Brothers, let's make things clear. Are you asking me to make decisions for my grandfather, or is it just Dr. Mathews?"

"Well... It's not a bad idea, Adam," Brothers said.

"I see. So that's how it is. Well... I'll make a

decision. I'll make one right now. This man," Adam pointed at the old heart specialist, "until my grandfather is able to decide for himself, is off of his case. If you feel the need to confer with him, by all means do that, but until Jacob Belle himself says so, he's not to treat him in any way. Is that clear? Is there any question as to what my wishes are concerning any of this?"

Silence blanketed the room. A silence that said understanding. Adam, once again, insisted on seeing his grandfather. He was not denied.

~*~

As Adam entered the hospital room, his grandfather opened his eyes. He smiled a small smile. Adam could see that he was weak, but he could also see that he had been underestimated once again.

"Doctors, would you leave us for a moment, please?" Adam requested when he saw that Brothers and Mathews had followed him.

When they had left the room, Adam motioned with his eyes for Maggie to close the door. She did. Adam leaned to over his grandfather.

"Can you hear me?"

He nodded his head slowly. Again... a tiny smile.

"You said something about not wanting that old specialist anymore. Do I have that right?"

He nodded.

"Should I dismiss him?"

Another nod.

"Is there anything else you want Maggie and I to do?"

Jacob Belle whispered weakly, "Amelia. Call her. Tell her... send her doctor."

"How do I do that?"

"Maggie," he said weakly.

Adam shot her a look.

"I can reach her through my father," she said.

"Adam, I think we need to let him rest."

Adam kissed his grandfather on his forehead.

"You rest. We'll be around if you need us."

A single tear formed in the corner of Jacob's eye.

Don't weaken, Adam. Control your feelings, he warned himself.

Then Maggie kissed him and said goodnight. She assured him that Amelia would be called and everything would be alright. They went into the hallway outside his room where the two doctors had been waiting.

"I need to talk with you, Dr. Brothers. In your office."

Once there, Adam shut the door before Mathews could follow.

"Grandfather wants him gone," he said, bluntly.

"I don't understand," Brothers said.

"Neither do I, but that's what he told me."

Brothers had no further objection. Clearly, he had placed Jacob Belle first—not Mathews. "I'll see if I can find another heart man to take a look at him first thing in the morning."

"I don't think that'll be necessary. He's asked Maggie to call someone in Chicago, an old friend of his, and ask her to send a specialist from there."

"He told you all of that? In his condition? Why... he's a bit tougher than Mathews thinks. Isn't he?"

"I assume that's exactly why he doesn't want Mathews."

"I'll see to it," Brothers said. Then he went out to the hall and dismissed the old doctor.

Maggie and Adam found coffee. Then they searched out a waiting area near Jacob's room where they could relax for a while. Mathews shot them a foul look as they walked in. He was just leaving.

~*~

Frankie Tucci was sitting in a chair by a slightly

opened window. He was blowing the smoke from a cigar out through the crack into the cool night air. He did not turn around.

"You the ones pissed in that man's cornflakes?" he asked. He turned. He grinned. He stomped the cigar out on the floor. Maggie rolled her eyes.

"You know, your grandpa never did like that guy."

"How are you tonight, Mr. Tucci?" Adam asked.

"It's Frankie," he said, "you're too old to be callin' me Mr. Tucci. That kinda shit was for when you was a teenaged punk. Ya outgrew that years ago. It's Frankie."

"Okay. Frankie. What're you doing here so late? There's really nothing you can do tonight. He's sleeping."

"I ain't here for 'im," he said. "I come down here for you. I thought I could answer some of your questions, about the Landing. I was there too you know."

Adam sat down on the sofa in the waiting room. Maggie sat beside him. Neither of them had considered Frankie Tucci as a source for Cobb's Landing information. It wasn't, after all, until Adam's last time at the diner that he knew Tucci had even been there, and he still didn't know how involved he had been—only that he knew about the buried bodies.

"How much do you know about the Landing?"

"About the early days? Nothing. About the end? All of it."

"Were you around when the bank was robbed? Because I never heard my grandfather mention your name, I mean in connection with the Landing story."

"Was I there? You bet yer ass I was there. You just don't know about me 'cause I wasn't Frankie Tucci back then."

"Well… who were you?"

"You remember your grandpa talkin' about a kid named Beletucci?"

"Wasn't that the kid who showed up just a few days before the robbery, the one who was hanging around with my grandfather and Amelia Cobb?"

"That was him," he said. "That was me."

"I'm not sure I understand," Adam said. He pulled a list from his pocket, the list that Maggie had written, the list of souls who had been buried at the Landing's cemetery. He searched it until he came to the entry he wanted. "It says here that someone named Frank Beletucci was buried in lot eleven at the Cobb's Landing cemetery."

"That's me too!" Tucci said. "Only that ain't me. It just used to be me. You see, when I was born I was Frankie Beletucci, the son of a mob strong arm. I ended up on the Landing 'cause my father took me there. He took me there kinda as a way a hiden' his real reason for bein' there. Everybody was supposed ta think we was there on vacation or something, only he was really there for a job. He was supposed ta hit Petruzzi for the Palanos—that is, if nobody got him first. He got a Petruzzi; only he got the wrong Petruzzi. He missed the old man and killed his wife. He never got the second shot off, the shot meant for Petruzzi. He got shot in the back of the head by Jordan Cobb hisself. I seen the whole thing with my own eyes. I'll never forget it. I don't think your grandpa will either. He seen it too."

"I got to the Landing about two weeks before the bank job," he started. "Did yer grandpa tell ya the bank job was a cover for the hit on the Cobb brothers and ta save Anthony Russo from the axe?"

"He said that it was a cover so Cobb could get his hands on the priest, or something to that effect," Adam said. "I kind of figured that the whole thing got a bit more complex than that, and that Delaney and friends had a double agenda thing going down."

"That's pretty much on target," Tucci said. "Anyway, when those guys in the cars, the bank robbers, left the Landing, me and your grandpa and Amelia, see, we followed 'em. Only when we got to the bridge we kinda give up. The car was way ahead and out a sight. We knew that they was headin' for town, but town was still a long ways off. We knew they'd be half ways back before we ever got there. We decided to wait for 'em at the old bridge. That was the only way in and out of the Landing. Anyway, when we heard the first car comin', we ducked into the thick brush. The car flew past us like a cat with its tail on fire."

It occurred to Adam that this old man, as he listened to him speak and watched the expression of excitement grow to epic proportions as he talked, that this guy would know exactly how fast a cat with its tail on fire would run.

"Amelia jumped out of the bushes just after the car went by," he went on. "We could see there was three in the car, Jonah Cobb, the driver, and Russo, the guy pretendin' to be a priest."

~*~

"Stop!" she yelled. "Uncle Jonah! Stop!" she shouted again, as she ran into the middle of the road.

Jacob Belle heard the sound of another car coming up on the bridge rapidly. He ran into the dirt road. He snatched Amelia practically off of her feet and they were back in the thick brush, hidden from sight in a flash. They all watched the bridge. A noisy vehicle approached. It slowed almost to a stop right in the middle of the bridge where all three of the youngsters could see its occupants.

"It's the sheriff," Jake said.

"What the hell is he doin' here?" Frankie asked.

"There's going to be trouble," Amelia said.

The truck started to move once again, this time real slow. The sheriff was looking for something—maybe them. But he couldn't be looking for them. How would he even know that they were around? The truck stopped and the sheriff got out. He went to the back and stared down the road behind him. He stared at the bridge.

"He's goin' ta set up a ambush," Frankie said.

"How do you know that?" Jake asked.

"Oh... it's an ambush alright," Amelia agreed. "I've seen it done before."

"Me, too," Frankie said. "I was with my dad just last summer, out west, and this is just how he done it. I was there. I seen the whole thing."

The sheriff looked hard at the spot where the kids were hiding, and for a moment they all thought that he was about to choose their hiding place for himself. Then, just as he was about to step into the brush, one of the deputies yelled for him.

"Looks real good ahead, Sheriff. Sharp curve. We can leave the truck in the road and the cars would never see it in time. We could even walk back a piece. Hit them from behind."

The sheriff went to have a look.

"Alright then, Louis," Morgan said. "Pull the truck around the corner. We'll set up a hundred feet or so behind it, in the brush."

The truck jumped forward as the deputy popped the clutch. One of the other two men who were standing in the back fell off. When he hit the ground the shotgun he had been carrying fired with a deafening blast.

"What the fuck?" the sheriff screamed. "God damn it, Thompson, can't you do anything without screwing up?"

He watched as his truck traveled slowly to the ditch and rolled onto its side.

"Louis! Watch what you're doin' for Christ sakes. Louis! Louis!"

Louis Prowell was dead. The blast from Thompson's shotgun had taken out most of the back of his head. Morgan reacted. Louis Prowell had been with him for twelve years... since he first started as sheriff of the tiny community. They had grown up together. They were friends. Factually, Louis had been Morgan's only friend. He had bullied everyone else into hating him and fearing him, and Louis Prowell had been the only one around who would not be bullied. Sheriff Morgan looked at the back of Louis Prowell's shattered skull, pulled his revolver from its holster, and shot Thompson cleanly between the eyes.

As Thompson staggered around for a moment before falling to his knees, waiting for his brain to tell him that the bullet from the sheriff's gun had put an end to his life, Morgan said, "That's better'n you deserve."

A rustling came from a few feet behind where the three teens, Jacob Belle, Amelia Cobb, and Frankie Beletucci, had hidden themselves in the brush. All three of them held their breaths and listened. The sound came closer. Then a large figure appeared. Amelia's mouth opened wide. A scream was coming. Jacob Belle could almost see it and at the same instant he could see Sheriff Morgan rushing to their position with his gun cocked and ready to fire. He grabbed the girl and slapped a hand over her mouth. When the figure came into view, the youngsters recognized it. Jonah Cobb.

"Ambush," he whispered.

"I know," Amelia whispered. "But who for?"

"Not sure. But I think...me!" Things were getting complicated. Amelia was in harm's way. "Stay low," he whispered, "and stay quiet." It was all he could do for now. It was too late to get the kids away from the danger. He would have to protect them right where they were. He watched. He waited. If the chance came, he would move the kids. With luck, the chance would not come too late.

With only two ambushers left in the game, Sheriff Morgan seemed to be having trouble coming up with a plan revision and, for a time, it looked as though he might turn his gun on the only help he had left. The two of them were running in circles. Yelling! Screaming! Out of control.

The sheriff waved his gun around aimlessly, while his lone deputy dodged it. Then the sound of the second sedan, the one with Delaney in it, came within earshot. It was too late for them to take up a hidden position so they simply pointed their pistols in the direction of the sound.

The battle lasted just seconds. The first of the good sheriff's bullets found its way into the forehead of Tommy Delaney's driver. As luck would have it, the car had already come to a stop so it didn't end up in the ditch along side the sheriff's overturned truck.

Another shot wounded the little queer who traveled with Delaney. The third round came from Delaney's own pistol and ended the life of Morgan's last living deputy.

The battle seemed to be over, as Tommy Delaney crawled carefully out of the back seat of his car. He stood. He holstered his gun. Morgan holstered his. Then Delaney approached the sheriff.

"Where's the other car?"

"It's either comin' or already gone past before we got here," the sheriff said. "Look at this mess. " Everybody's dead."

"Not quite!" Delaney said.

Then he shoved his gun into the sheriff's midsection and pulled the trigger. He watched the terror in Morgan's eyes, as he sunk to his knees. Morgan had a firm grip on the barrel of Delaney's pistol. As he weakened, his hands slipped loose.

"Now everyone's dead," Delaney said.

Delaney put a gloved palm on Morgan's forehead and pushed him backwards to the ground. Then he returned to his car. He pulled the dead driver from his seat and flung him into the ditch. Then he got in behind the wheel and sped off, heading for the main compound of Cobb's Landing.

Tommy Delaney's face was void of emotion throughout the entire event.

Jonah Cobb's face showed disgust.

~*~

"Excuse me, Mr. Belle," the nurse interrupted. "Your grandfather is asking for you. I'm afraid he won't go back to sleep unless he sees you. Do you mind?"

"Of course he won't sleep. I'll tuck him in, nurse"

Adam got up and headed to his grandfather's hospital room.

Maggie followed.

When they entered Jacob's room Adam was delighted to see color in the old man's face, more color than he had that afternoon in his apartment.

"Well, you certainly look better than you did a while ago."

He motioned towards an I.V. that hung from a chrome hook near his bed.

"They've been pumping me full of some liquid shit. It's supposed to make me better. I think it just adds color to my cheeks, so I'll look like I feel better."

"So you don't feel better?"

"Maybe a little," he admitted. "Listen," he said changing the subject, "I wanted to see you before I turned in. I can't remember, did I ask one of you to call Amelia Cobb for me?"

"Yes. You did. Maggie said she would find her number at her father's office and call in the morning."

"Do it tonight," he insisted. Then he started to cough violently.

The nurse rushed to his bed.

"He's had enough. You two will have to say goodnight."

He pushed at her hand, and shook his head from side to side to let her know that he did not want Adam and Maggie to leave just yet.

The nurse insisted.

He stopped coughing and then told her "NO!" in a loud and firm voice. She got the message. His coughing returned, and then subsided once more. When he had caught his breath, he told Adam he wanted the call to Amelia made that evening.

"Tell her I need her heart doctor here in the morning."

Then he told Maggie the number and sent her to make the call.

"Can't trust these doctors with this. Only heart doctor here is Mathews. Might as well let me die. Same thing."

He closed his eyes.

Adam stayed with him for awhile. He fell asleep.

Then Adam went to find Maggie. He caught up with her in the waiting room where they had been listening to Tucci's account of the Cobb's Landing war. She was sitting on a plastic-covered sofa, crying.

He held her until they were both asleep. And that's where they were when morning came.

Chapter Eighteen

An ancient doctor entered the waiting room where Maggie and Adam slept. He was not quiet. He slammed a clipboard down on the coffee table just inches from Adam's ear.

If they thought their night's sleep on the plastic covered hospital waiting room furniture seemed harsh, the rude awakening surpassed it. And the doctor who gazed down on them, aside from his attire—white coat—stethoscope hanging around the neck—didn't look like a doctor at all. *You've got to be kidding,* Adam thought. *Mathews looked more capable.*

Maggie squinted her eyes against the sunlight shinning through the waiting room window.

"Who are you?" she asked.

"I'm Doctor Lang."

Adam sat up. He looked the old gent over. His trousers appeared to have permanent wrinkles in them, like they had never seen an iron, or even a dryer. *This can't be right!*

"I'm sorry," he said. "Who did you say you are?"

"Dr. Lang. I'm your grandfather's heart specialist, that is if you are Adam Belle."

"I am," Adam said. "How did you become my grandfather's doctor?" *Oh yeah! The call that Maggie made to Amelia Cobb, the call that was to summon her doctor from Chicago. Don't tell me this be the guy?* he silently questioned.

"The company sent me," he explained.

"Which company?"

Adam wiped the sleep from his eyes. He attempted to

focus, then to sit up straighter—not working. Stiff muscles fought him all the way. *You win! Permanent slouch*, he told them.

Dr. Lang reach out and pressed on something on one side of Adam's neck. It sent a wave of pain down his spine like a bolt of electricity. He winced. He felt like screaming like a little girl. He opened his mouth to do just that. Then he noticed it. The pain was leaving. The stiffness was subsiding. He relaxed.

"That better?" the old doctor asked.

"That was fantastic," Adam said.

"The Cobb's Landing Foundation," he said. "Amelia Cobb sent me."

"Excuse me?"

"The company who sent me," he said, "it s The Cobb's Landing Foundation."

Adam was still foggy, and he was skeptical.

"Why did they send you?"

"To look after Jacob," he explained.

He looked at Adam, as though his being there should have been sufficient explanation in itself.

Adam looked at Maggie. She was giving him the same look as the doctor. He gave it up.

"Are you here for his cancer or for his heart?"

"Both," he said as he shuffled over to Maggie's side, reached a hand out towards her neck, and with a long bony finger pressed on something sending her into an instant silent terror. Tears began to fill her eyes. Then she relaxed. The color returned to her face and she looked refreshed.

"We think they're related. We think the cancer, or maybe the medication, is causing the heart problem."

"Can we go in and see him?" Adam asked.

"I'm afraid not. Perhaps tomorrow," he said. "I've given him something. He'll be out of it for most of the day. We have to do extensive testing, and he'll be much better off if we keep him as sedate as possible."

"What tests?" Adam asked him.

"A variety of tests, Mr. Belle, all designed to tell us more about Jacob's total condition. That's all I can tell you for now."

"A variety of tests?"

"A variety."

"Such as?" Adam asked.

"I told you. I'm not prepared to discuss them with you at this time. Now if you'll excuse me, I have important work to attend to, for your grandfather," the old doctor said, looking challengingly over the top of his eyeglasses. Then he moved towards the room's exit.

Adam walked to the window to check on the weather. While there, he watched Dr. Lang's reflection in the glass as he left the room. He watch Maggie's as she came up behind him.

She had been reading his face. She knew his thoughts. "I know this man, Adam," she told him as she wrapped her arms around his middle. "He's treated your grandfather before. He knows what to do for him. Come! Buy me breakfast at Tucci's."

She hooked an arm through his and led him from the waiting room. Lang was in the hallway looking through Jacob Belle's medical chart. Adam glared suspiciously at him for a second. Maggie pulled on his arm until they turned a corner and the old doctor was out of sight.

~*~

"Frightening! You're getting more like Jacob Belle every day," she said.

"Is that old man going to be able to help?"

"I don't know, Adam. But I do know... if he can't, nobody can, according to both Jacob Belle and Amelia Cobb."

"Surely there are younger, more knowledgeable... well... maybe not more knowledgeable, but probably a lot less set in their ways doctors out there. You know. Guys with more up to date skills and a whole lot less of the almighty—I'm the one in charge so mind your own business type attitude."

"Is that the way you saw him?" Maggie asked.

"Yep!"

"Humph!"

"You didn't see him that way?" Adam asked as they arrived at the car.

He fumbled with the keys, trying to get the passenger's side door lock to release. It didn't seem to work.

Maggie reached in and pulled the button up. "You didn't close the window last night," she said.

She got in and pulled the door closed. Adam went around to the other side and got in behind the steering wheel.

"He really didn't say anything that should have upset you, Adam. I'm not sure I understand."

"It's not what he said. It's what he didn't say. Even more, it was the way he didn't say it."

"What?" she asked.

"What do you mean? What?"

"I mean what. What! What the hell are you saying, I mean, because I really don't have a clue what you're saying, or trying to say."

"Attitude! That's what I'm talking about. He talks down to us. He doesn't tell us anything and he does this little 'I'm a God and you are nothing' act. And he's holding back on what we need to hear like it's precious information that someone of his caliber can comprehend, but would be way over our heads. Where does that come from?"

"His position, I would imagine," Maggie said.

"As a doctor?"

Adam pulled the car to the curb in front of Tucci's Diner. They both opened their doors at the same time. Once out of the car Adam folded his arms and leaned over its top. He rested his chin on his arms. "Well?"

"As a mobster. Not as a doctor," she said.

Then she turned and started towards the entrance to the diner. Adam stood there for a moment, leaning on the car's roof.

"Coming?"

~*~

Frankie Tucci spotted them immediately. He rushed to them, placed himself between them, and hooked an arm through both of theirs. "So, how's Grandpa?" he asked. "How's that old doctor?" he asked without waiting for an answer to his first question.

"Don't ask," Maggie suggested.

"Pissed you off already, did he?" Tucci said. "He's good at that. Don't worry, though. He's every bit as good at doctorin' as he is at pissin' people off. Come! Let me fix you some breakfast. You two love birds sit over there." He pointed at the table where he and Jacob Belle always sat.

"I'll get somethin' for us ta eat. Then I'll tell you about the sheriff."

"The sheriff?" Adam asked. "I thought the sheriff was killed by Delaney. I thought he got his at the ambush site."

He did not answer. He just walked off in the direction of his kitchen as though he hadn't heard Adam. Maggie and Adam sat at the table and sipped silently at the two cups of coffee that he had placed there when he saw them park. It was not until their cups were in need of a refill that he returned with food.

"Just shot. Not killed," he said, as he placed the platters in front of them. "He musta been hurtin', that's for sure, but he weren't dead yet." He picked up the coffee urn and refilled their cups. "He crawled back out of the ditch after Delaney got back in the car, and he started limping his way to the landing. He was leakin' blood somethin' awful, from what us kids could see. We all thought he'd run out before he ever got all the way

back, but the sheriff was tough. He took a lot a killin'."
He sat down across from Maggie. Then he continued.
"Now Delaney needed to get back to the landing. He had
to try to protect the priest who weren't really a priest at
all."

"I'm confused," Maggie said. "From all I've heard of
the story he was some sort of a henchman. How did he
pull it off? How did he get away with posing as a
priest?"

"Gould...well Russo was his real name...was almost
a priest. He went to the seminary 'til he flunked out in
his last year. That's how he could fool folks into thinkin'
he was a real priest. But really? He was a hit man who
worked for the Rosetti family. And they was hooked up
wit the Palanos, a rival gang from the west coast, the
same gang my dad was wit. It was always Petruzzi they
wanted dead. It was an old grudge. Everyone figured it
was time to settle it, and for the gang who did the
settling, the pay was the Landing's liquor connection.
With Petruzzi out of the way, they all figured takin' over
would be a snap. Of course they was way
underestimatin' the Cobb boys.

"Well...Russo, according to my grandfather, had
been around here since the beginning of Cobb's landing.
Why hadn't he made a move before?" Adam asked.

"Well, that's kinda the way things worked out. You
see, the Palanos made their first move on Petruzzi back
in Chicago, before Cobb's Landing. Right after Russo
took the boss before Angelo Petruzzi. It all turned into a
war between the Rosetti family and the Palanos for one
reason or another. Anyway, the hitter they sent for
Angelo Petruzzi got killed by a Rosetti man. Guess who
it was?"

"Anthony Russo?" Adam guessed.

"Anthony Russo," Tucci confirmed. "And that's
when the Rosettis sent him here. Not to get Petruzzi or
Cobb though. Just to hide him from the
Palanos—'course that was before the Palanos and the

Rosettis were joined at the hip. Neither gang even knew where Cobb's Landing was before that. And Russo endin' up here?... Luck. That's all. Dumb luck!"

"What happened when Russo got to the Landing?" Adam asked. "Did your dad kill him right away?"

"No," Tucci said. "There was way too much excitement by then. Jonah Cobb, before he come lookin' for us kids, put the priest with Petruzzi and Jordan Cobb. Anyway, when Jonah Cobb got to us kids is when all the shootin' at the ambush started."

~*~

"Keep down and keep quiet," Amelia's uncle Jonah commanded.

He pushed the kids down, one by one, until their faces were in the dirt. Each of them felt as though they might suffocate. They all wiggled loose enough to see what was happening, but everyone kept quiet.

When he felt it was all over with, Jonah Cobb let them up.

They all watched as the sheriff labored to his feet and stumbled off around the corner out of sight. Then he led the kids back to the compound and deposited them at the Jake's cabin.

"Now the three of you stay put. You hear me? You just stay in this cabin till this is all over."

Then he set out to find his brother, to see what else might be taking place. By the time he got to Jordan's quarters, the interrogation of Anthony Russo had been completed. The young priest lay on the floor in a pool of his own blood. He held his face in his hands. Tears ran freely from his swollen eyes.

"He don't know nothin'," Beletucci said.

Beletucci, who was at the Landing for a vacation with his son, had been recruited that afternoon by Petruzzi, for his well-known talent of being able to extract information from anyone. There had been a saying among mobsters of the day, 'if Beletucci couldn't get information, there was none to be had'."

"He don't know nothin'!" he said again. "He ain't no danger to nobody."

Jordan Cobb looked at Beletucci, suspiciously. They had Anthony Russo. Russo knew a lot. He just wasn't talking.

Keep a close watch on Beletucci, Cobb warned himself.

Amelia Cobb, Jacob Belle, and Frankie Beletucci peered in through a small window in the back side of Jordan Cobb's bedroom. The view of what was going down inside was lousy. All of the action was taking place a room away, and beyond a partially closed door. And a curtain, one of those cheesecloth types that did not block everything completely, distorted the scene, just the same.

"I can't see," Amelia said.

"Sh!" Frankie Beletucci warned. "They'll hear you. My dad's got ears like a hawk."

"What the hell are you little shits doin'?" Ellen Petruzzi asked, as she staggered around the corner of the building. "Sneaky little spies," she yelled. "Get the hell outta here!"

She tripped on a small tree root that was poking out of the ground. She fell flat on her face.

Jacob Belle bent down to help her.

"Get the fuck away from me, you dirty little urchin!" she said, as she pulled her arm from Jake's grasp and stumbled to her feet. Then she disappeared around the corner of the building.

"Kill him anyway," Petruzzi ordered. "If he don't know nothin', we sure don't need him. Kill him!"

"No!" Beletucci shouted.

Petruzzi, who had already started towards the door—he liked to order the assassination of others but he never liked to witness them—turned to face Beletucci.

"What the fuck is this?" he asked excitedly, as he

stared down the barrel of Beletucci's handgun. "What the fuck are you doing?"

"My job." Beletucci said. He smiled. "Palano wants you dead. He don't give a shit about him." He gestured with his handgun towards the priest. "You're my job."

Beletucci liked to take things slow. He preferred to make his victim sweat a bit. In his line of work, finding pleasure was difficult. Watching someone who knows he's about to die squirm a bit first? Now, that's enjoyment—about all of it he'd ever get from his job. But this time, the delay would be a mistake. He had underestimated Jordan Cobb. He hadn't counted on what would happen next.

Cobb jumped across in front of Beletucci just as he fired, knocking Petruzzi to the floor and altering Beletucci's aim in the process. The bullet whizzed within centimeters of Cobb's right ear and through the wall just beside the window. It lodged itself in the drunken Ellen Petruzzi's left temple.

The woman died instantly. She didn't so much as whimper. But she did fall against Cobb's cabin and made enough noise to attract the attention of the gunman.

Beletucci changed his focus. He looked out the window. Cobb saw his chance. He pulled his own gun and fired one shot into the back of Beletucci's head.

Frankie Beletucci's eyes opened wide. His mouth opened wider. Jacob Belle instinctively wrapped his hand tightly over the Frankie's mouth to muffle the scream.

Jordan Cobb heard something. He turned. Amelia Cobb pulled Jake and Frankie to the ground. She knew what would come next. This was the mob. The mob never, never, let the son of a man who had been executed by one of their own, accident or not, necessary or not, live to take revenge. This was the way things were. And it wouldn't matter if it were her father or a total stranger. Frankie was doomed.

Amelia had the responsibility for her friend's life and she would share that responsibility with the only other person that she could trust at that moment. She would share the guarding of Frankie Beletucci's future with Jacob Belle. Together they would protect him.

They stayed low, crawling their way to cover away from Cobb's cabin. Then they ran.

~*~

In the tiny town, the undertaker was busily preserving the heavy frame of Mavis Charnley, the woman who had been killed by Tommy Delaney's shot into the air at the bank; the shot that was intended to get the undivided attention of the patrons. Mavis and her husband Karl lived in the apartment above the bank. While the undertaker worked, most of the rest of the town's population were gathered at a town meeting. They were planning steps that needed taking. Something had to be done. Most were angry, not just because of the loss of one of their own, they were angry that it had come to this. They were furious with themselves. Why hadn't they acted before? Everyone knew what went on at the Landing. They simply ignored it—easier that way. It was a disgrace. Now, at this meeting, they would form a group, a vigilante group. They would go to this Landing. And they would put an end to all of this.

"How many of you have rifles?" the town's mayor asked.

All of the men, twenty-two altogether, raised their hands.

"Here's what I suggest," the mayor continued. "Everyone go home and get your guns. We'll meet back here in one half hour, and we'll go out there and we'll clean that place out once and for all."

~*~

On their way back to Jake Belle's cabin, both Amelia and Jake comforted their friend Frankie, as best they could.

"What's happened to him?" Bill Rihle, the Landing's bartender asked, as he came face to face with the three kids on the trail.

"He fell!" Amelia quickly said.

She hoped Rihle would not question them any further. He didn't, but he did look at them curiously enough to plant a seed of doubt in the minds of both Jake and Amelia. They realized that it would not take long until someone figured out that they had seen the action back at Cobb's quarters.

Their path took them past the front door of Delaney's cabin. They saw that it was empty. They entered. They hunted for guns. They found two. They hunted for ammunition. When they had found it, they left.

They changed their route. They would no longer go to Jacob Belle's cabin, because they reasoned that the rest of them, Amelia's father included—especially Amelia's father—would guess that they would go there.

They chose to hide their friend in the root cellar. He would be safe there. Only the kitchen staff ever entered the root cellar and they had all disappeared as soon as the shooting started.

They could not go directly to the new planned hideout, though, because it was openly visible from where Ellen Petruzzi's bloody body lay. They needed something to take everyone from the area—a diversion of sorts—perhaps near the greenhouse. That would be far enough from the cellar and in the opposite direction.

When they came near the greenhouse, they found the exact diversion they needed. They came face to face once again with Bill Rihle and Bill Rihle had them figured out. And Bill Rihle had his own advancement to see to. He figured that all he needed to do to get himself solidly into the good graces of both of the Cobbs and Petruzzi was to rid them of the dangerous Beletucci boy.

He aimed a pistol at Frankie's forehead.

He didn't hear the shot from the gun that Jake Belle held tightly in his young hands, the same hands that shook uncontrollably before the bartender's lifeless body ever hit dirt. Then Jake's heart pounded. The realization that what he had just done was something he could never take back, that he could never outlive, seemed too much. His only relief from the pain and guilt that was now relentlessly hammering his spirit was the sight of his true friend, Frankie Beletucci, looking at him with gratitude and his girl, Amelia Cobb, looking at him with admiration.

~*~

The group from the village, the vigilante gang, had been formed and was now headed towards the landing. At the same time, a tiny airplane flew over the treetops that surrounded the airstrip. It touched the ground seconds later. Soon the plane's engine sputtered to silence and its pilot was out, running, not walking, towards the Landing's lodge building. His shouts for Jordan Cobb as he ran did not go unnoticed.

Cobb hurried towards the runway at the first call of his name. The two men, Cobb and the pilot, nearly ran into one another along the path. "What's all the yelling about?" Cobb shouted at the pilot.

"There's a mob, I'd guess about fifteen or twenty well-armed men in the back of trucks headed out this way," the excited pilot yelled back.

"BELLE! JAKE BELLE!" Cobb shouted at the top of his lungs.

"I'll get Frankie back to the cellar," Amelia told Jake. "You see what my dad wants. Hurry!"

Jake did not move. He was still shocked from shooting the bartender between the eyes. He had heard his boss call for him, but he could not make his feet work.

"Hurry!" Amelia shouted again.

Jake finally found the will to move. He set out in a dead run in the direction of Cobb's call. Soon, he stood beside his employer awaiting his orders. He prayed silently that his boss did not know what he had just done, that he had killed another human being.

~*~

Tucci's new waitress approached the table where he sat telling his tale of Cobb's Landing to Adam Belle and Maggie Bartell.

"Excuse me sir. You have a phone call," she said softly.

"Who the hell's callin' me now?" Tucci asked. He did not sound tolerant. He hated interruptions of any kind, but the phone, he hated most of all.

"It's not for you sir," the waitress said. "It's for Mr. Belle. It's someone from the hospital."

Chapter Nineteen

"Hello," Adam said into the payphone that was located near the checkout station. It was hard to hear through the surrounding noise. He put a finger in his opposite ear to block outside sound. "Hello!" he repeated.

"Is this Mr. Belle?" the caller asked.

"Yes. This is Adam Belle."

"This is Nurse Jennings over at the hospital," the caller said. Adam wondered, *Could she be a descendant of the nurse named Jennings who served as Cobb's Landing's only medical staff back in nineteen thirty one? Was she related to the nurse who gave my grandfather the rubdown the morning after the wreck of the plane that brought Amelia Cobb to him?* He wanted to ask but fought the urge.

"Yes?" he said.

"Everybody shut up!" Tucci yelled. "This man's tryin' ta hear."

Adam recalled his teen years. Old man Tucci had always bossed his patrons around. He hadn't thought, though, that he bossed the adult customers: just the teens. Everyone in the place quieted.

"Doctor Lang wishes to see you, Mr. Belle," the nurse said, "you and Miss Bartell. Oh. And Mr. Tucci, too, if he's available."

"Tell him we'll be right there."

"We need to go," Adam said to Maggie and Frankie who were both standing beside him waiting for a report.

"Call me and let me know what's up," Tucci said.

"You're to come with us," Adam explained. "Lang

264

wants to see you, too."

Tucci's eyes immediately dropped. Adam tensed. Tucci knew something, something not good, and Adam could sense it.

"What?" he said. "What's that look for?"

"Nothin'! Come on. Let's go," Tucci said. He headed towards the door.

~*~

The long-faced, old doctor met them at the hospital's front entrance. He led them to a small waiting room just a few steps down the hallway from the main reception desk.

Adam felt weak.

Maggie squeezed his hand. She held on tight. Then they sat in fake leather chairs for a long time and stared at one another.

Lang broke the silence. "There's no kind way of telling you this," he started.

Tears, with the knowledge of what was coming next, began to well up in Adam's eyes.

"The disease has progressed too far. There's little we can do. I'm afraid our good friend Jacob will be leaving us soon." The old man looked down at his dusty brown wing tipped shoes. "I'm sorry," he said. "I'm so sorry." He rose from his chair and began to walk out of the room.

"How long?" Adam asked.

"Weeks," Lang said without turning around, "maybe only days. It's hard to tell for sure." He walked into the hallway a few more feet. Then he stopped. He turned back to look at them. "I took him off the sedatives. He's alert. You can see him, if you'd like."

~*~

"What's with all the long faces?" Jacob Belle asked

265

Adam, Maggie, and Tucci, when they entered his room. "We all knew this day was coming, and we knew it would come soon."

"That don't make it easy, Jacob," Tucci said.

"Ah, hell," he said, "I'm getting a bit tired of listening to your old worn-out stories every morning anyway, ya old bastard." He looked at the three of them. "Anyway, nobody said when I'm going, did they?" He paused for a moment. When no one answered he continued. "Ah…come on. I ain't dead yet, and I'll have none of you treating me like I am. Now cheer up and get me the hell out of here. If they ain't going to do anything for me, then I don't need to be here."

"I quite agree." The voice came from the doorway. It was Doctor Brothers. "Other than the money I'll be losing, there's absolutely no reason for you to be cooped up in this stuffy place. I've already signed your release, Jacob. You can go home. I will come to your place every morning for a while, just to check on you."

"You're just after the money," Jacob told him.

"Of course I am," he admitted. "I'm making payments on this, you know." He smiled and pointed at the Rolex on his wrist. He turned and walked away.

Maggie and Adam waited in the hallway while nurse Jennings helped Jacob dress. Tucci had business in the neighborhood so set out on foot. Maggie took the moment to ask about something that troubled her.

"Adam, how is it your grandfather was so obviously sick last night, and looks and acts so vibrant now?"

"Drugs," Adam said. "I had a good friend back in Chicago. He had a heart condition… no… it was a heart disease. Incurable. Only hope was a transplant. Anyway, I visited him for months while he waited for a donor. Poor bastard sometimes could hardly talk. He looked more dead than alive. Finally, one day, he decided waiting for some other poor bastard to die so he could have his heart just wasn't his thing. He took himself off the list and checked out of the hospital a day later. It was the drugs. They stopped giving them to him. Next day, he looked great."

"How long did he live after that?"

"That was three years ago. Far as I know he's still kicking."

~*~

Adam tried to talk his grandfather into moving in with him and Maggie (although Maggie still maintained a place of her own, she lived with Adam at his house these days) but Jacob Belle had been on his own forever, and had no intention of changing that now, not even temporarily. "Take me home," he insisted. "The day I can't do for myself, you can either bury me or stick my ass in one of those nursing homes. You do what ever you like. Only if it's one of those homes, get that cute little nurse to take care of me. That Jennings girl who helped me dress. I remember another nurse named Jennings. At Cobb's Landing. She was nice to me too. But this one's better looking."

Adam laughed. It was the first time he felt like laughing in what seemed a long time.

"Say!" Jacob said. "Did Tucci tell you more about the Landing? I asked him to fill in some of the blanks for you."

"Yes he did."

"Did he make any sense?"

"His story follows. Just one discrepancy."

"Discrepancy?" he asked.

"Yeah! He said Tommy Delaney's queer partner was shot in the ambush. I thought you said he might still be alive."

"That's right. He did get shot." he said. "But he didn't die. Everyone thought he was dead. The rumor is, though, he crawled out of the woods and got help from someone in the town. Then he disappeared."

The car came to a stop in front of the bank. Jacob

opened the back door and got out onto the sidewalk. He leaned in Maggie's window.

"I want to go to the Landing."

"When?" Maggie asked.

"I don't know," he said. "Probably in a day or two. After I get my strength back. I'll see the two of you at Tucci's in the morning. We'll decide then."

~*~

Adam Belle did not sleep well that night and it showed.

"You look like shit," Frankie Tucci told him as he struggled with his chair at the breakfast table.

"Where's my grandfather?" Adam asked. "Have you heard from him this morning?"

"Right behind you, dumb ass." Jacob said, as he approached the table. "I had to go to the bathroom. Is that alright with you?"

"He didn't sleep so well," Maggie explained.

"No shit," Jacob said. "I can see that in his eyes."

Frankie Tucci's young waitress broke up their snappy conversation. She delivered breakfast plates piled unusually high with food.

"Christ," Adam said. "Who's going to eat all of this?"

Jacob Belle grabbed a fork and began shoveling from plate to mouth like a fireman feeding the coal furnace of an old locomotive.

"He eats like this every time they stick 'im in the hospital," Tucci explained. "I think they try ta starve 'im in that place."

"The food they serve all starts out as a powder," he said as he shoveled. "Nobody with taste buds can eat it. I don't care what happens. Don't take me there anymore."

He left no space for comment. He just kept on talking around the bites of his breakfast.

"Tucci, how far did you get in the Landing's story? Did ya get to the part where you're dad got it?"

That's right! Adam thought. *Tucci's old man was the hit-man, Beletucci, there to whack Petruzzi.*

"When did you drop the first part of your name?" Adam asked.

"The day I got killed," he said, "the same day my pop got hit, and Billy Brooks, and a whole bunch of the others. When your grandpa was called by Jordan Cobb, a whole bunch of shit come sliden' down from the pile."

Jacob seemed content to let his friend continue. He shoveled food and listened.

Tucci went on.

~*~

When Jake arrived beside Jordan Cobb, he realized his silent prayer, that Cobb had not found out that it was he who killed the bartender, had been answered. The two of them set off for the bridge in the same car that had brought Tommy Delaney back from the botched bank robbery. He filled his young apprentice in as they drove.

"It seems the whole goddamned town is on their way out here," he said.

"Are we going to fight them off by ourselves?" Jake asked.

"No! We're going to burn the bridge."

"What good will that do?"

"It'll at least slow 'em down. It'll give us time to get ready."

Cobb looked at the boy. The thirty-eight sticking partway out of the top of Jake's trousers caught his eye.

"I see you've come prepared."

"Huh?" Jake asked.

Cobb reached across the car and snatched the pistol out of Jake's pants. He held it to his nose.

"Been fired, too. Who'd you shoot, Son?"

He laid the gun on the seat between them. Jake grabbed it and stuck it back in the front of his trousers. "I found it," he explained. "It was on the trail up by the greenhouse."

He sat silently. The car bounced over some fresh ruts that had been left behind by a recent rain. When they had cleared the rough spot in the road, he spoke again. "I've heard a lot of shooting today. When I saw the thing just laying there I thought God must have left it there for me to find, you know, kinda like he was looking out for me or something."

"You think God gave you a gun?" Cobb smiled at Jake's naivety. *Youngsters!* He thought. "I doubt it, boy. That looks like one of Delaney's guns. This God of yours, he wouldn't happen to look anything like Tommy Delaney would he?"

"No, Sir." Jake answered.

The car rounded the last turn before the bridge. Jordan Cobb slammed on the brakes. He swung the door open. He could hear engines in the distance. It had to be the vigilante group from the town.

"Come on, boy. We need to hurry."

He started to pull gas cans from the back seat. There were four of them in all, two on his side and two more on the Jake's side.

"Grab those cans."

Soon, the two of them were on the bridge, splashing gasoline over its timbers until all the cans were empty. Cobb didn't just want it on fire; he wanted it destroyed. They let the cans lay.

"They'll explode when the fire reaches them. That'll help."

They ran to the Landing's side of the bridge. The first of the trucks carrying the heavily armed men from the town was rapidly approaching. As soon as they were clear of the bridge, Cobb struck a match. He threw it at the gasoline-soaked timbers. It went out before it landed.

"Shit!"

He struck another.

Same thing.

"Shit!"

He struck a third—his last. He threw it at the bridge. The flash that followed removed the eyebrows of both Cobb and Jake Belle.

A truck came to a stop, just inches from the fire. Cobb and Jake could see that several men were standing up in the back of the truck. The shooters took aim and were about to spray bullets in their direction. They ducked for cover.

They heard an explosion. They felt a large chunk of debris fly past, just over their heads. It landed directly on their car. Then they saw a man, flames bellowing from both of his legs, as he flew almost gracefully by them. They both sprang to their feet and rushed towards the flaming man. They rolled the burning body until there were no more flames. It was too late. He was dead. His neck was broken. His head was turned in an unnatural position; one that would not have been possible had the neck not been broken. They rolled him once more just to be sure and that's when they saw it. Half of the man's skull was caved in.

Jacob Belle puked on the spot.

Jordan Cobb, accustomed as he was to mob violence, seasoned as he was to the sight of blood and guts, felt like joining the boy. He thought perhaps he had simply had enough for one day. "Jesus Christ," he uttered softly.

One of the Landing's guests, a slight man, with an almost albino lack of pigmentation to his thin skin, got into a truck that sat idling in front of the lodge. Amelia could see him watching her and Frankie Beletucci, as they tried to duck into the underground root cellar where they were to wait out the fighting in safety and meet up with Jake Belle as soon as he returned.

"He's watching us, Frankie," Amelia said. "We've got to do something."

"What should we do?" Frankie Beletucci asked.

"We have to kill him," Amelia answered.

"We have to kill him?" Frankie questioned.

"Come on, Frankie, don't sound so shocked. You were raised mob. You know how things are. Either we kill him or he rats us out to save his sorry self. Then it's us they'll be hunting. We have to kill him, Frankie."

Frankie Beletucci snatched the gun out of Amelia Cobb's hand. If there were to be some killing done, by God, he'd be the one to do it. He was the man. Men didn't let little girls do their killing for them.

With the gun cocked and ready to fire, he ran in a zigzag pattern at the idling truck. The pale man watched, stunned look on his face, probably trying to figure out just what the crazy kid was up too.

At fifteen feet away Frankie raised the arm that held the gun, took aim, and plugged the man just behind the left ear. He kept running past the truck and into the woods, out of sight of anyone who might have heard the shot and come out to investigate.

Amelia knew two things, and both of these things told her that she should stay put. She knew that Frankie would likely circle and come up on her from the back, and she knew that Jake Belle knew that the two of them were making their way to the cellar. That is where he would go to find them as soon as he got free of whatever it was that her father had him doing. But she felt a bit vulnerable in her position. Should anyone come out of the lodge, she would be standing there all alone, an easy target.

That was an odd feeling. She had never before thought of herself as a target, but this day, with all that was happening at this place, and the rate at which everything was happening, she could not only imagine herself as a target, she knew for a fact that she was a target. Everyone was. Her father's enemies, and Petruzzi's enemies, had seen to that. And girls weren't exempt. Not in this war. Mrs. Petruzzi, lying there in a pool of blood outside her father's window, proved that.

And, in a war like this, a young lady's life would do when her father's life was unavailable.

She eased back, a step at a time, careful not make noise. She kept her eyes on the main door of the lodge. Once in the thick brush beside the entrance to the root cellar, she felt safe again.

Shots rang loud and echoed long. They came from the lodge and preceded two running men. The first man was Amelia's uncle Jonah. He seemed to be bleeding from his right shoulder. He ran to the idling truck with the dead albino in it. There was no time to drag the corpse from behind the steering wheel so Jonah Cobb shoved it over in the center of the seat. As he got in, the second man ran towards him. It was Tommy Delaney. He didn't appear injured. Tommy jumped over the bed of the already moving truck and scrambled to get in on the passenger's side. The third man, the man with the gun, was Sheriff Morgan. He took aim at the back window of the truck and fired one shot. He missed.

Amelia took a step back. Her foot landed on a dry twig.

Morgan turned in the direction of the snap and fired instinctively.

Amelia screamed out with pain. The bullet hit her in the chest, close to her heart. She fell to the ground.

Frankie Beletucci arrived just in time to catch her.

Morgan could not see into the brush but judged from the scream two things. One, that the victim was Amelia Cobb, Jordan Cobb's only daughter, and two, that he, Sheriff Morgan, was a dead man.

Jordan Cobb and Jake Belle thought they heard a scream following the latest barrage gunfire. As they ran towards the sound, a fast moving truck forced them to dive for the thick brush beside the road.

"You alright, Boy?" Cobb yelled out.

"I'm ok," Jake shouted back. He got up, dazed but unhurt, and moved to join Cobb once again. "That sounded like Amelia," he said.

"I know, Son," Cobb said softly. "Let's move." He picked up the pace.

Morgan flew past Belle and Cobb like a bolt of lightning. "Morgan?" Cobb shouted. Morgan didn't answer.

The pilot who had flown in just in time to see the vigilante group heading towards Cobb's Landing ran along side of Petruzzi towards the brush where Amelia lay bleeding, just as Jake and Jordan Cobb entered the clearing behind the lodge. Frankie Beletucci disappeared into the woods when he saw them.

"Jesus!" Cobb uttered when he arrived at the spot where the girl laid. "Not her!" he said, his voice shaky. "Who did this?" he yelled at the top of his lungs. "Who the fuck did this?"

Jake knelt beside the girl and began to cry. He held her hand and kissed her on her forehead.

"Who?" he asked her.

Cobb knelt on her other side and took her other hand.

"Daddy," she whimpered.

"It's okay, baby. It's going to be okay," Cobb promised his daughter. "Who shot you?"

"The sheriff."

Cobb ordered the pilot to fire up his engine. Then he asked Petruzzi to take his daughter and get her in the plane.

"What do I do with Ellen?" Petruzzi objected.

"This young man will take care of her, won't you, Boy?" he asked Jake.

He did not understand the grief that Jake Belle was undergoing at that moment. His summer, with the influx of guests and the growth of problems and the constant babysitting that was his function where the Petruzzi's were concerned, took all of his work hours and his free time as well. The time for him to be made aware of the flowering relationship between this youngster and his only daughter had been swallowed up by tasks that seemed, as he looked down upon Amelia lying there with her blood spilling out on the ground, unimportant. He was a smart man, a man who caught on easily once he paid attention. He looked into the teary eyes of Jacob Belle and he could see there, the love that this youngster had for his daughter, and then he looked into the fear-filled eyes of his injured daughter. She was not looking to her father to put an end to her misery, to stop her pain. She looked to this young man.

Cobb knew at that moment that he had missed all that was of value in the summer of thirty-one. He had missed it completely.

"Can you do that, Jake?" he asked.

"Yes, Sir."

Angelo Petruzzi picked the girl up, cradled her gently in his arms, and began walking in the direction of the airstrip.

Jake and Amelia did not release their grasp on each other's hand until their arms would not stretch any further.

Cobb placed his hand in the middle of Jake's back, just between the shoulder blades, and guided him towards the burning bridge.

"Don't take off without me," he yelled over his shoulder at the pilot and Petruzzi. "I won't be long."

He watched for a moment, until the three of them disappeared around a bend.

"Son," he said turning his attention back to Jake, "I'll need you to stay on here and keep an eye on things while I'm gone. Can you do that for me?"

Jake told Cobb that he had no other place to go, but that he had no idea what he should do.

"I don't think there'll be much of a problem. Just clean up around here. Those who aren't dead will be gone. Just keep the place in order until I return. It'll be just a short time. When I get back, we'll bury the bodies.

I think then I'll spend the winter in Chicago. Maybe we'll open the Landing again in the spring. You stay on here and we'll keep on paying you. Can you do that?"

"Yes, Sir."

Jake thought of asking about his friend Frankie Beletucci, but thought better of it. He had learned enough about the ways of the mob this summer to know that it was better to not bring his friend into the light, that he might be able to protect him, if he just let it be. He said nothing.

"Where did that Beletucci boy get off to?" Cobb asked.

"He's dead." Jake said, unaware until that moment that he could lie with conviction. "His body is up by the greenhouse. Want to see it?" he asked, knowing that Cobb was in a hurry to get on the plane with his daughter.

"No," Cobb said. "He seemed a nice kid. I know you were friends. He deserves a better burial than the rest of these stiffs. You see to it and I'll pay the bill. The rest of this bunch, we'll just stick in the ground. I have to go now, Boy. You go find my brother. He'll stay here and help you."

He turned and ran off in the direction of the airstrip.

A tear-filled Jake Belle watched as his employer, the man who had sent for him, met with him, talked him into coming to this place, and changed his life forever, walked off into the thick brush that lay between him and the airstrip where he would very likely disappear from his life forever. And he would take with him the one good thing that young Jake had gotten for his all of the misery and mayhem that this terrible day had brought: his cherished Amelia.

He watched until he could see nothing, not even the movement of the rustling brush that Cobb had left in his wake as he hurried to join his wounded daughter, the frightened and nervous pilot, and an unfeeling mob boss named Petruzzi who, it appeared, could not even bring himself to grieve for his own murdered wife. Belle felt sorry for Petruzzi. He felt a great loss over Amelia. He felt concern over the probability that his boss would not be returning. And he knew that he could not wait for Cobb's return, even should it actually come, to bury the bodies. He and Frankie Beletucci would have to see to it.

He turned to make his way towards the bridge, to find Jonah Cobb, to see if he was still alive, to see if anybody was still alive.

~*~

Jonah Cobb had pulled the truck onto a side road, one that had seen little use, more of a trail that could be used to haul things to the back entrance of the greenhouse when necessary. He and Delaney got out of the vehicle and covered it with brush. Jonah stared at Delaney. *I should shoot the prick now. He's the enemy. I know it.* They watched as Sheriff Morgan ran past and smiled briefly at one another. *I'll wait. Shoot him later. Might need him to fight beside me.*

"Tough son-of-a-bitch ain't he?" Delaney commented. "I shot him good. I know I killed him. I don't know how he's still moving around that way. You'd think he'd run out of blood, sooner or later."

"He's running on hate, hate for you and hate for me, and hate for having his life ended. And his spirit won't let him quit till he gets us. You watch and see," Jonah Cobb said. "Now, we can't stay here long. That bunch from the town, sooner or later, they'll figure a way in here and they'll find us."

"Well, no shit, Cobb!" Delaney said. "All they got to do is drive over the bridge. I don't see what's keeping them now."

"There ain't no bridge. I'm sure there ain't," Cobb said. "My brother, if I know him, would have set fire to it the minute he got wind of vigilantes heading this way. He built this place here, right where it's at because of that ravine. That's the way he does things. He makes sure there's either a good way out, or a good way to stop others from getting in, usually both. That bridge is burning down as we sit here."

Delaney sniffed the air. He smelled smoke. "I guess you're right," he said. "Only real problem for now is that Morgan is locked in here with us. I think we'd better figure out something before he figures out that he missed us. Maybe we'll get lucky. Maybe the bridge will still hold us and we can make a run for it. Maybe we'll be able to run the sheriff over and finish him off. Maybe the guys from the town gave up and went home."

Jonah Cobb thought that there were far too many maybes in Tommy Delaney's half-assed plan. He looked around their position for another answer. Then he heard the small plane, as it took off and flew low over the trees. It was certain, Delaney's plan was a lousy plan but, even more than that, it was now the only plan.

"Let's go," he said.

"What about him?" Delaney asked, pointing to the stiff in the center of the truck's seat.

"Leave him there," Cobb said. "If the sheriff survives long enough to take another shot, he might aim at him instead of one of us." *Him or you!"* he added silently.

Jordan backed the truck out and headed it toward the burning bridge.

~*~

Jake Belle hadn't gotten three paces before he heard the rustling in the brush. He drew the gun that he had taken earlier from Tommy Delaney's arsenal. He aimed carefully at the movement of the branches. He was about to pull the trigger.

"Don't shoot! It's me, Frankie Beletucci," the youngster said, as he emerged from the bushes, hands held high in the air.

"No! It's not!" Jake yelled at his friend. Then, in a

much softer voice, he began to explain. "From now on your name is Tucci, not Beletucci, get it?"

Frankie did not seem to get it. Jake thought that it must have been all that had already gone on, that the days horrors was making his friend slow-witted. He would explain.

"They're going to kill Frankie Beletucci if they find him. Think about it. You know that's true. You know who we're dealing with. Frankie Beletucci died here today. We'll bury Frankie Beletucci beside his father, and you can go on living as Frankie Tucci. Ok?"

The message sunk in. "Ok," he agreed.

He stood there beside his friend. He thought for a time before he spoke again. "Jake," he finally said, "Sheriff Morgan shot her."

"I know," Jake said. "Let's go find Jonah Cobb. He'll know what to do. Only when we find him, you get out of sight. He's mob too. He'll shoot you."

The two boys started to run in the direction of town, thinking that the other Mr. Cobb had to have gone to defend the Landing from the vigilante gang. When they rounded the last bend in the road before the bridge, the spot where the sheriff's overturned truck and the grossly twisted and bloody bodies of its dead passengers lay, they saw the sheriff. He was standing just in front of them, his back turned towards them, his arms held straight out, both hands tightly gripping his pistol, and they stopped dead in their tracks. The sheriff's gun fired. The boys flinched. The back window of the truck ahead of them shattered into hundreds of tiny pieces and slowly fell into the truck's bed. The truck's driver slumped over the wheel. His foot must have automatically pushed the accelerator to the floor because the truck sped onto the burning bridge and fell, together with most of the structure's flaming timbers, into the creek below. The boys watched the sheriff walk towards the ravine. They saw the gang of vigilantes watching their sheriff from the other side of the gully. They watched as Tommy Delaney crawled over the edge of the bank and stood, only to come face to face with Morgan's speeding bullet. He was knocked backwards into the ravine he had just emerged from. Then they watched as the sheriff turned to face them.

Morgan took aim.

Both boys pointed pistols.

They fired.

Morgan fell first to his knees, then to the ground, dust rising as he hit. He lay there in a hideous pile, not ten feet from the shaking youths.

"Is that Jacob Belle?" one of the vigilante group asked.

"Yes, Sir," Jake yelled out.

"Are there any more of them over there?"

"No, Sir. They're all dead," Jake shouted back.

"You alright, Jake?"

"Yes, Sir."

The vigilantes, all of them thinking they saw the man from the ravine shoot their sheriff, turned and began their long journey back to the town. No one had seen the boys shoot.

~*~

"I gotta take a piss," Frankie Tucci said, as he slammed his empty coffee cup on the table. Everyone, Adam, Maggie, and Jacob Belle jumped.

"Jesus, Tucci," Jacob said. "Jesus!"

"Well, I gotta piss," Tucci said again.

He stood and shuffled off towards the restroom.

Chapter Twenty

Lunchtime had come and gone. Frankie Tucci was away at the men's room. Jacob Belle had decided that he had enough for one day. He needed a nap.

Adam Belle thought it rude to leave while their host was away, but there was urgency in his grandfather's tone. Good manners or bad. It mattered not. Jacob had to go home. Adam and Maggie would return to make their apologies later. Perhaps they could even persuade Tucci to continue with the story.

By the time they reached his apartment, Jacob seemed to have gotten a second wind. He felt like talking. They all sat at his kitchen table for a time. Maggie made sandwiches and iced tea while Adam and Jacob talked small talk.

Then Jacob got up from the table and went over to the window. He looked to the street below. Adam and Maggie both awaited complaints about the missing traffic signal, but none came. Instead he said, "It's twenty-three degrees Celsius."

Adam moved to the window and stood beside him. He wanted to know what that was in Fahrenheit. The sign switched to read '73 F'.

"It's supposed to be even warmer tomorrow. I think I'd like to go to the Landing, if you have the time," Jacob said.

Adam looked at Maggie. She nodded.

"We have the time," he said.

"You two need some information from me."

"We aren't here for a nap, are we?" Adam asked.

"No. I just thought we needed a little private time, time to discuss a few things that involve only us," he said.

"Would you two like to be left alone?" Maggie offered.

"No, you stay," he insisted. "You're family too, what there is of it at any rate. You need to hear what I have to say as well. This is about what happens next, about what happens after I'm gone."

"Do we really have to talk about this?" Adam asked him. "I don't want to do this now. I don't know if I'll ever be ready to do this."

"You heard the doctors, Adam. Now, I plan to stick around for some time yet, but we already passed the time of guarantees. This has to be done. Let's just go over a few things and get it over with." He looked at Adam and Maggie. No one appeared to want an argument.

"The company wanted me to make sure that you would take over my duties. Are you willing to do that?" He waited for an answer. None came.

He dug into a long description of the job, its duties—money—the importance of family—the mob and all its local holdings. There were many. Adam was amazed at how much of the little town was under the control of the mob.

"Is that something you can handle?" he finally asked.

"I'm still not completely sold on working for the mob."

"Don't look at it as working for the mob then. Look at it as preserving the Landing, preserving history, the history of this area; mine and Amelia's history. Look after Cobb's Landing because of what it meant to me, not because it belonged to the mob. Do it, Adam, because I asked you to. And do it because that is where I want you to take me when I go. And there's one more reason, Adam. The Landing and what happened there needs to be protected from the authorities. Me and Amelia and Frank Tucci committed crimes there.

Murder. And more. Soon, they won't be able to get me. But what about Amelia and Frankie?"

He made a powerful argument. He knew he had. He knew a request to be buried at Cobb's Landing would bind Adam to the place. He knew his grandson would protect him as long as he lived, and he would do the same for Amelia and Frankie.

So...finally...Adam agreed. Now he wanted the conversation stopped. He did not want to think about his grandfather dying.

~*~

"You once told me that you were told that Amelia Cobb had been killed at the Landing. Who told you that?"

"Her father, Jordan Cobb," he said.

"Then he did come back?"

"No. I never saw him again. He sent me a note with my pay. I cried for weeks. It hurt for years, even after I found that it hadn't been true."

"That was at his funeral. Wasn't it?"

"Yes. At his funeral. Amelia had been told that I had been killed as well. When her father died and she inherited the job of managing the Cobb's Landing Foundation, Angelo Petruzzi's ill-gotten gains, she found that there was a caretaker at the landing and that he was on the payroll. No name, of course. There had never been a name, just an envelope with money to be deposited in the bank. I drew my pay from that account each month in the early days. It was later that things changed and my income came directly from the company's local holdings. Anyway," he continued, "it was when she sent a dispatch to the caretaker of Cobb's Landing notifying that person of the death of Jordan Cobb, and to invite that person to his funeral, that I discovered she was still alive."

"That is so sad," Maggie said as she wiped at a tear.

"It was sad. And it is my greatest regret," he said. "The two of you promise me something. Promise me that you will guard against anything like that ever happening to you." He didn't wait for them to answer. "I do need that nap," he said. "Will you take me to the Landing tomorrow?"

"We will." Adam promised him. They said their goodbyes, left him to nap, and returned to Tucci's to explain their disappearance. Then they went home to relax.

~*~

It was still dark out when Adam woke up the next morning. He felt something. A disturbance. He couldn't explain it. He simply felt it. The clock read "4:28." He got up and made coffee. The first pot he drank...alone.

"I tried not to wake you," he told Maggie, when she joined him.

"I can't sleep anymore without you there beside me. What do you make of that?"

"I think it must be love."

"Well then... I guess it's alright," she said. She kissed him, and then went to the counter to pour herself some coffee. "How's yours?" she asked.

Adam slammed the quarter-cup he still had, and held the empty out for a refill.

"How come you're up so early?" she asked.

"Couldn't sleep."

"Hungry?" she asked.

"You know, I think I am."

"Then I'll fix us some breakfast, a big breakfast. You have a lot of paddling to do today. You'll need the extra calories."

Whatever his uneasiness had been, it disappeared as soon as Maggie was up. The rest of the morning; breakfast, Maggie packing an enormous picnic and all of the usual things they took with them to Cobb's Landing, and Adam packing the car and strapping the canoe down on its roof, went like clockwork. Soon they found themselves parked in front of Tucci's, Jacob Belle already in the back seat. Adam found himself excited.

"Would somebody see what's keeping that old idiot?" Jacob asked, impatient to get on the water. He no sooner said it and Tucci was at the door. "It's about time!"

~*~

Adam stopped paddling, as usual, when they passed over the top of the truck that pinned Jonah Cobb to the lakes floor and guarded the entrance to Cobb's Landing.

"I need to ask something of you," Jacob said as he looked down at the ancient truck. "I want you to find a way to get Jonah Cobb out of there and I want you to give him a proper resting place at the Landing, with the others. And don't forget to put me there, too. I'll be happy there. It's where I belong."

No one had to answer him. It was rhetoric—an order—not at all a request.

They paddled on in silence, each of them studying the shoreline, Adam, looking for things to explore; Maggie, looking to see what Adam was looking at; Jacob and Frankie Tucci, looking for memories. It seemed only moments until the bow of the canoe was pushing onto the shore of Cobb's Landing.

"Home," Jacob Belle murmured.

~*~

"If Jordan Cobb never returned to the landing, and Jonah Cobb was killed on the day of the war, who buried all of the bodies?" Adam asked as he pulled the canoe on land.

"We done that," Tucci offered, "me 'n your grandpa buried 'em all. It took us most of a week to get it done."

285

"That must have been an awful experience for the two of you, I mean, you were just kids." Maggie said.

"We woke up as kids that morning," Jacob said, "but we went to sleep as men that night; men seasoned by war, by blood, by killing when killing had to be done, and by burying those who we had killed."

"Besides," the less poetic and more practical Tucci added, "dead bodies ain't really nothin'. They're just things, like furniture or rocks or somethin'. You don't really feel for 'em."

Adam thought about it. Tucci was right. He once came across an accident on the highway, and to him the bodies didn't look real. They looked like mannequins. Not humans. *I wonder if the soul leaving the body causes that?*

Then he thought about the men who died at Cobb's Landing, the men his grandfather and Frankie Tucci buried that week. *If any of those men ever had a soul, they gave it up long before that day. They were gangsters, criminals, killers. Dead men with no soul. They wouldn't look real. Would they?*

"There's a grave marked with Amelia's initials," Adam said. "What's that about?"

"I did that," Jacob said. "Made me feel better at the time."

"And the little one by the lodge?" Adam asked.

"Elizabeth."

Adam helped his grandfather out of the canoe. Then he and Maggie unloaded all that they had brought with them: the cooler filled with cold beverages, the wicker basket filled with food, extra blankets for just in case (Maggie had thought of their last visit as she packed).

Jacob and Frankie busied themselves with a slow walk down their memory lane; their personal voyage through their colorful youth. When they returned, they chose to sit together on a bench in front of the bathhouse. When Adam and Maggie offered to join them they told them they wanted to be alone.

"Just want to sit and think. Don't feel much like talking. You two kids explore the Landing. Us old guys... all we'll do is slow you down," Jacob told them. "Go! Have fun."

They did.

As they reached the path to the old greenhouse, Jacob shouted, "LOOK OUT FOR POISON IVY!"

~*~

"How long is the walk to where the old bridge was?" Adam asked Maggie, when they had arrived at the greenhouse.

"Two miles, if we take the main road," she said. "We can cut some of that off if we can find the back road in here."

"Would that be the road where Jonah Cobb and Tommy Delaney hid from Sheriff Morgan?"

"That would be the one," she said.

She probed around in the underbrush for a time.

"This look like old tire ruts to you?"

Adam looked them over and agreed. This was the road. They began to follow it—mistake—it took forever. It would have been quicker to go back to the main compound and follow the longer path to the old bridge. But, eventually, they did find the bridge, its ruins anyway, not much to look at. What hadn't burned had rotted to nothing.

The journey did answer one lingering question for Adam, though. He wondered why the vigilante group from town didn't find a way to help the boys that day. As he looked across the ravine he had his answer. It had been impossible. The ravine was deep and wide. It couldn't be crossed without the bridge, not if the water was rapid enough to have carried Jonah Cobb and his truck all the way to Jesse Lake. Folks hadn't been as heartless as he had thought.

On the walk back, the couple found the rusted metal

that Adam had seen from the canoe on their last visit to the Landing. It lay in a ditch just around the corner from the bridge, half-buried under brush and leaves and dirt. Sheriff Morgan's overturned truck. And near it, a shoe. Probably blown off the foot of one of the deputies.

"You suppose there's still a foot in there?"

"I don't know. But I don't think I want to know either," Maggie said as she pulled him away from the shoe.

Adam looked down at the shoe. He glanced at his watch—noon—better get back. He'd check to see if the shoe was empty another time. They started the two-mile trek along the overgrown road to the main compound of Cobb's Landing. When they broke into the clearing, Jacob Belle and Frankie Tucci were still on the same bench where they had left them hours before.

They approached.

Frankie Tucci dried an eye as they came close.

Grandfather Belle was leaning on his friends shoulder.

"He went to sleep. His heart just quit beating, Adam," Frankie said.

Now tears were running freely down his cheeks. He wiped at them.

"Your grandpa's gone, Son."

Chapter Twenty-One

As they stood on the picturesque shore of Cobb's Landing on a sunny summer afternoon, with a warm breeze wrapping around them like an invisible blanket protecting them from whatever harm might chance their way, Maggie and Adam had but one regret. Jacob Belle, Adam's grandfather and the person who was solely responsible for them being there, the man responsible for there being a them, would not be present to witness what would take place that day. They were there, at Jacob's beloved Cobb's Landing, to add a tiny piece of what would become their history to the already rich and intoxicating history of this fascinating place and its extraordinary breed of people.

Adam had, on that day, a great excitement welling up within him; but a great sadness as well. The excitement was caused by this being the day that he would keep his bargain with Maggie Bartell by declaring publicly his undying love and loyalty to her by affirming his vows in the presence of all of those spirits who will forever occupy Cobb's Landing, and those beings still among the living who held those spirits in such high regard. The extreme sadness was caused by the simple fact that his grandfather, Jacob Belle, was no longer one of the living beings. He had become one of the occupying spirits.

Adam would miss him at their wedding. Maggie would miss him at their wedding.

They would miss him… always.

~*~

Neither Maggie nor Adam had considered how small their wedding would be back when they first agreed to hold it at Cobb's Landing, but small it was. Maggie, for her maid of honor, had chosen a cousin, Heather Newberry, who was not her cousin at all but a cousin of her adoptive father, Mayor Buckley. Mayor Buckley, naturally, would walk her down the isle, or more correctly, down the grassy lane that had been chosen to serve as the isle.

Adam had ventured out early in the week by himself. He had brought an ancient reel mower, the kind without a motor, and had cut a wide path leading from the lodge, where his bride would change from canoeing clothes into a wedding dress, to the bath-house on the shore, where the celebration would take place. Both of them wanted the view of the lake as they vowed their love to one another, and they wanted, as a backdrop for any photos that might be taken, the picturesque setting of Cobb's Landing.

Adam's best man would be a bit of a paradox. He hadn't been a close friend. Most of the time, they didn't even like each other. What he was, was a lack of options; chosen partially because Adam knew no one else—his friends from high school, those he actually came to remember, had all moved away—and partially because of their joint connection to Cobb's Landing. He chose Leonard Morgan to stand with him.

~*~

Maggie and Adam were the first to reach the landing, long before anyone else. They stood, watching out over the water as a small rowboat rounded the tip of the peninsula. In it, manning the oars, was Leonard Morgan. The sight amused Adam.

Morgan's passenger was the preacher who would marry them. *Don't tell me history doesn't repeat itself,* Adam thought as he recounted his grandfather's story of the night Leonard Morgan's great-grandfather, the sheriff, sat mid-lake spying on Cobb's Landing through field glasses with Anthony Russo (Father Gould) as his passenger. *That's an old boat. Could be the same one.*

Moments later, another craft, a canoe, pulled around the bend. It carried Maggie's cousin and maid of honor, Frankie Tucci, and the mayor, Maggie's father. As it touched land, the sound of an airplane filled the ears of those present. Frankie Tucci nearly capsized the canoe trying to get out when he heard it. He knew who it was—Amelia Cobb. He had thought to invite her when nobody else had. He had told Maggie weeks earlier that he had a surprise for her wedding day. Amelia Cobb was that surprise. Frankie ran towards the old airstrip.

What the wedding that was held at Cobb's Landing that day lacked in quantity of guests, it made up for in quality of guests. Royalty attended. It was a wedding to be held in the company of a king and a queen. Frankie Beletucci, the man Adam and Maggie had grown to know through their adolescent years as Mr. Tucci of Tucci's Diner, the closest and most loyal friend of Adam's grandfather and the guardian of all of the children who were fortunate enough to have grown up in this tiny part of the world, was the king who reigned over their union. Amelia Cobb, the love of Adam's grandfather's life and the sole reason behind his undying efforts to protect and preserve this great place, this treasured piece of all of their histories, was the lady who had always been the one true queen of Cobb's Landing and was now their queen, the queen of their wedding. Maggie and Adam were honored. Majesty witnessed their joining.

~*~

Adam did not know who the newcomer was. It was the excitement of the day. It kept him from thinking about anything but his soon-to-be wife. He only knew that, there, standing arm-in-arm with Frankie Tucci, was a handsome lady who said nothing, just smiled at the bride and groom.

It was after the ceremony that she approached. It was then that she spoke.

"Congratulations my dear great-niece," she said as she put her arms around Maggie.

"I didn't know you'd be here, Aunt Amelia."

"Of course I came. This is the union of the Cobbs and the Belles. I couldn't miss that. It's what Jacob and I hoped and planned for all our lives. And you, young man," she said to Adam as she clasped his hand. "You're the spitting image of Jacob Belle. When he was about forty, we couldn't have told you apart." She studied Adam's face. *Regrets? Sure. But also a certain pride.* "Welcome to the Cobb family, my dear new great-nephew." She pulled him close and kissed him on the cheek. It was a gentle kiss. It was a Cobb kiss. And, in it, he could feel her pain. Her losses. But also, in it... he could feel Maggie.

A tiny tear came to his eye. He brushed it away.

When Amelia Cobb pulled back from him she handed Adam a large brown envelope.

He asked her what was in it.

"It's a wedding gift. And it's the rest of your life. Walk with me to the cemetery."

She pushed her arm through the arm of Frankie Beletucci and began walking.

Maggie and Adam followed. And when they arrived at the tiny burial spot that had until just weeks ago been almost completely grown over, she walked up to the newest of the graves. Jonah Cobb was the name carved in the headstone. Adam had kept his promise. He'd had Leonard Morgan help. Together they had managed to pull the old truck out of the water. But they did not find all of Jonah Cobb. All that remained was his wallet and his pocket watch, and a few bones. They were buried here. As a memorial.

Upon the headstone, Amelia placed a single rose from the bouquet she had held tightly throughout the ceremony, crossed herself, kissed the fingers of her white gloved hand, and placed the hand on the headstone. "Uncle Jonah," she whispered.

Then she went to the other fresh grave. On its headstone was the name Jacob Belle. It was the only stone in the cemetery that bore a picture. It was an old black and white photo, the kind with the crinkled edges with the date printed in black on the white boarder, and in the photo were a teenaged Jacob Belle and a small framed, freckled, reddish haired beauty with hardly any tits named Amelia Cobb.

She looked at the photo and smiled, knelt on the ground beside him, placed the remainder of her flowers on the grave, kissed the headstone and said, "Soon, Jacob, very soon."

Amelia Cobb started to turn away. Another headstone caught her attention.

"Who did this?" she asked, her eyes filling with tears.

"I did, Ma'am," Adam told her. "With Leonard's help. I hope it's alright."

She looked down at the small headstone and the tiny grave that lay beside her beloved Jacob.

Elizabeth Cobb-Belle, it read.

"It's perfect."

Then Amelia Cobb walked in silence to the small airstrip, boarded her plane, waved goodbye, and flew off into the sunset like a dream whose end had come.

That was the last time any of them saw her alive.

~*~

Eleven months later Adam and Maggie, with the help of Leonard Morgan, would bury her with her beloved Jacob; their daughter, Elizabeth nestled between them.

The envelope that Amelia Cobb gave Adam that day contained the deed to Cobb's Landing, papers that

293

granted him and Maggie ownership to other properties and businesses, including a small bank which had once been the target of the robbers from the Landing, and an appointment to the directorship of an organization called The Cobb's Landing Foundation, whose main function had been to hide the ill-gotten fortune of Angelo Petruzzi from the federal government while Petruzzi served out a prison term that he would never come to outlive.

The Cobb's were the only ones to have known of the money since Petruzzi had come to realize that he had been ratted out by one of his family members and he did not know which of them he could trust.

Now Maggie and Adam were in charge of Petruzzi's fortune.

Now Maggie and Adam were the keepers of Cobb's Landing.

They have brought the place back, as nearly as they were able with the aid of Grandfather Belle's collection of old photos, to its original condition; to the way it had looked in the early thirties when Jacob and Amelia had shared their first love together.

They did it in their memory.

They did it for them.

But mostly, it seems, they did it for themselves.

The End

ABOUT THE AUTHOR

Duane Schwartz

Duane Schwartz, born and raised near Minnesota's Mesabi Iron Range, lives a quiet country life with his wife, Betty, where they enjoy a variety of hobbies: hiking in the woods, motorcycle touring, classic cars, and, of course, writing.

Schwartz is a published short-story writer who has been practicing his trade for many years. *Cobb's Landing*, his debut novel, was inspired by a walk in the woods where he and his wife stumbled across a deserted prohibition-days resort. From that experience, his novel grew.

Currently, Schwartz is working on his second novel, *Calumet*, a story of the boom days of a now forgotten mining town. He expects to complete this work and publish yet this year.